The Road to Astroworld

Astroworld, Volume 2

Charles Harvey

Published by Wes Writers and Publishers, 2025.

THE ROAD TO ASTROWORLD

First edition. September 10, 2025.

Copyright © 2025 Charles Harvey.

ISBN: 978-1878774187

Written by Charles Harvey.

Table of Contents

The Road to Astroworld
A Novel
by
Charles Harvey

* * * * *

PUBLISHED BY:
Wes Writers & Publishers
The Road to Astroworld
Letters from a Life Broken by Trauma and Survival
Copyright © 2025 by Charles Harvey
Rev. 2026 Charles Harvey
From the Publisher

Published by **Wes Writers and Publishers**
Houston, Texas
ISBN: 978-1-878774-09-5

"Normally, we'd have ushered him out.
But I told the elders to lead him to the Sinner's Chair.
Strap him down."
— *The Road to Astroworld*

Prelude

Promise's Dream . . .

Promise and her brother Jonathan sat close as the Ferris wheel spun through white clouds beneath a blue sky. The sun, the color of a balled-up yellow cat, threw a blanket of heat over them. Warm, dusty air blew in her face and stung her eyes. She reached for Jonathan's hand, which clutched a bouquet of white roses.

"Big Mama is going to hell," he whispered in her ear—

then vanished into the clouds, the roses spilling across the gondola's floor.

She picked one up, but a thorn pricked her finger. She flinched and threw the bouquet down.

The Ferris wheel groaned and came to a stop—

in front of a window.

Behind the billowing white curtains stood a clown, with silver dollar eyes and tufts of red hair sprouting from his skull. He shook his head slowly, mournfully, as if her presence brought him sorrow. In front of him, a table of mixing bowls. He scooped and slapped brown dough with his wide hands. Cinnamon-colored dust floated like smoke.

Out of that dust stepped a thin young man.

White lights buzzed like insects and lit a stage where he sang into a large microphone. His teeth dazzled like diamonds. The wind lifted his blue silk shirt—revealing festering purple bruises that lit his chest like fireflies. Sweat and tears flowed down his face, gathered at his sharp chin, and splattered the floor.

Girls with angel wings rushed toward him, screaming, "Sugar Face, we love you!"

Promise stretched out her hand to touch him—but he drifted away.

The angel girls twisted, morphed into flocks of black birds, and flew toward the sun.

Suddenly, Promise lurched forward. She stumbled. A bus roared down the street, swerving through cars and crowds. She beat her fists on the driver's back, screaming at him to stop before he killed someone. The louder she screamed, the faster he drove.

A shadow fell over her.

Arms pinned her down.

"Be still, gal, before you hurt yourself."

Her grandmother's voice.

Rough hands shook her.

"Turn over on your side."

Promise brushed sugar crumbs from her cheek, nestled her hands between her knees, and drifted back to sleep.

Big Mama shuffled back to bed.

Prologue

Elder Ella Brazille, Bishop Overseer – Sept 21, 1992

I been a leader of the Lord's flock a mighty long time. I started when folks said it was scornful for a woman to lead in the church. Some still think so. A few won't let me bury their loved ones or marry them. I can be co-pastor—but not the "real" pastor.

Well, I am where He put me. And I see plenty of reasons why He did.

Now Sister Sharon's granddaughter, Promise—
Lord, that child is of the devil.

I saw her right after she was born and knew something was wrong. Her eyes were closed, but it wasn't no angelic sleep. It looked like death. You might say you can't tell much about a baby, but I believe you *can*—you can see peace in their rest, like the Lord is inside them. And I do believe He is, in every newborn. But the devil? He usually comes later.

In Promise, I believe he came right away.

I don't recall Sharon saying the baby had died, so I touched her cheek. It was warm. But her countenance—cold. Like her soul was in another world.

Sister Sharon brought Promise to church when she could, like she did all her grandchildren, when her daughter Marsha let her. Now, Marsha is another one who needs prayer. God can't be pleased with her, having lost all her boy children to violence or sickness. By the time Sharon joined my church, her children were teenagers, and it was too late to get them to come to service unless she nearly beat them down. And that ain't the way to the Lord.

Now I do believe in not sparing the rod, but the rod must be applied when the flesh is still supple. You strike old flesh, you just harden the heart. I once suggested putting Promise in the Sinner's

5

Chair when she was five. Sharon agreed, but said Marsha would throw a fit—and maybe have all of us jailed.

****

The Sinner's Chair

The Sinner's Chair ain't no joke.

One day I was reading in the paper that Texas was retiring its newest electric chair. They'd already stopped using both of them when they started giving folks the needle. The old one, "Old Sparky," went into the prison museum. The newer one was up for sale. The governor was selling off excess inventory—that chair was listed alongside five hundred thousand jars of government peanut butter and a truckload of canned peaches.

I folded up the paper and went to sleep. But the Lord woke me not five minutes later.

He said, "Buy the chair."

"What, Lord? The electric chair?"

He said yes.

Next day, I borrowed my husband's truck while he slept and drove to Huntsville. There it was, sitting in a warehouse between towers of peaches and stacks of peanut butter. I told the men I wanted the chair, not the peaches. I reckon they figured I was in the pie business. But I said, "No sir. I'm in the *preaching* business."

They looked at me like I was crazy. But I paid cash: one hundred nineteen dollars and forty-seven cents. They threw in two cases of peaches anyway.

It rained something fierce as I drove back to Houston. The straps and buckles clanked like slave chains. I thought, *Lord, is this the devil trying to crash me?* But the Lord said, "Ella, you drive. I'm washing the devil out of what's in the back."

When I got home, my husband refused to touch it. "Aaron," I said, "are you gonna drive to work with an electric chair strapped to your truck?"

He said he'd walk.

None of the men would touch it.

7

I had to call my sister and her lady friend to help unload it.

That chair is solid oak. Heavy as the tree it came from. We set it square in the center of my church.

The next Sunday, God's house *overflowed*. Folks came from miles to gawk at that chair. Money flowed into the collection plates. News cameras came. MAD WOMAN PREACHER BUYS ELECTRIC CHAIR.

Then, a month later, the church caught fire.

It burned from the back almost to the center—right up to the chair.

God spoke again: "This ain't no sideshow. This is for purging sin."

It took all the money I made to rebuild the church. And it took a long time to get a sinner to sit in that chair.

Then one night, the Lord sent Daniel.

He could barely walk. Most days he crawled, but that didn't stop him from drinking. Men gave him liquor just to watch him do his "belly crawl" imitation. But that night, he crawled into my sanctuary like a snake.

Normally, we'd have ushered him out. But I told the elders to lead him to the Sinner's Chair.

Strap him down.

There was no electricity in that chair. All the wiring had been stripped out. I even signed a paper saying I could never hook it up. But when Daniel sat down, he went to *bellowing*. He jerked against the straps like the chair was alive.

I preached. The saints prayed. We danced around him.

A smoky haze rose up. He screamed. Foam poured from his mouth. Pee ran down his legs. But we kept praying. Those were demons coming out.

Finally, he slumped over.

We let him sleep in that chair. Next morning, God had released the straps. Daniel walked out of that church on two feet.

He came back two Sundays later in a suit, clean-shaven, and gave his life to Christ.

That's the story of the Sinner's Chair.

****

Now, back to Promise.

Like I said, I wanted her in that chair at five, because I knew she wasn't right. That girl had no emotion. Didn't cry at any of her brothers' funerals. Well—maybe a few tears at Jonathan's. But I wonder if those were for *herself.* She ran off the day of his service to some amusement park. We had to postpone everything to find her.

And that's when she met one of the devil's snakes. The Leaky Eye Rapist.

He raped that child.

Evil going into evil, I thought.

She came back near-catatonic. They tried psychiatrists, psychologists. Nothing worked. Mind stayed locked.

Marsha relented and let Sharon bring her to church. We strapped her in the Sinner's Chair. Prayed over her until we near passed out. That child stayed motionless the whole time. Not a squeak.

Finally, just after midnight, a tear slipped down her cheek.

Sister Sharon shouted. Thought it was the miracle.

We unstrapped her and saw blood on the back of her dress. Some saints thought it was further evidence of God's purging. I was too tired to argue.

She started talking again. Seemed obedient.

But her eyes—

There was no starlight in them.

She laughed sometimes. But the light didn't reach her soul.

I began to wonder if the Lord had led me right. Some folks need to stay locked inside themselves. It's a good prison for them.

I prayed—and turned Promise over to God.

THE ROAD TO ASTROWORLD

Chapter 1—Sugar Water

Promise

Promise sat up in bed and yawned. Streaks of sunlight shot through the Venetian blinds and warmed her room. A mirror nailed to the wall reflected twinkling red and blue lights.

"The police! The police!" she shouted, bouncing out of bed. "They got the Leaky Eye! They got the Leaky Eye!"

Her shoulders sagged as she peeped through the blinds. A cop stood with one foot on the bumper of his car, writing a ticket for a man on a bicycle. Nowhere in sight was the Leaky Eye, arms raised to the sky, gray water pouring from his eyes—as Promise had imagined.

She sighed and raised the blinds. The window felt cool against her nose. It was fall. The sky was brilliantly blue. Trees near the broken swings had turned orange, their leaves glowing like bits of fire. Sunlight danced off the red brick duplexes lining Lyon's Avenue two by two like rows of glazed cakes. Across the yard, LaKeisha Ann's shaggy mutt bounced on three good legs, spinning in circles, chasing its tail.

Promise raised her skinny arms and snapped her fingers like the girls on Soul Train.

"Astroworld, Astroworld, baby girl," she chanted, dancing around the room.

Someone grumbled outside her door. She paused and listened as feet shuffled down the hallway. The bathroom door creaked open and slammed shut.

"This is a good day," she whispered to herself, relaxing at the sound of running water. "Just like my name. Goodday."

Her flimsy pink robe hung off her body like a net as she searched for her doll. She sighed and buttoned it up. Her hand brushed against a stiff white dress hanging from the doorknob.

She ran to her cigar box on the dresser. Inside, next to a half-eaten peppermint stick, lay an old copper penny with a hole in the middle. Uncle Bobo had sworn it came from a dead man's pocket—and that it brought good luck if you breathed into the hole in Abe Lincoln's face.

Promise held it to her lips and whispered, "Please, Mama, let me go to Astroworld. Please, Mama, let me go to Astroworld today." She said it a third time for good measure and ran to her mother's room.

"Mama, can I still go to Astroworld today? You said so last week."

Marsha paused in the middle of combing her hair. A clump of coarse strands stood up from her head like a rooster's tail. Promise avoided her mother's sharp eyes, glancing instead at Nettie—curled up on a towel across the bed, drooling. Nettie smiled and grunted. Her chest swallowed Sweetie Pie's plastic face. One of the doll's discolored eyes bulged out.

"Nettie is killing Sweetie Pie."

"Nettie ain't hurtin' that doll. I swear, sometimes you act like you don't have as much sense as she does—asking some foolishness about Astroworld. You know today is Jonathan's funeral."

Promise winced. Marsha always compared her to Nettie when she was angry.

"But Mama, I'm tired of going to funerals," Promise whispered. "The police got Daddy all chained up between them. Sirens be screaming. People crying and hollering..."

"Those men aren't police. They're prison guards."

Promise didn't respond. "All them gangs be standing outside the church puffed up like they gonna bust. And you, Mama—you always crying. If we went to Astroworld, we'd be happy."

"Promise, there won't be no gangs at this funeral. Jonathan wasn't that kind of boy."

"You can say that again," said a nasal voice through the wall.

Marsha rolled her eyes toward it and sighed. She looked back at Promise.

"Let me fix your hair. I told you to tie it up in a scarf last night. It's all over your head."

She scooped a dollop of grease into her palms, rubbed them together, and smoothed Promise's stiff hair. Using the small end of the comb, she curled a single bang and slicked it down with more grease. Promise's forehead glowed like polished wax. The rest of her hair she combed neatly to her ears.

"I haven't seen you shed a single tear for your brother," Marsha said, voice lower now.

Promise stared at the floor and didn't answer.

"He mentioned you in the letter he wrote before he died."

Marsha stopped combing, rummaged through the cluttered nightstand, and pulled out a folded sheet of lined paper. Her hands trembled as she began to read.

Dearest Promise,

Little Sister I love you with all my heart, but I'm going to leave you soon. You must be the light of hope in this family. That's what Promise means—hope. Take care of Mama, Big Mama, and Nettie. You are the grown one now who must help Mama see after things. Help her with the dishes and cleaning. I hope to see all of you in heaven one day. I pray that the Lord understands me more than Big Mama thinks he will and that he won't send me to hell for who and what I loved. I love Mama, you Promise, Big Mama, and Nettie more than I loved anything else. That ought to give me some credit with the lord. Promise, be good always.

Love,

Your Brother Jonathan

P.S. Mama, give David my sapphire cufflinks

As Marsha read the letter, Promise fidgeted and twirled a string on her robe. A faint odor of smoke drifted in through the window. She turned her head.

Jonathan's cot lay in a heap near the smoldering trash pile, waiting for the garbage men—or for Big Mama to burn it. Just a few days ago, she'd stared out that same window watching sparks rise like red fireflies while Big Mama torched the sheets Jonathan had soiled.

"Mama, I did cry for him," Promise said, looking up.

"When?" Marsha snapped.

"When you wasn't looking."

Marsha sighed, folded the letter, and picked up her brush. She dragged it through her hair with fast, rough strokes.

"Go eat some cereal. Then get ready for the funeral. I got something for you to do. Mama's already ironed your dress."

"LaKeisha Ann never has to go to no funeral."

"LaKeisha Ann's mama was blessed with only girl children. No hard-headed fools to go get themselves killed—or die from AIDS," Marsha muttered.

"A flock of gals—" came Big Mama's voice through the wall, "even them older gals is having girl children now."

Marsha glared at the wall, then back at Promise.

"Don't ask me nothin' else about Astroworld. You hear me?"

Promise shifted her weight from one foot to the other.

"Mama, when they gon' catch the Leaky Eye?"

"I have no idea. The Leaky Eye is the least of my concerns this morning."

"Why he do nasty things to Paula?"

"Because he's a devil," Marsha said.

Big Mama appeared in the doorway. "And Paula's mama ain't had no better sense than to let that gal wear makeup and strut around like she grown. And what's all this talk about goin' to some carnival? You forget your brother's funeral is today?"

Her thick gray wig sat like a crooked hat. Her bifocals were as cloudy as waxed paper. She clutched her flowered robe tight across her chest like she was trying to keep evil out. Thick brown stockings were knotted just below her knees, smothering her legs.

"Promise ain't but eight, Mama," Marsha said. "I'm trying my best to teach her."

"Well, you better teach her quick. Else that imp will be burying you before your time—and skipping off to Astroworld."

Promise hated when Big Mama called her an "imp." LaKeisha Ann had told her an imp was a scrunched-up little black devil with horns, a long tail, and a home underground.

"Why Big Mama call me a imp? I don't got no tail."

"Well stop actin' like you do," Marsha said, "and act like you got some sense."

"I wish I did have a tail."

"Stop sassin' your mama, girl! I'll take a switch to you this morning—you need a tail-whippin', that's what you need!" Big Mama shouted.

Promise huffed and snatched Sweetie Pie from Nettie's arms. She darted past Big Mama's raised hand. By the time the two women called her name, she was already through the living room.

"Funerals," she snorted.

Her dead brothers smiled from tarnished gold frames on the coffee table. She stuck out her tongue at them—then stopped cold. The spot where Jonathan had vomited when he died still marked the floor like a foot-shaped cloud in the blue linoleum. All the ammonia in the world hadn't lifted it. Big Mama had scrubbed and scrubbed, but Marsha had told her, "Shoulda left it alone. Time would've covered it up."

Promise climbed onto the couch and crawled across it, careful not to step on the spot. LaKeisha Ann said it was bad luck to walk where someone died. Not even Big Mama made her step on the place where Jonathan had thrown up something green as grass.

She plopped into a chair at the kitchen table and slammed Sweetie Pie into the one next to her. The doll stared back through one cloudy eye. Promise picked it up by the foot and shook it until both eyes popped open. Then she tossed it back in the chair.

Behind her, the refrigerator buzzed like a trapped insect. The stove made quiet popping noises as it cooled. The ceiling above it was cracked and parched like old skin. Bits of wallpaper curled and hung down. Brown stains dotted the wall like freckles.

The dinette table was littered with broken crayons, a coloring book, Big Mama's red coffee cup, and Nettie's blue eyeglasses. Promise swept her hand across the table, pretending to knock it all to the floor. She imagined stomping on Nettie's glasses until they turned to blue dust.

A thump on the wall rattled the dishes in the sink.

Promise wrinkled her nose and stuck out her tongue in the direction of the noise. On the other side of that wall lived LaKeisha Ann Jackson and her family—three girls, a mama, and a daddy who worked at the welfare office. Just a few days ago, she and LaKeisha Ann had argued over who was the cutest rapper: Sugar Face or Pretty Fat Ed.

"LaKeisha Ann, how can Pretty Fat Ed be cute? He got a big ol' stomach."

"He cute 'cause he got a cuter face—and more money."

"Sugar Face got the most money. He paid a million dollars for his car. And the girls in my class say he the cutest."

"You and them hoes don't know nothin.'"

"He got eyes just like Sweetie Pie."

"You tired of carryin' around that ol' ugly doll."

"Sweetie Pie ain't ugly."

"She is. Sugar Face's eyes is gray—but not cloudy like that ugly thing," LaKeisha Ann said, pointing at the doll.

"Then your old mangy dog is ugly."

"At least Chester's real. That doll ain't real, silly bitch."

And with that, LaKeisha Ann slammed the door to her side of the duplex.

Promise picked up Sweetie Pie and walked over to the sink. She opened a small flap in the doll's back and filled the tiny reservoir with water. After closing the flap, she cradled the doll in her arms and gave it a firm squeeze. Water squirted from its eyes and trickled down its plastic cheeks like tears.

"LaKeisha Ann don't know nothing," Promise muttered, rocking Sweetie Pie gently.

From next door, the Jacksons' TV blared until someone turned it down. Promise glanced at the small television in her kitchen—perched on a stack of phone books atop the drainboard. The screen was dark and greasy, like an old mirror. But when you turned it on and jiggled the rabbit ear wrapped in foil just right, a burst of color, laughter, and noise sprang from that drab box.

All summer long, commercials for Astroworld spilled out of the screen—kids with their arms flung high on looping roller coasters, clowns letting toddlers honk their red noses, people stuffing hotdogs and sodas down like pigs at a trough. Every week Uncle Bobo had promised tickets, but Jonathan's sickness had swallowed up the whole summer. Marsha either cried or drank while Bobo chauffeured Jonathan to and from the hospital in Mr. Fritz's Lincoln—without Fritz knowing. Big Mama cleaned, prayed, or cuddled Nettie. No one had time for Promise. No one had time for Astroworld dreams.

Now it was fall. Today was the last day before the park closed.

Promise longed to turn on the TV, but Big Mama had forbidden it. "The whole house got to act like it's dead because Jonathan is dead," Promise thought bitterly.

From the other room, Marsha and Big Mama's sharp voices drifted in, making Promise's skin prickle.

Suddenly, the garbage can squeaked. Promise jumped and snatched the broom from the floor. She slammed it against the can. It let out a metallic gong, and a rat screeched as it scrambled up through the lid and vanished behind the stove.

"Be quiet in there!" Big Mama hollered.

The rat reminded Promise of the woman who kissed her the night before at Jonathan's wake. The woman had worn a brown coat, its loose black belt swinging behind her like a tail. Promise remembered bits of what she'd said:

"Poor baby, you done lost your last brother... Marsha, try not to take it so hard... Child, even rich boys die from AIDS... The white woman I worked for, her son died from the same thing..."

Her breath reeked like Bobo's when he was full of wine and tried to kiss her. Promise watched her mother frown as the woman fawned over them. She thought Marsha might slap her, but instead, Marsha pulled Promise close and brushed powder off her cheek.

"Miss Ella, my mother is over there," Marsha said quietly, pointing to Big Mama, who was being fanned by her church sisters.

"Why do people gotta talk so much?" Promise asked Sweetie Pie. "Why couldn't they just look at Jonathan and sit down like I did?"

She poured cereal and milk into a chipped white bowl. The milk overflowed and puddled on the table in the shape of a clover. "Big Mama said rivers of milk and honey flow through Heaven. The honey might be okay," she told Sweetie Pie. "But a waterfall of grape soda would be better—unless the milk was chocolate."

All that talk about lions and lambs lying down together didn't excite Promise. One of her favorite TV shows was Wild Kingdom. The lions chasing their prey looked more fun than the lazy ones she'd seen at the zoo, flopped on sand-colored rocks.

"If we lived in Heaven, we'd make the lions eat up the Leaky Eye, wouldn't we, Sweetie Pie?" She imagined herself and Jonathan, dressed in long white robes, scooting across the sky in search of the Leaky Eye, ready to pelt him with heavy stones.

"Mama, do I have to die and go to Heaven before I become an angel?" she shouted toward her mother's room.

No answer.

She picked up a piece of paper and scratched out the letters S O L in red crayon. She held it in front of Sweetie Pie.

"Why Big Mama say Jonathan gonna burn up if he didn't save his soul? I thought only bad people got burned up when they die. Jonathan wasn't bad like the Leaky Eye. He made us laugh, didn't he, Sweetie Pie? He even made Mama laugh when he acted like Big Mama in church."

"Ooh Sala! Ooh Sala, Whoo Whoo! Loose me, Devil! Whoo! Whoo!"

Promise whooped around the kitchen, mimicking her grandmother speaking in tongues. Sweetie Pie's pale blue eyes seemed to follow her around the room.

"What you doing in there, gal?" Big Mama's sharp voice cut through the wall. "Don't make me come in there with a switch."

Promise crept back to her chair.

"Pig Latin dipped in collard green juice—that's all that whooping and hollering is. Jonathan was right. Big Mama is the Devil herself."

She dipped her spoon into the cereal. The milk was warm now, and the flakes had turned to mush. She pushed the bowl away and watched a roach scurry toward the spilled milk. Big roaches fascinated her—especially the ones with long, twitchy legs. She liked to pull off their legs and watch them spin helplessly on their backs.

Just as she reached for the bug, rain suddenly crashed against the window like a string of broken beads. Promise jumped, then peered through the curtain at the bullet-sized drops streaking the glass. She snapped her fingers and did a quick dance—maybe the rain would cancel the funeral. But the joy faded as another thought hit her:

"No Astroworld either."

She moped back to the table and rested her face in her hands. Sugar crumbs scratched her elbows.

"Sugar water," she muttered.

The pantry door squeaked when she opened it. Big Mama grunted in the next room, so Promise eased the door shut. She slipped over to the sink and pretended to be interested in the dirty dishes in case Big Mama came stomping in.

A tiny bell tinkled—Sweetie Pie's tear reservoir had emptied. Promise put a finger to her lips and mouthed, "Hush." The bell went quiet. Big Mama coughed and fluffed her pillows. Promise knew she was "resting her nerves."

Quiet as a whisper, Promise tiptoed back to the pantry and twisted the lid off the glass sugar barrel. A jelly glass held half sugar and half water. She wanted ice—Promise loved crunching into cold, sugary cubes—but the house was too quiet for that today. Noise usually hid her "mischievous ways." A siren outside could muffle the clinking cookie jar lid. Loud music could drown out the crash of broken glass. Even Big Mama's gospel records gave cover to the "cuss" words Promise sometimes shouted when she thought no one could hear.

But today? No such luck. So she settled for sugar stirred into plain water.

As she sipped the milky syrup, LaKeisha Ann's warning echoed in her head—something about sugar being dangerous.

Listening to her had earned Promise a lick upside the head.

Earlier that week...

"You can die from eating too much sugar," LaKeisha Ann had said. They were sitting on the back porch, sipping sugar water they'd swiped from Promise's kitchen. Ants floated and flailed in the sticky syrup.

"How sugar gonna kill you? It tastes good. That's what they make candy out of," Promise said.

"They say my Big Mama had too much sugar in her. That's why she died. Why you think they call it Sugar Die Beats?"

"You said your Big Mama had heart attacks."

"I'm talking about my other Big Mama."

"Girl, sugar can't kill you."

"Eat that cupful then," LaKeisha challenged.

"I did last night. I drank a whole cup."

"I didn't see you."

"You ain't gotta see me do everything. You didn't see me have a baby either, but I had one."

"Your Aunty had that baby. It wasn't yours. You don't even know how to have a baby. You probably think you sit on a toilet and have one."

"I had it for my Aunty. And I ate a whole bowl of sugar too. Ask my brother Jonathan."

"I ain't asking your stinky brother nothin'," LaKeisha Ann snapped. Then she hopped off Promise's porch and slammed her own screen door.

That night, Promise volunteered to make Big Mama's coffee. She dumped the whole sugar bowl into the mug and stirred it until it looked like black syrup. Then she stood behind Big Mama and waited.

Big Mama took one sip, spat it out, and slapped Promise with a dishrag. "You damned fool!" she barked. "What you trying to do—kill me?"

But she didn't die. Not even close.

****

"LaKeisha Ann don't know everything," Promise said as the last bit of sugar water scratched her throat.

"Gal, you hurry up with that breakfast. I can hear you moping in there. I'm countin' to ten!"

Promise stuck her tongue out at Big Mama's room.

"I wish I had two of them lucky pennies," she whispered. "One to make Mama take me to Astroworld. The other to make Big Mama die."

The roach kept lapping at the milk. Another joined. Their antennae twitched like beacons. Promise picked up Big Mama's coffee mug and flipped it over them. One of the legs got caught between the table and the rim of the cup. She pressed her ear to the china and listened to the bugs scratch and flutter.

Chapter 2 -Mamas and Daughters

Promise stared out of her bedroom window, brooding after being chased from the kitchen. Sweetie Pie sat at her feet, squashed in the belly where Big Mama had stepped—startled—after righting her cup and sending roaches flying.

The rain had stopped, leaving spots the color and shape of fish scales on the glass. Down Lyon's Avenue, past the dip that scraped the underside of cars, the American and Texas flags fluttered in front of her school like red and blue handkerchiefs. A line of school buses wormed through the U-shaped driveway. Her classmates, jostling like frenzied bugs, vanished one by one into the open sides of the buses.

A white speck in the distance—Mr. Wicks, the principal—stepped into the street and raised a stop sign. Cars halted. The buses, arms and heads hanging from their windows, rolled forward. The last bus paused to let Mr. Wicks hop on before it scooted away.

Promise scooped Sweetie Pie off the floor and picked up a broken comb. The doll's eyes rattled as Promise raked the comb's wide teeth through its tangled hair.

"If Big Mama wasn't here, Mama would let me go to Astroworld. We both could go, Sweetie Pie. LaKeisha Ann says they got all kinds of good stuff to eat—Now-Laters of every kind. Grape, orange, strawberry, cherry, even banana. They got ice cream and mountains made out of sugar. Hot dogs as long as Lyon's Avenue. You hear me, Sweetie Pie? As long as Lyon's Avenue."

She twisted some of the doll's hair around her fingers and wound it into a roller, which sat crooked on Sweetie Pie's forehead.

"Don't got none of Big Mama's nasty food—collard greens, ox tails, pig feets. LaKeisha Ann says Astroworld would go outta business if they served that kind of food. And boys are made outta oxtails, she says. I wonder why Big Mama ain't turned into a boy yet—she eats that mess all the time, huh, Sweetie Pie?"

She laughed softly, then grew quiet.

"LaKeisha Ann says at Astroworld, you can drive a real car, and if you bump into somebody, they won't jump out and kill you."

Promise stared at the doll and sighed, remembering how Big Mama had nearly ruined her eyes with Pine-O-Pine. Nettie had dropped the doll in the toilet and then acted like it belonged to her.

"Ol' Big Mama always got to mess up things—like she almost messed up your eyes and the floor where Jonathan threw up. She said LaKeisha Ann was lying about Astroworld. And then she messed up more stuff by makin' Daddy go to jail and stay a long time."

She paused, her voice low now.

"All I did was ask her if she'd ever been to Astroworld, and she slapped me for sassin'. Daddy said, 'Don't you hit my child, black bitch!' And he slapped her. Big Mama run out the door like she got shot, and the police came and took Daddy away. Said he messed up a 'peroll' and had to go back to jail."

She frowned. "That don't make no sense. Daddy wasn't being bad. He didn't mess up no stinkin' 'peroll.' All he did was call Big Mama a bitch and slap her. Now he's in jail five years."

"LaKeisha Ann says people'll be wearin' shoes that can fly and babies'll be born in microwave ovens by the time Daddy gets outta jail." She grinned. "All Mama says when I tell her what LaKeisha Ann says is, 'Lord ham mercy.'"

"Lord ham mercy."

Why grown folks always saying that? You say it to Big Mama and she hits you for sassin' her. When I get big—just a little bit bigger than her little self—I'm gonna look right in her old black face and say "Lord ham mercy" a hundred times. I sure will. I'll fix her.

"Gal, you grease your legs yet?" Big Mama hollered.

"I'll tell her when to grease her legs," Promise heard her mother say.

"Lord, I'm just trying to help out."

"Well help by fixing Nettie's hair. I ain't got time to fool with her this morning."

"Come on, darling. Come to Grammy," Big Mama cooed to Nettie like she was calling a puppy.

Promise propped Sweetie Pie against the pillows on her bed so the doll stared straight at her. She scooped up some Vaseline and slapped it on her legs.

Big Mama love ol' cross-eyed, retarded Nettie. Always takin' her in her lap. And Nettie's bigger than me. Nettie can't do nothin' but grunt, and sometimes she forgets how to use the toilet. She got to wear a diaper like a baby. Sweetie Pie, even you don't pee on yourself. Nettie too old for diapers. But Big Mama don't say nothing about that. And when Mama's mad at Nettie, Big Mama say it ain't Nettie's fault Daddy punched Mama in the stomach when she was carryin' her. Ain't Nettie's fault at all, she say. Then she turn her lip up like she gonna laugh. But she don't. She start all that "come to Grammy" stuff after Mama slams her door. But me—let me do something bad and Big Mama handing Mama a switch or belt—or trying to hit me herself.

"Mama, can I wear my yellow shorts under my dress?" Promise hollered.

"All my boys. All my boys gone," she heard her mother cry out.

Promise paused at the sound of her wailing, then slipped on the stiff white dress Big Mama had ironed. She shoved her feet into bunny slippers—one missing an ear—and reached for her comb. That's when she saw it: a small slip of paper on her card table desk. The permission slip Marsha had signed for her to go to Astroworld.

A gold star glimmered in the corner. She had made all A's. That meant she didn't have to pay the one-dollar "School Bus Fee." Five points of the gold star pointed right at the word ASTROWORLD. Another tip pointed at Marsha's scrawled signature.

"September 19, 1992," Promise read, tracing each letter and number. It was supposed to have been Jonathan's birthday. But he had to up and die three days ago on his cot and ruin everything—just like he ruined the floor with that green vomit.

She folded the slip and tucked it in the pocket of her dress.

From the doorway of Marsha's room, Promise watched. Mrs. Jackson dabbed her mother's forehead with a rag.

"God has him. Your burden has been lifted," LaKeisha Ann's mother said.

Big Mama was busy plaiting Nettie's hair into big corkscrews, pinning them with hairpins.

"I hope God has him," Big Mama said. "I got on my knees every night praying he'd find God and a good wife."

"Mama, please," Marsha whimpered.

"He boo-booed all over hisself and made the whole house stink. LaKeisha Ann called our house the 'stink-house.'"

Everyone turned. Promise stood there, words still hanging in the air.

"Girl!" Mrs. Jackson snapped.

Big Mama's glasses swam with tears. Her mouth flew open like she was being strangled. She gripped a fistful of Nettie's hair and reached toward Promise.

"Stop, Mama," Marsha said, raising her hand.

"Did you hear what that imp just said?"

She turned to Mrs. Jackson, who shook her head slowly.

"This house been lacking discipline. That's the problem. None of them ever got the whippings they needed. And now you gonna let that girl get away with that mouth?"

"Promise, take off those shorts from under your dress."

"That's all you gonna say?" Big Mama looked at Mrs. Jackson. LaKeisha Ann's mama just shrugged and scratched her scalp. "A good whipping would do that girl some good this morning."

"Mama, all you think about is beating somebody."

"Well, it must've done some good. You and your sisters and brothers all living and never been to jail—except Bobo."

"We living all right. Lena in the nuthouse. Bobo's a drunk and a thief. Arthur Lee don't come 'round. And Susan..."

"Susan had sense to get her education and marry well. Married a preacher. Kept her dress down, too."

"That's what you think. You ever wonder how she paid for all that so-called education?"

"What you mean by that?"

"Nothing at all, Mama. Like marrying a preacher and running a daycare is all that."

"Well, it's better than what you married—and all them afflicted children you had."

"Afflicted?"

"All your kids had something wrong with 'em. Little Bobo couldn't sit still. Poochie had bad asthma. Promise act like she ain't even in the world sometimes. Look at her, dressed like she going to play in the mud, not a funeral."

"All my children by one man."

"Hah! One man, you say. A half-man, if you ask me. Everything on Suliman's side is dead or in jail—including him. And Lord, don't mention them sissy cousins of his."

She snapped a rubber band around a plait. Nettie squealed.

"One man—yeah, right."

Marsha sighed and looked out the window. Mrs. Jackson twisted the rag in her hands and stared at the floor.

"Mama, I don't want to fight. I'm burying my last boy child today."

"If you'd put that boy in Church, he might be living today. All your boys might be living."

"Mama, Church don't stop AIDS. Church don't stop drive-bys. Church don't stop nobody from stabbing you for your chain."

"You told Poochie not to wear that chain. If there was more God around here, he'd have listened. Little Bobo wouldn't've been selling dope. And Jonathan wouldn't've been practicing no abomination."

"Mama, some preachers are sissies. Jonathan came into this world that way. I could tell when he was little."

"That's when you should've beat it out of him! The devil get in them young and twist their souls inside out. You hear me? Inside out."

Big Mama wagged her finger at Mrs. Jackson like she was preaching.

"Maybe God ain't meant for everybody," Marsha shot back. "Or maybe He takes naps. Or gets him a woman. Maybe He don't care when some poor nigger gets shot, gets AIDS, or gets hung from a tree."

Big Mama dropped the comb. Her mouth opened and closed like a fish's. She jammed her fist in her palm and closed her eyes.

In her heart, Marsha smiled. She had landed her blow.

But Big Mama wasn't done. She opened her eyes and picked up the comb.

"I thank the Lord for waking me every day—for giving me strength to endure—"

"To endure! He takes away our children and our men and we women are left to goddamn endure!"

"Promise, run to Kwong's and get the white roses they ordered for me," Marsha said. "And take off those shorts before you leave this house."

"Mama, can I buy me some candy?"

"One piece—just one. Bring my change."

She folded the money and tied it in a white handkerchief. Then she pinned it to Promise's undershirt, next to her chest.

"Don't take that money out until you get to the store. You hear me?"

"You sending that girl by herself? That Leaky Eye got hold of Paula not too far from here."

"It's daylight, Mama. And I'm sure Bobo and his buddies are hanging around that old house. He can watch her."

"If he ain't too drunk. And what you need flowers for anyway? All his so-called friends sent raggedy flowers to the Funeral Home. Looked like a white woman's garden party instead of a wake," Big Mama said.

"Mama, why they call it a wake? Jonathan didn't wake up. Poochie didn't either. Or Little Bobo," Promise said.

"Hush that stupid talk," Big Mama snapped.

Mrs. Jackson put a hand on Promise's shoulder to guide her away. Promise pulled back.

"Mama, Jonathan said he wanted white roses in the casket. It's bad enough I can't buy a dozen. And now I gotta listen to you and God both criticize."

"I'm not criticizing, Daughter. The flowers'll be nice. But shouldn't he be buried in a suit?"

"Mama, I'm not doing this again. He begged to be buried in them jeans and that sweater."

Big Mama turned toward Promise. "Didn't your Mama tell you to go to the store? What you standing there with your big lips poked out for?"

Mrs. Jackson swept Promise out the room. They paused at the door and listened.

"Well, the sweater is pretty, I guess," Big Mama muttered. "But he won't get into Heaven with all them earrings. But I suppose he wanted that too."

"Mama, some folks get burned up when they die."

"The worst of sinners still get buried in a suit. What will my Church think?"

"Damn your Church! That's my child. I'd bury him naked if he wanted it!"

"I should have some say. It's my insurance helping bury that boy."

"Helping, Mama. Helping. Once I get Jonathan's policy from work, I'll pay you back."

"It's not the money. It's the principle. A man should stand before God with dignity."

"God made us buck naked, and I suspect we'll return to Him that way. God might be a freak for all we know."

Big Mama stared. The vein in her neck trembled like a worm. She got up and straightened a photo of Jonathan in his graduation gown. His smile beamed.

"I wish I could find a good, needy church to will my land to."

"I wish you would too," Marsha said.

"Anybody who talks trash about the Lord don't need His land."

"Maybe they don't want it."

"I'll say this, Daughter: if you'd raised these children on that good Louisiana dirt instead of this boxy apartment, they might've grown up right."

"Children grow where they grow. And die where they die."

Marsha pulled the lacy frock over Nettie's head. The child screamed as the fabric covered her eyes.

Big Mama watched. "A good piece of land where that child could see nature might help her more than that special school learning about blocks and circles."

"Well, Mama, the city's all about blocks and circles. Not pigs and chickens."

"Oh, the city's got pigs, Daughter—two-legged diseased pigs. Walking around killing with knives and disease. On the land, we kill the sick animals quick. Ain't no long dying."

Marsha paused. Her nail scratched Nettie's neck as she fumbled with the tiny button. She knew what Mama meant by "long dying."

"I thought you loved Jonathan."

"He was my rock. I named him after David's friend in the Bible. But I didn't have to like his funny ways."

Marsha chuckled. "Mama, you ever think what kind of friend David and Jonathan really were?"

"The Bible ain't got trash in it, Daughter."

"Nah. I guess not. People just got funny ways of living. And funny ways of dying too. Like your first husband. He died on the land, didn't he? That good ol' country land near the place you ain't lived in fifty years."

"He died at a carnival, Daughter. A carnival—just like that Astroworld Promise is all stirred up about. A carnival."

"And Susan's the reason he died there. That half-white bitch. And you got nerve to talk about my afflicted children—my sissy boy. You got your nerve."

Big Mama stomped out. The screen door slammed. Promise and Mrs. Jackson hurried through it just ahead of Big Mama's balled-up fist.

Marsha had won the battle.

Chapter 3 – Goose Steps

"Where you going, goose?"

Promise stopped. She had just run through the gates of Paradise Gardens and was striding briskly down Lyon's Avenue, her head high. Her Uncle Bobo and his friends loitered on the porch of a sagging shotgun shack. The porch dipped like the belly of an old boat. Two crooked columns held up the roof, leaning into each other like tired drunks. Bobo rested on his elbows between them, stroking his chin with one hand and holding a Styrofoam cup in the other. His pals, dressed in frumpy clothes, circled him, all grinning at Promise. One man wore a dark blue bus driver's uniform; the silver badge on his chest gleamed like a razor blade. A bright green bottle sat on the banister, catching the sun like a jade offering. The men had already taken a few sips. Their loins were humming and they were ready for some female amusement.

The air was ripe with rain, sweat, and fruity wine when Promise planted her hands on her hips. She looked at the grinning men and felt something swell inside her. Their attention was on her, and she leaned into it—acting "womanish," as Big Mama would say. At the same time, she turned up her nose at their "old man" clothes. They were at least thirty and dressed silly, she thought. Not a single one of them looked as "fly" as Sugar Face in his glittering jackets and gold chains. Her favorite singer wouldn't be caught dead in a yellow suit or a T-shirt with a big black X on the front. And he sure wouldn't be hanging around a shack, drinking wine.

She dismissed them, mostly. But they were still men, and that meant something. They brought out her sass. She needed their attention—it lifted her.

She looked Bobo in the eye.

"Don't call me no goose."

34

"You was stepping mighty fast there, Pee. Big Mama ain't riding her broom behind you, is she?"

"You don't see her, do you?"

"I don't need to. I can tell she around, the way you flying down the street like a goose." Bobo stuck out his neck and flapped his arms. The men howled, slapping their legs.

Promise frowned at Bobo's belly, shaking like a pillow. His thick, ginger-colored neck had forced his collar open, and the flaps fluttered like tiny wings. When he laughed, his cheeks puffed and his chauffeur's cap slipped down over his eyes.

Pumpkin head, Promise thought. Her older brother had been nicknamed after this uncle and had the same giant head. She was glad she wasn't a boy—or named Bobo—or else her head might be huge, too.

She glanced at her uncle's scooped-up-in-the-back red car parked in front of the house. One of the rear tires was missing a hubcap. She skipped over to the car and peeked through the dark-tinted windows. Boxes hid beneath sheets in the back seat like they were playing hide-and-seek. A toilet leaned crooked in the corner.

"Why you got a nasty commode in your car, Bobo?" she asked, scrunching up her nose.

"That's grown folks' business," he said, tilting his cap to hide his eyes. His friends snickered. "Besides, that commode's clean as a whistle."

Someone snorted.

Promise caught a glimpse of her hair in the window's reflection and frowned. She smoothed her bangs, then puckered her lips like she was checking invisible lipstick.

"Where Mr. Fritz's car? He fire you for being drunk?" she asked, watching their faces in the glass.

The men glanced at Bobo and laughed.

"Bobo, I didn't know you was married," one of them teased.

"Watch out, Pee. I'll take my belt off."

"You do, and your pants gonna fall down. Where my Sugar Face CD and poster?"

"It's coming, Pee—same as that ass-whipping from Big Mama."

"Everything always coming," Promise said with a sigh. "Including them Astroworld tickets. But Big Mama says she gonna beat you if you show up at Jonathan's funeral smelling like wine."

"I'm a grown man, little lady. Big Mama ain't beat my ass in thirty years. And I'm still working on them tickets."

"Yeah, yeah," Promise said, wrinkling her nose again at the commode before skipping up the porch steps.

"Where you supposed to be going anyway?" Bobo asked.

"Down to Kwong's to buy some roses."

"Roses for what?"

"Mama gonna put them in Jonathan's coffin."

"Marsha and her ideas."

"It was Jonathan's idea."

Bobo stared at her for a moment, then shrugged and poured himself a drink. When he set the bottle down, another hand reached for it.

"Bobo, I sure am sorry about your nephew."

"Thanks, man. Yeah, he was a good kid. Just got caught up in the wrong lifestyle."

Bobo looked like he was about to spit.

"How he catch the AIDS?" Promise blurted.

Bobo cut his eyes at her, then at the men. Promise ducked her head. His bloodshot glare told her she'd asked the wrong question. The men stared at their feet. Then up at the sky, like they were trying to figure out what it was. A woman in tight pants passed, and they craned their necks like she'd just landed from the moon. Sirens wailed in the distance. The men refilled their cups and glanced around, waiting for someone else to speak.

The man in the yellow suit cleared his throat.

"Speaking of Mr. Fritz, Bobo, didn't the Leaky Eye get his wife?"

"Naw. She slipped right out that nigga's greasy hands. Ain't no bigger than a matchstick—just slipped through."

"She was lucky. He killed one woman just down the street. I wonder why he kill some and let some live?"

"He'd kill 'em all if he had time."

"The nigga close to getting caught. That's why he killing 'em now. Desperate."

"You reckon he's a nigga, Bobo?"

"Fool, the news says he is. Besides, can't no white man sneak in here and kill a Black woman. Somebody would've seen him."

"News can lie. A white man could put on blackface, look just like a nigga. I seen a movie about that. I don't think the Leaky Eye is no nigga. I think he's a white man in blackface who got a thing for Black women."

"Ain't nobody seen nothin' white on the Leaky Eye."

"Well, I doubt they are staring at him with their eyes wide open. He ain't gonna let nobody do that. The women who do catch his eyes in the dark say he got gray eyes. Ain't none of us got gray eyes."

"Your Aunt Susan got gray eyes, don't she, Promise?" Bobo nodded at her. "Since you wanna be all up in grown folks' conversation."

Promise thought of her aunt's piercing gray eyes set in a face the color of school desks—and how those eyes always made her look down at the floor. She studied a bug crawling nearby instead of answering.

"Your sister look like a white woman, Bobo," the man in the yellow suit said. "Everybody say the Leaky Eye's face is like dirty dishwater, the way them eyes streak."

"A nigga on my job got runny gray eyes," said Two Jack, the bus driver. "Guess what they call that nigga behind his back?"

"What?"

"Good Coon."

"Now why they call him that?"

"'Cause you know how a coon wears a black mask—like a robber? Well this nigga look like he wearing a white one. Some kind of chemical accident when he was a boy. Burned him all around the eyes. He wear shades all the time. Even when he driving the bus at night."

"Why they let a half-blind nigga drive a bus?" Bobo asked. "Bet he don't drive through no white neighborhoods. Shows how much white folks care about us. We got the Leaky Eye *and* a blind man behind the wheel."

"I didn't say he was blind. The bus company got regulations," Two Jack said.

"Fuck regulations. Maybe that nigga is the Leaky Eye."

"Hell no. That man scared of women. His wife got a ring in his nose big as that hubcap." He pointed to one lying in the gutter. "He come to work with knots on his head, face scratched up like a chicken got to him. I know he ain't no rapist."

"The New Brotherhood is patrolling for the Leaky Eye," said the man with the X on his shirt.

"Them niggas ain't shit," Bobo spat.

"Aw, I wouldn't say that," Neck said, locking eyes with him.

"Why? You a member?"

"The New Brotherhood comes straight from the old Black Panthers."

"What good did they do? What happened to the so-called revolution? Cops and the FBI shut that shit down."

"Well, I take exception, Bobo. I think the Panthers did a lot of good. Made us proud to be Black men, for one."

"Where that nigga at on that old ass shirt you wearing?" Bobo pointed at Malcolm X, frowning between the big X on Neck's shirt.

"Well—"

"Well, my ass. Anytime we try to rise up, the Man puts his foot on our necks. As long as we kill or rape each other, he don't give a shit. That's why these gangs everywhere. That's why that Leaky Eye bastard's roaming free. Let him touch a white woman—just one—and the cops'll find him faster than stink finds shit. Mark my words. New Brotherhood, my ass."

"Why he like to raise up women's dresses, Bobo?" Promise asked suddenly.

The men stirred, uncomfortable. Once again, they looked to the sky.

"Promise, you ask one more question—you hear me, little girl?" Bobo warned. "You worse than a cop. Just stick close to home so he don't try to raise your dress up."

"You watch," the man in yellow said, "Leaky Eye's gonna end up looking like a white man from one of them old-timey minstrel shows." He didn't bother pouring a drink—took a swig straight from the bottle. The others followed suit. "You'll see. He gonna look like a greasy devil. Greasy. That's why Fritz's wife slipped away from him. I wish she coulda seen his belly or his ass. We'd know the truth then."

"I wonder what a fine Black woman like her see in Fritz?" asked Two Jack, the bus driver. "He's bald and pink as a baby."

"Well, shit, just open your eyes," Bobo answered. "All of us put together couldn't come up with five thousand dollars if our asses depended on it. If my mama hadn't had that dollar-a-week burial policy, you think Marsha coulda buried her boy? Hell no. I ain't got no money. But Fritz? That crooked stock market shit he's in? Earn five thousand in a day. I drive that motherfucker to five different banks. You hear me? Five." Bobo fanned his fingers.

"He should've let you use his car today for the funeral," the man in yellow drawled. "Could've saved y'all some money."

"I damn sure asked him—and he damn sure told me no. Marsha had to pay extra for a limousine. Or else I'd be driving my folks around in that raggedy-ass car. Stingy motherfucker. Don't want a bunch of niggas in his ride." Bobo hurled his chauffeur's cap on the ground.

Promise eyed the cap and wanted to put it on. She liked to perch sideways on the couch arm at home and pretend she was Bobo, driving Mr. Fritz's long black limousine. Sometimes the grown-ups played along. Mostly, they told her to hush all that "whoosh whoosh" noise she made, mimicking the car's quiet purr. This time, she let the cap stay where it fell. She didn't want another scolding from her uncle.

"Well, that wife of his sure is a nigga," the man in the yellow suit said.

"She don't think so—claims she's from Brazil or somewhere."

"Money ain't everything," Neck retorted. His Adam's apple bobbed like he was swallowing an egg. "Five Fritzes couldn't equal the size of my you-know-what—or match the motion of my ocean lapping between some big brown thighs."

"Aw, Neck, women ain't thinking about all that no more. Cold cash rules the world."

"I bet they think about plenty when Leaky Eye's going to town on 'em. Woo! Wee!" Neck grabbed his crotch and held it.

"Nigga, you sound like you rootin' for the Leaky Eye."

"He doin' what we oughta be doin'. Only we oughta be doin' it to white women. You ever try to get with Fritz's wife?"

"Hell no, not that scrawny-ass thing."

"I bet she misses a good Black man in the midnight hour."

"She got plenty of fur coats to remind her of our Black asses. He don't let me drive her unless he's in the car. She drive herself in that Jag he bought her."

"I'd drive her—drive her right out of them furs and jewels. Drive her into my kitchen, cookin' beans, rice, and pork chops. Fatten her ass up."

Promise stared at Neck's bobbling throat as he drawled. He winked and flashed a mouthful of crooked gold teeth. She looked away.

"Well, I better get on down the road," Neck said, slipping off the porch like a snake. He glanced at Promise and winked again.

"I don't like him," Promise said as he made it halfway up the walkway. "He got something stuck in his throat, and he nasty."

"Probably a chicken bone," said the man in the yellow suit. "Y'all ever seen that nigga eat fried chicken? Don't be nothin' left but the box."

"Yeah, and I bet that ain't all he can swallow—with a neck like his. They tell me him and your neph—"

The bus driver stopped mid-sentence.

Bobo and the man in the yellow suit turned toward Two Jack. Bobo stood up.

"Him and my nephew what, nigga?"

"Nothing, Bobo. Nothin' at all."

Bobo glared at Two Jack. The man shifted from foot to foot. He looked at the man in yellow, who stared down Lyon's Avenue. Promise watched him too. He dropped his gaze to the ground.

"I say let's have a drink to nothing," the man in yellow said, slapping Bobo and Two Jack on the back.

"Don't let your tongue outrun your brains, nigga," Bobo muttered, reaching for the bottle. "Yeah, let's drink to nothin'," he spat.

"Whatever the Leaky Eye is, one thing's for sure," said the man in yellow, "he's slippery as an eel."

"Slippery for sure. One woman said he had on white and got her in a cemetery—in the back of a hearse. Another said he had on a bus driver's uniform."

Their eyes landed on Two Jack.

"What the hell y'all gazin' at me for?" Two Jack asked. "I told y'all about that nigga with the runny eyes!"

"We just sayin' what we heard—like you said what you heard," Bobo said.

"Whoever he is," added the man in yellow, "he's a tiger who can change his stripes."

After a few more swigs from the bottle, Bobo noticed Promise sprawled on the bottom step.

"Say, Pee—who dressed you this mornin'? Got you lookin' like Raggedy Ann with bunny shoes, a wedding dress, and yellow shorts."

"It ain't no wedding dress."

"I'd say Nettie dressed you if I didn't know better."

"Nettie ain't dressed nobody. Mama's dressin' her after she clean the slobber off her face. I ain't goin' to no funeral—I'm goin' to Astroworld."

"Astroworld? Pee, is you crazy? I told you I was gon' get us tickets."

Promise shrugged. She got up and studied a poster stapled to a tree—the same X and frowning man printed on Neck's shirt. The X reminded her of the line on the permission slip where Marsha had signed her name, granting Promise approval for the field trip.

She held the slip of paper up to Bobo's eyes. He glanced at it, then waved it away.

"Marsha signed that before Jonathan died."

"She's still gonna let me go."

"Marsha ain't doin' no such thing, little lady. And even if she was, the school buses gone already. We saw 'em leave earlier. How you gonna get to Astroworld?" Bobo asked.

Promise glanced at Bobo and his friends grinning at her. She hunched her shoulders. She remembered Mr. Wick holding up the red stop sign, the buses crawling away from school.

Just then, a rumble and snort behind her. A yellow-and-white city bus passed. Its tires churned through a puddle and splashed Bobo's car.

Promise snapped her fingers. "I'm gonna catch a city bus."

"Promise, you ain't never caught a bus by yourself in your life. But I bet you catchin' crawfish with them toes right now."

She looked down at her soaked bunny slippers. Her mouth opened, then shut. She jerked her feet out the water and sidled over to Bobo's car, pretending to be interested in the old toilet in the back seat.

"Look at little Miss Nettie who don't know how to stay out of mud puddles," Bobo hissed.

The back of her neck burned with shame. A tear slid from the corner of her eye. She wiped it with her sleeve, turned from the car, and headed down the street.

"Big Mama said you better pull up your pants and don't be showin' your dirty drawers at the funeral," she called over her shoulder.

The men on the porch howled. A passing car drowned out Bobo's reply. Down the sidewalk, Kwong's Market squatted like a red cinder block.

Promise kicked a tin can and sent it rolling. The can came to rest in a patch of grass. She raised her foot to kick it again, but a strip of yellow police tape—twitching like a cat's tail—caught her eye. She followed the tape's trail over broken glass and beer cans. The end was attached to a dwelling hiding behind a clump of bushes, sitting far back from the street, as if it didn't want to be bothered with anything happening on Lyon's Avenue.

The shack leaned against two planks bracing its right side. A mass of posters clung to the left side like a swatch of old bandages. In the front yard, weeds lay flat as if a giant foot had stomped them. A large hole pierced the wall next to the front door, and two huge planks were nailed crisscross over the opening. Police tape fluttered weakly from the hole like streamers from a long-ago party.

Promise took one step forward and stopped.

She thought of all the talk floating around about the Leaky Eye—

He sleeps curled up in empty houses like a snake.

He hangs from the ceiling like a bat.

The liquid from his eyes burns you like acid...

She leaned against a tree and looked back toward her uncle and his friends. They laughed and passed the green bottle around. They had forgotten about her.

She turned, picked up a stick, and crept into the yard. The ground, softened by the morning rain, was littered with paper and tin cans. Rags blotted the yard like wet skins. A hospital gurney leaned on its side against a tree, its legs sticking out like metal bones. Promise struck the gurney with her stick—it answered with a dull clang. She darted behind a tree and peeped out in case a head popped up in the window.

Nothing.

The windows stayed dark and silent. Promise let out her breath.

"Hey, hey," she called out.

Leaves shimmied in the wind. She shouted more "Heys" before stepping onto the porch and peeking through the hole. Darkness inside was sliced by slivers of light sneaking through gaps in the planks. A pile of rags took up one corner. A rusty box spring lay on the floor, a blue rubber glove tangled in its coils. Footprints covered the dusty floor as if people had been dancing. As she tilted her head to check the ceiling for bats, Promise heard a scraping noise in the yard.

She yanked her head from the hole and turned.

Neck stood in the yard, watching. The thing in his throat moved like he was swallowing.

"What you doin' up in here, little Mama?" he drawled.

"Ain't doin' nothing."

"Aw, you doin' something all right."

Neck started toward the porch, stepped in some muck, and cursed under his breath. He stomped on a rock to knock the mud off his shoe, then scraped both feet on the bottom step as he climbed. Promise backed away, watching as he poked his head through the hole. The hole seemed to suck him in—one leg bone, one arm bone at a time.

Clouds of dust danced around his feet as he kicked trash aside. Promise watched him bend and pull the glove from the box spring. He held it up to a shaft of light and scratched his finger across the rubber. He examined his nail.

"Blood."

He stared at Promise and threw the glove on the floor, then kept poking around.

"You know who was in this house the other day?"

Promise shrugged.

"The Leaky Eye had him a woman in here. The police wore that glove when they examined her body."

He let out a high-pitched screech.

"Woo! Wee! I know she had a time with his business. Woo! Wee!"

He looked back at the hole where Promise had stood.

It was empty.

Promise didn't stop running until she stumbled into the legs of boys dribbling and passing a basketball between them.

"Watch out, Little Mama," one boy said, steadying her by the shoulders.

She peeked around his waist just as Neck stepped out of the yard. He paused in the middle of the street and stared in her direction, then disappeared between two row houses.

Promise threw away the stick she'd been holding and continued down the street. Her shoulder brushed a smooth surface. She stopped and frowned.

It was the garish red mural of the smiling Kwong family. Their oversized teeth made her feel like she was about to be attacked by a pack of monkeys. When she was smaller, Jonathan had to hold her hand or she'd run into the street to escape the mural.

Promise reached her hand upward, as if expecting Jonathan to grab it.

Then she remembered she was alone.

Chapter 4 – Pete

Sunlight streamed through the bathroom window, warming his thick red back. Cold water gushed from the faucet into the sink, cooling his sore knuckles. The tiny mirrored tiles above the sink broke his face into a grid of small squares. Each reflected a reddish face with a white circle around the left eye.

Pete's left eye was like a water ring set in mahogany. Oddly, the pupil remained a natural brown. It was the right eye that the chemical "accident" had turned gray.

Sometimes he wondered if he was the devil. After all, the devil was red as cayenne, just like the pictures he'd seen all his life.

Blue nylon panties lay crumpled in the basin, soaking up water. A bitter taste rose in the back of his throat. He hocked and spat into the toilet. Shaking the water from his hand, he picked up the razor and began shaving from his chin to his Adam's apple. Pete mumbled, watching himself in a small round mirror that stuck out from the wall on an accordion rack, like a big silver eye.

"I cut that bitch's laugh off right quick. Should've had a mirror like this one—so she could've watched her eyes bug out."

A hard thump rattled the bathroom wall like a bird slamming into it. Pete nicked himself.

"That nigga and that goddamn basketball."

He rinsed the blood and gnat-sized whiskers down the drain and dabbed his chin with tissue. Then he sat on the toilet. Someone knocked.

Pete reached for the panties. The doorknob rattled but didn't turn. He relaxed—he had remembered to lock it.

"Pete, what are you doing in there? Hurry up," Jackie's voice called through the door.

"I'm doing a number two."

"Oh? I didn't see you take anything last night. Are you sure you're not doing something else?"

"Jackie, I'm shitting and shaving."

"You don't have to talk like you're in the gutter. Just hurry up. I think Shadrach's invited Ashley to breakfast. And I have a plane to catch later today."

He listened to her house shoes flap down the hallway.

That damned woman, always prying.

Another loud thump landed next to his head. Pete grabbed his chest.

"That damn ball again."

He banged on the wall. But he knew Shadrach couldn't hear him. Probably had those headphones glued to his ears, arms flailing as he dribbled and shot. Pete imagined him flopping around like a puppet on strings.

He glanced over at the panties. A tingling sparked in his loins. His body tightened. His lips parted.

****

The woman had come right up to his car and leaned in the window. It was still daylight, though the sky was fading from blue to deepening azure. Her breath reeked of peppermints and shit. Pete flinched and backed away.

Cars zipped along the freeway in the distance like mice. But down in the Bottoms, winding under the overpass, men circled slowly in old cars, eyeing the girls who mingled along the cracked sidewalks near abandoned shacks.

Pete had already made several loops. His silvery, catlike eyes scanned the dark corners. A misty rain blurred his windshield, and his eyes began to burn. He stopped the car, dug in the glovebox for his drops and pills.

The drops calmed his eyes. The pills quieted the whining in his head. He squirted, blinked the haze away.

Then—she was there. Teeth flashing through the mist, eyes fixed on him.

Sometimes it was eyes. Sometimes teeth. Sometimes a thin chain around a slender neck. That's what caught his attention.

He never remembered them getting in.

It always broke like a dream. Screams snapped him out of it. Arms clawed at him. Hot air rushed his face. A mouth twisted in terror.

Then silence. A long sigh. Pete stood, dusted himself off. He jammed panties or socks into his pocket and picked his way through trash back to his car. Drove home listening to jazz—usually *Bitches Brew*.

"Don't cry, baby. It's gonna be all right."

He looked at the woman's broken teeth.

She must think I'm the one crying.

His car door creaked shut. The old Lincoln's engine rumbled.

Then: laughter.

Pete looked down. One hand gripped his limp dick. The other held a pair of blue panties. The woman leaned back on her elbows, skirt thrown over a rusty box spring. Her thick thighs opened and closed with the breeze. Her breasts hung like sacks of lemons. Her head jerked back as she laughed.

"Is that the best you can do, sweetie?"

That was the last thing she said.

****

"Shaking her head like I was a damn baby," Pete muttered. "Shook it 'til I turned that laughing into crying. Then she knew who the man was."

He stared at the bathroom wall.

"One day I'm gonna let this bitch know who the man is. She gonna suck my dick and know her place. Yeah. She gonna suck her husband's dick like a bitch oughta."

Pete stroked himself, picturing Jackie's lips wrapped around him. His shoulders tensed. His mouth opened, letting out a soft animal cry. His loins and thighs trembled, then went slack.

He wiped his hands on the panties and stood. Stuffed them into the front of his underwear, right next to his dick.

He picked up his dark glasses.

****

"My God, you sure can stay in the bathroom a long time. Don't you know I have things to do? And why do you have on your work uniform? It's Saturday. You're supposed to cut the grass and watch Shadrach."

Pete sat down at the breakfast table. Jackie poured him a cup of coffee.

"I got called in for overtime. That boy's old enough to watch himself a few hours." Pete sipped and set the cup down.

"Yes, he's old enough to get himself into a world of trouble with that girl."

"You want him to get in trouble with a boy? He's supposed to have a girlfriend."

Jackie turned. "I told you what I found in his room. He's having sex, and I don't want him to get into any trouble."

"He ain't the one gonna get pregnant."

"You don't give a damn about our reputation." Jackie banged her spatula into the skillet, scrambling an egg.

"You worry about a reputation. I just know this house note ain't gonna pay itself."

"Oh, like being Dr. Cook's assistant isn't work?"

"Try trading shuffling papers for handling twenty tons of steel on wheels. That boy's teeth cost us fifteen hundred dollars this month and—"

"Our son. Our son. Can't you call him that for once?"

"Mama's baby and daddy's maybe."

"He is your son. How many times have I had to say that these sixteen years?"

"As many times as it takes to make me believe there's a drop of my blood in that nigga—unless it got there through my brother, who you admire so much."

"That's a damn lie. He's your child."

"He might be my uncle's. You wanted to name him Lazarus. Didn't think Pete was good enough."

"You're a dripping-eye liar. Don't try me this morning, nigger. Trying me because you ain't shit. You didn't have sense enough to fight for your part of Heavenly Rest. I wanted to name him Lazarus because the doctor couldn't hear his heartbeat one day and thought he had died. I slapped my belly in anguish, and that woke his heart up."

"Yeah, yeah. It's a wonder he got good sense, as hard as you slapped."

"If I recall, you was in a nut house when our son was born. Voices or motors or something whining in your head. My mother named him Shadrach—for all I went through carrying and birthing your child, nigger! Don't you lie and try me this morning."

Pete looked at Jackie's bent back as she leaned over the stove. She wore a black tunic blouse and skirt. He was reminded of the black rubber apron his uncle used to wear while working on the dead.

She'd brought up his hospitalization and his uncle's funeral home—as if they were proof of his failure, just another way to keep his dick limp and useless.

It had been a small, two-man operation with hired help as needed. Mostly it was just his uncle and jazz music drowning out the embalming machine's mournful hum. The real dirty work was done in the "back room."

It wasn't the smells or the blood or the shit from last bowel movements swirling down the toilet that made the work dirty. The dirt was in the man doing it.

His uncle preferred working on male corpses. The back room door was normally kept locked. But Pete had walked in one day and caught his father's brother with his pants down, rubbing between the legs of a young man killed robbing a store.

His uncle, startled, threw a bottle of formaldehyde. It missed but shattered against the wall and sprayed Pete's face. He almost lost his right eye. He let the lie be told—that he'd been playing with chemicals and one bottle broke and exploded.

Pete sighed. He'd tried to tell Jackie the real story, tried to explain why he let his brother take the business. But all she saw was a dumb nigger driving a bus, while dollars and "reputation" slipped through her fingers.

Jackie turned and scooped eggs onto his plate.

"What you sighing about?" she asked, holding the skillet a few inches from his face. The heat made his left eye twitch and steamed up his shades. She stared for a moment before turning back to the stove. Pete picked up his fork and cut off a piece of egg.

"I wish you would let Lazarus rest."

"He is resting quite peacefully—while your brother is running things. Arlene said they have three funerals today. Money you could be making."

"That freak can have it."

"That's your attitude about everything. Just roll over and show your belly. I'm glad I have sense enough to drive things around here. You barely have sense enough to operate that bus."

Pete picked up his glass of apple juice. It reminded him of piss on a concrete floor. He set it back down.

He heard the faint sound of a whining motor.

As it grew louder, he rubbed his eyes behind Jackie's back. He didn't want her to see—she'd make him call his boss and say he couldn't drive. When his eyes acted up, colors blurred, and sometimes he bumped into things. The noise came with bad weather and left a bitter taste like grape seeds. It wasn't just an annoyance—it was a force. A living, breathing thing that guided his hands and feet. When the motor finally ceased, soiled undergarments remained behind for him to wash.

Pete shifted in his chair. The whining motor in his head needed punishment. He looked at Jackie's back.

"So, you think our son needs that talk?" he asked.

"I told you a week ago. What are you waiting for?"

"I'm waiting for you to drive things."

Jackie turned. "Don't be a son of a bitch this morning."

"Maybe the panties belong to him."

"How dare you say that."

"What color were the drawers?"

"They were pink."

"Lacy?"

"Stop asking me those damned questions. They were women's drawers. I found them balled up in the corner of his closet. They probably belong to Ashley."

"Could be that some of my uncle's funny ways got passed on to our son. I caught the man in some women's drawers one time."

"I don't believe that lie. I'll talk to the boy myself."

"You gonna talk man to man with him?"

"Nigger, what's wrong with you?"

"You oughta let your principal talk to him if you ain't man enough. I know she is."

"What you say, nigger? What did you say?"

"You been spending a lot of time with that dyke."

Pete barely finished the sentence when Jackie rushed at him. She grabbed his collar, held the spatula high, and smacked him on the head. The air whistled as her arm came down again, striking another blow that rang in his ears.

She tightened her grip.

Pete closed his eyes and winced. Blood rushed to his dick. Jackie's screams drowned out the whining motor.

"Oh Jesus, Jesus," Pete moaned softly as Jackie struck him again.

The front door slammed.

Jackie held him another moment, then let go of his collar and returned to the stove. Smoke filled the kitchen. She opened a window.

Their son came bouncing in. A white girl trailed behind him. Shadrach kissed his mother at the stove.

"Hello, Mrs. Chesterfield," the girl said cheerfully. Her blond ponytail bounced with excitement.

"Hello Ashley," Jackie replied with a dry cheeriness that barely masked her mood. "Pancakes coming right up."

She didn't turn around.

Shadrach and Ashley turned to grab seats at the table—then froze.

Pete sat there, wiping grease from the top of his head.

"Oh," Shadrach said quietly. "This is my father, Pete."

"Hello, Mr. Chesterfield. I don't think we've met before." Ashley stuck out her hand and bumped a glass on the table. It rocked but stayed upright. Pete said nothing, keeping a steady gaze on the girl. He felt a swelling between his legs as his dick pressed against the panties he'd stuffed in his underwear.

Ashley stood for a moment, confused about what to do with her hand, until Shadrach pulled out a chair and punched her lightly on the arm. She giggled and plopped down beside him. The braces in her mouth glinted, making her appear babyish. The girl smiled brightly, shifting her eyes between Pete and Shadrach.

"I got this gold star for working so much overtime. That's why—"

Jackie interrupted. "Ashley, do your parents know Dr. Cook?" She cracked an egg into the pancake mix.

"Mama, Ashley and me—"

"Ashley and I," Jackie corrected.

"Ashley and I don't have time for politics this morning."

"You're never too young to care about the world you live in."

"Aw, Mama."

"'Aw Mama' nothing. Dr. Cook is going to put a computer at every kid's desk. They'll be able to dial into a database and ask all kinds of questions. I'm her assistant campaign manager."

"Wow!" Ashley said. "Do you get to be on TV?"

"Only if the camera is turned the other way."

"Aw, Mrs. Chesterfield."

"Yeah, Mama, didn't you used to model?" Shadrach asked, hoping to steer the conversation away from Dr. Cook and school.

"I used to be a lot of things." Jackie paused and cut her eyes at Pete. "But I love kids, and Dr. Cook has good ideas for teachers and students. That's why this convention in Las Vegas is so important."

"Dr. Cook can do anything a man can do," Pete said quietly.

Ashley giggled, then stopped. Jackie clenched her teeth and breathed hard. Shadrach looked at his father as if he were a stranger. Pete smiled at Ashley. She caught a glimpse of herself in his shades. She wasn't sure if he was looking *at* her or *through* her. Her eyes drifted to the gold star on his name badge. She absently pulled her blouse together.

Jackie brought over a plate of pancakes and set them noisily on the table. Pete's eyes dropped to his belly.

"Mama, how long are you going to be in Vegas?" Shadrach asked.

"Until the cows come home," Pete answered.

"Long enough for me to help somebody do something good and worthy in this world," Jackie shot back.

Pete and Shadrach looked at each other. Shadrach wondered how he could weather a weekend in the house with a man who was virtually a stranger. He couldn't remember riding in a car alone with his father, or them holding hands crossing a busy street when he was small. And when he *did* see the man's eyes, they were either vacant or smoldering with hostility.

"Mama, how long?" Shadrach pleaded.

"Until Sunday. I'll be back Sunday night. Dr. Cook has to make a report to the Board on Monday. We'll have to write it up on the plane, for sure. You'd think they'd give us more time."

"I want to go with you."

"Shadrach, you can't come to Vegas. This is all business."

"Stop worrying your mama, boy."

"Pete, it's the first time I've ever left him."

"Well, I'll be here. He's acting like some bastard orphan."

"Pete!"

"All I'm saying is I'm here. And we can do that bonding thing that's so popular now. Just father and son and some hot dogs."

"There won't be no hot dogs. I cooked Sunday dinner already. Fried chicken, mustard greens—"

"What's wrong with hot dogs on a Saturday night? While you and Dr. Cook are doing your thing in Vegas, me and the boy can be bonding over hot dogs. Wrestling comes on tonight."

"Shadrach doesn't need to watch that trash. Dr. Cook says there's too much garbage on TV polluting our kids' minds."

"Well, ain't nothing wrong with wrestling. I remember when you and I used to wrestle."

"Your wrestling days are over, brother."

"That's what you think. I'll bet *your* wrestling days ain't over either."

Jackie glared at him. She put down her forkful of pancakes and got up from the table. Ashley and Shadrach ate in silence. When they finished, they bounded up the stairs toward Shadrach's room.

"Leave the door open, Shadrach. You know I'm going to be picking up your dirty clothes this morning," Jackie shouted.

Her eyes fell on Pete. "You ain't much of a man, but you try to get me any way you can. 'Dr. Cook can do anything a man can do. My wrestling days ain't over.'" She mocked him.

Jackie picked up the steaming coffee pot and held it in Pete's direction. "If that girl wasn't here this morning, you coon-looking son of a bitch..." She gripped the pot before slamming it on the counter. Pete looked down as Jackie passed him on her way to their room.

"Your uncle was right about you. You have a streak of something ugly deep in your heart."

"He should know," Pete said to her back.

****

Pete stood at the bottom of the stairs, listening. Ashley's squeaky laughter tumbled from Shadrach's room. His mind's eye conjured the image of her panties—white as cotton, with lace around the thighs. The voices returned.

"You know the kind women wear. You carry them balled up next to your dick. You wipe your filthy eyes with them. Men know these things—know them in a natural way. There's something in your heart this morning."

Whitish tears ran down his face. He dabbed at them with a wadded tissue from his pocket.

He climbed one step and froze.

"Not now, fool," the voice warned. "Your son is up there."

Pete stared at the shadow of the girl's ponytail bouncing against the wall. Rain ticked against the window like a thousand tacks. He wished the door had been pulled to—just a sliver of an opening would be enough. Enough for one eye.

Carnal thoughts clawed inside him. His groin thickened. Milky tears streaked his cheeks.

He wondered what a white girl might smell like. Lavender and vanilla? Would she yield quietly—or scream and claw at his eyes—eyes already ruined?

"What are you standing there for? Don't you have a bus to drive this morning?"

Jackie's voice cut into his thoughts.

Pete turned. Jackie stood, glaring at him.

"Put your shades back on and use those eyedrops. Your face looks like somebody spit on you."

Chapter 5 – Kwong's Market

Promise pushed through the smoke-colored doors. A malodorous combination of sour pickles, grape bubblegum, onions, and a decaying rodent greeted her.

Why Mama gotta send me to stinky Kwong's?

Why not Stop N Sack's? They got flowers. And they don't watch you like a tiger ready to eat you. You can even see yourself on that TV up on the wall.

Mrs. Kwong rose from her milk crate seat as Promise passed the counter. This was her habit—get up when someone walked in, then sit and stare with eyes hidden behind oversized sunglasses. The kids called her "Jack-in-the-Box Kwong."

Her son, "Little Kwong," sat unsmiling in a tall high chair beside her. A cowbell stood upside down on his tray like a sentinel. Promise wanted to stick her tongue out at him, but couldn't tell if Mrs. Kwong's eyes were watching behind those dark lenses.

"I see Little Promise is holdin' her water today," Mrs. Kwong said as Promise passed.

Promise hunched her shoulders and wandered down the aisles, picking up items and putting them back. Mrs. Kwong and her boy kept a sharp eye on her. Promise knew exactly why.

****

It was a Saturday morning.

Promise, LaKeisha Ann, and Paula from across the courtyard were playing jacks when LaKeisha suddenly stood up, hands on hips.

"I want me a peppermint stick and a sour pickle," she declared.

"Where a scrub like you gonna get money from?" Paula asked.

"Hoe, just how much money you got?" LaKeisha shot back. She dropped to her knees, bounced the rubber ball, but missed her "threesie."

"My boyfriend gonna give me some money tonight." Paula scooped up three jacks.

"It's my turn!" Promise shouted. The older girls ignored her.

"Ol' Jimmy Crick ain't got no money—with his skinny legs and big-nose self," LaKeisha scoffed.

"He *do* got money! He sellin' crack for the War Boys. I'ma kiss him tonight and he gonna give me some."

"Them War Boys ain't givin' Jimmy Crick nothin'. They'll kick him in the booty or shoot him first."

"First off, his name ain't no Jimmy Crick—it's *James Creekmore*. He half white, so ain't nobody gonna kick or shoot him nowhere."

"Child, please. Them War Boys would kick a white policeman's booty."

Promise reached for the ball and jacks after Paula missed, but LaKeisha snatched them up.

"It's my turn!" Promise screamed again.

"Here, silly bitch!" LaKeisha flung the jacks in Promise's direction.

Promise scooped up one jack. "Paula, how come James gonna give you money just for kissin'?"

The girls looked at each other and laughed. At eleven, they were already women who *knew*. They called each other names to feel "womanish." They had smelled exotic seafood in their blood and kissed boys. Fine hairs were sprouting beneath their arms and between their thighs. Promise, at eight, was tolerated mostly because her older brother gave her money to buy the giant sour pickles and NowLater candy they craved.

"You's a silly bitch," LaKeisha said.

"It feels good, baby," Paula added.

"I kiss Jonathan. Don't feel nothin'," Promise said.

"Jonathan your brother, fool. It gotta be a man not kin to you. Child, you green as *Irish Spring*. And it gotta be a *real* boy. Not no sissy boy like Jonathan."

"Jonathan ain't no sissy!" Promise snapped.

"Silly bitch, shut up. We gotta figure out how to get some candy. Your brother give you any money?"

Promise shook her head. "But I can go get my lucky penny."

"Shut up, silly bitch. That voodoo don't work," LaKeisha sniffed.

"How we gonna get candy with no money?" Paula asked.

"We can steal it," LaKeisha said.

"Girl, is you crazy? How we gonna steal outta *Kwong's*? They got that little boy sittin' up there with that bell in his hand."

"If our Mamas was gone, we could sneak to Stop N Sack. It's easy to steal from there."

"Well we can't. Some fool'll tell on us."

"I wish I could take that bell from Little Kwong and beat him upside the head with it—him and that ugly fat rat face of his."

"My Big Mama say he a big fat rat the Kwongs grew and put clothes on," Promise offered.

"Girl, your Big Mama ain't got no sense," LaKeisha said.

"Oh, I got it!" LaKeisha snapped her fingers.

"What? Make Promise do the nasty with Little Kwong?" Paula teased.

"Naw, fool. Mrs. Kwong wouldn't let him. Besides, Promise wouldn't know how to do the nasty with *herself* in the mirror. But here's the deal—we all go in the store..."

"Mister Kwong say only two kids at a time unless they got they Mama."

"Child, Sidney the Butcher there today. Ol' Man Kwong gonna be too busy doing the nasty with him."

"How two *men* do the nasty?" Promise asked.

"Ask your sissy brother," LaKeisha retorted. "Now, when we go in, I'ma walk to where they keep the ol' squished-up vegetables. It's the biggest part of the store, and everyone can see me. You two stay by the candy. I'm gonna scream like I saw a rat, then say it ran up my dress and pull it up to my panties. While I'm screamin', y'all grab candy and run."

"What if Little Kwong ring his bell?"

"He gonna be too busy lookin' at my panties. He ain't gonna look at y'all."

"Oooh girl, you too much," Paula said.

"Honey, I don't watch movies for nothin'. Every time a boy sees a half-naked girl, his thing stick out."

"Naw it don't. My brother turn off the TV when girls wearin' swimsuits come on," Promise said.

"Silly bitch, ain't nobody stuttin' your sissy brother. Just don't mess up my plan," LaKeisha said.

"All I got to say is I hope your draws is clean," Paula hummed.

"Shut up, silly bitch. At least I *got* some on."

****

A little later, the three girls stepped into the store. Luck was on their side.

Mrs. Kwong barely looked at them. She was glued to the TV. Little Kwong dozed on his perch. Mr. Kwong was nowhere to be seen. A few shoppers lingered in the dim aisles. LaKeisha drifted toward the fruit and vegetables. Paula and Promise hung by the candy, pretending to watch TV.

LaKeisha reached a pile of sweet potatoes, then let out a screech. She danced and fanned her dress. Shoppers craned their necks. Paula glanced once and started stuffing candy in her pockets.

Promise stared, amazed at LaKeisha's nerve. She was actually showing her blue underwear with yellow daisies. A bell rang.

Promise turned to see Little Kwong's glittering eyes.

Paula darted out the door. LaKeisha yanked Promise's hand to pull her out too. But Promise stood frozen.

LaKeisha let go and shot out the door.

A buzzer buzzed. A loud click.

Promise snapped out of her trance and ran. But the door was locked.

Her thin arms couldn't budge it. A hand grabbed her shoulder.

Mrs. Kwong.

In one hand, she held a small black box with two red buttons. She pointed it at Promise, who stood trembling with her back against the glass.

A vibration.

The door didn't move.

Promise felt warm water trickling down her leg.

Mrs. Kwong smiled and clicked the box again.

Promise was locked inside.

*****

Promise found herself in the back of the store staring into the meat case. For the longest time, she'd believed meat was "pieces of dead people" and refused to go near the steaks or planks of ribs. She never connected the meat on her plate with the flesh oozing blood in the Styrofoam trays. It wasn't until she saw Big Mama ring a chicken's neck and strip off the feathers that she accepted meat came from live animals.

Kwong's thin steaks didn't ooze blood but looked blackened and clotted. The ropes of ground sausage lay coiled like skinless snakes. Promise wrinkled her nose and stuck her tongue out at the rock-sized ham hocks and knotted oxtails wrapped in yellowish fat. Sometimes, a mouse or two scampered over the chunks of cheese.

Her favorite item in the case was the giant hog heads that stared dead-eyed.

The first time she saw them, she was four and holding Jonathan's fingers. He suddenly placed her hand against the glass—right over a hog's big snout. She screamed and fainted. For days, she recoiled from Jonathan. It took weeks of candy and popsicles to win her back, and even longer for her to trail behind him to the store again.

She wasn't afraid of the hog heads today. Two of them sat in the case. One looked smug, as if staring out into a world of lesser beings. The other appeared drunk, its tongue hanging from its mouth. Promise shook her fist at them, then turned and shook her backside. Someone grunted.

She jumped, startled, and turned to meet the blinking eyes of Sidney the Butcher.

"Go 'head on, Miss Pee—shake your stuff," Sidney teased.

A hot flash of shame surged through her. She slid to another section of the meat case, pretending to examine the bacon. But Sidney's high-pitched voice grated again.

"Hey Miss Pee, what time's your brother's funeral?"

"My name is Promise Suzette Goodday," she said firmly. She hated being called Pee. It reminded her of a toilet. Even LaKeisha Ann never called her that. Silly Bitch, maybe—but never Pee.

"I didn't ask your name, Miss Thing. I asked what time the funeral was. One o'clock or two?"

"It's at two. At St. John Divine Lord Jesus Christ Holiness Church on Bishop Street." She rose on her tiptoes and fluttered her eyelashes at him. Sidney's eyes never stopped blinking. LaKeisha Ann had dubbed him "Turn Signal Sidney."

"I ain't ask you all that. I know the name of the church and where it's at. And you better get off them tiptoes before you hurt yourself. You ain't no ballerina."

"Why you always talk like my brother, calling people Miss Thing? My Big Mama says men ain't supposed to do that."

"Miss Thing—your Big Mama a man?"

Promise shrugged. She knew the answer, but didn't follow Sidney's logic. Was he crazy?

"You mean you don't know whether your Big Mama's a man or a woman? Lord have mercy," Sidney cackled.

"Naw, my Big Mama ain't no man!"

"Well then, how she know how a man supposed to act?"

Promise had no comeback. She wished LaKeisha Ann were here—she always had words that turned Sidney's blinking eyes watery and his skin red as a sweet potato. But all Promise could do was gape.

"You be sure and tell Marsha Sidney the Butcher sends his sympathy. And tell your Big Mama I grieves over her loss. That'll make her feel good." His eyes paused blinking for a moment as he chuckled, then picked back up like a strobe. "Can you remember all that, Miss Pee?"

Promise nodded and turned away.

"Why Jonathan gotta be friends with Sidney?" she thought. "He ugly and his eyes don't stop blinking. The War Boys ought to shoot him with their Uzis."

She walked down an aisle past jars of pickled pig's feet, wrinkling her nose as if she could smell the vinegar. At the flower cooler, she paused. Bright red lilies and pink carnations greeted her. A small bundle of vivid white roses stood upright in a plastic tube, bound in yellow string. Stalks of celery and parsley were tossed in among the flowers, like a little garden. A red milk carton with a cow in a garland of roses smiled at her.

The display struck Promise as something sacred. The sight filled her with longing. The money pinned to her chest scratched her breastbone.

Astroworld!

The word blazed across her mind in a vision. The amusement park was everything LaKeisha Ann had promised: candy, soda, cherry ice cream, and mountains made of sugar. "Hot dogs as long as Lyons Avenue."

Promise turned from the flowers and bounced over to the soda cooler. She plunged her hand into the cold ice water and pulled out a can of grape soda. At the counter, she unpinned the handkerchief from her undershirt.

"NowLaters," she said, pointing to a square pack of grape candy.

Mrs. Kwong rose from her milk crate and leaned over. Promise flattened both palms on the Formica. The handkerchief with the money bloomed in her left hand. Mrs. Kwong squinted at it like a suspicious cat. She grabbed the corner and picked at the knot with her fingernails. When that failed, she used her teeth. Promise frowned but said nothing. At last, the money freed, Mrs. Kwong held it up to the light. Satisfied, she grabbed the candy from the rack.

"Ah, good girl, Promise," she said.

Promise remembered what LaKeisha Ann said: *"I bet she got a sideways crack in her ass from sitting on that crate all day."*

Promise looked up and smiled as Mrs. Kwong rang her up.

"Do your mama want her flower too, Promise?"

Promise flinched. "Shoot. Mama must've told her about the funeral. And about the flower."

She stared into Mrs. Kwong's mirrored shades—and swore she saw Jonathan. She'd seen her reflection a thousand times, never thought she looked like anyone but herself. People said she looked like Big Mama. She always denied it. She used to cast spells with her lucky penny on anyone who said she looked like Sharon Pearl Jones.

But here, in Kwong's Market, Jonathan's large bright eyes stared back at her through the glasses.

"Promise? You okay?" Mrs. Kwong asked.

Jonathan's voice echoed: *"Girl, if you want to keep Big Mama's switch off your back, you better learn how to lie on your feet."*

"Oh!" Promise said. She looked directly into the spot she thought held Mrs. Kwong's gaze. "Mama just want some change now."

Mrs. Kwong looked puzzled. "Are you sure?"

"Yes," Promise said. "She gotta pay her insurance man. But he gonna give her a check." That part was true.

"Ahh. Okay. Poor Marsha. Take the flowers anyway. Tell your mama she can pay me when she cash her check, okay?"

"Yes, ma'am," Promise replied politely.

Mrs. Kwong went to the cooler and carefully removed the white roses in their plastic sleeve. She twisted newspaper around them and pressed them into Promise's arms. The flowers felt cold and sticky on her skin. She let them drop to her side.

Mrs. Kwong bagged the candy and soda along with the change.

Outside, Promise's shoulders dropped. *"Girl, you sure worked that lie,"* she heard Jonathan say.

She peeked into the sack. The money was crushed against the cold soda—a tangled mess of bills so green they made her swoon. She had to hold on to the wall to steady herself.

"Cold cash!" she sang, remembering her Uncle Bobo's favorite phrase. "Cold cash! Cold cash!"

Chapter 6 – The Number 10 is Never Late

Pete reached the end of the line. Route Number Ten stopped at a freight train switching yard—Settegast. He stared out the windshield at the maze of steel rails and gravel. Locomotives pushed and pulled boxcars, tankers, and gondolas. There weren't as many men on the job anymore. When he first started driving this route, the yard had been alive with overalled men jumping between cars, coupling and uncoupling boxcars to locomotives and cabooses.

Now? That work was done by some invisible force in a tower with black-glass windows. The cabooses had been abandoned to weed-choked sidetracks. A few men still roamed the yard with walkie-talkies, but they were just arms and legs for the ones in the tower.

The Tower of God, Pete thought.

To his left stood Jack's Market—a low-slung store with flickering yellow lights claiming it was open. The place looked dead. The windows were dark. The one-eyed owner (also named Jack) was likely thumbing through the tattered dictionary he kept near his Bible, lips moving as he sounded out words. Pete used to wonder where all those words were going, but his uncle had once told him, "A man of few words is a wise man." That had settled it.

More importantly, Pete knew he could buy a beer there and guzzle it behind the bus without anyone calling the company to snitch.

He stepped down from the bus and walked to the far side, hidden from both the store and the tower. He pulled out his dick and took a long piss. When his bladder was empty, he gave himself a hard shake and paused. His meat still dangled from his trousers. He stood still, shadowed by the side of the bus. A patch of weeds swayed behind him. Beyond that, the boulevard hummed with traffic.

A breeze could part the weeds, and someone driving by might catch a glimpse.

That idea excited him.

But today, the air was still. Even the sun ducked behind a bowl-shaped cloud.

He wasn't worried about Jack seeing anything. That man's one eye was probably trailing his own finger along the page, brushing over words like *ego*, *fuck*, *fusion*, *pussy*, *topiary*, on its way to *zealot*. Pete imagined Jack's dick pressed to the edge of the counter, leaking in time with the syllables.

He looked toward the black-glass tower. *Maybe they saw me*, he thought. *Maybe they're up there with their rods out too—jerking off together on a glass floor slick with lust.* If a woman was with them, she'd ruin the mood. Unless she was a dyke—then she might just bang on the window and high-five him.

But Pete didn't trust women. Their dignity, their pride—it was all a performance. All women were whores.

To prove that, he reached into his back pocket and pulled out a pair of panties. He'd taken them from his last victim. She had been happy to suck his dick for ten dollars—until she laughed at him. She ruined everything with that laugh.

He thought he'd called her Jackie.

The panties now lay in a yellowed heap at his feet.

If there's a dyke up there, he thought, *she's probably enjoying these too.*

He began to stroke himself, pulling and jerking like something irksome clung to him. His body trembled. Eyes closed. When he finished, he sprayed the panties. As his breathing slowed, he lit a cigarette and let the sun dry his dick.

He thought again of Jackie.

Hope her plane crashes into the Grand Canyon.

****

"Well, one thing's for sure," Jackie said after he rolled off her, "you're not the Leaky Eye."

His dick flopped against his thigh, limp as a dead chicken's neck. Nothing had happened—just him puffing and scraping against her belly while she stared at the clock, willing it to ring.

All he heard was ringing in his head and some whore's voice begging him to stop.

****

Pete looked down. His trousers were still open. The panties on the ground were dotted with wet spots the size of dimes.

Jackie done taught that boy I ain't no man, he thought. *A good ass-beatin' might set him straight. Lucky my Uncle ain't around. He'd have his finger up his ass or his dick in his mouth by now. And that white gal flouncing around my house, looking at me like I'm some kind of zoo coon. Him talkin' proper like some kinda faggot. I'd stop all that dental work, too. Let that nigger's teeth grow crooked like snake bones.*

His head buzzed. *If that bitch was in a grave next to my Uncle—or better, lying broken at the bottom of the Grand Canyon—my eyes would clear up, and the whining in my head would stop.*

Ever since I married her, my troubles started. Shouldn't have gotten her pregnant with that bastard.

He spat next to the panties and kicked them under the bus. Then he zipped up.

Back on board, Pete gave the rail yard one last glance before pulling away. The bus rumbled beneath the tower's shadow as he spoke aloud to no one.

"Be back in a couple hours."

Then quieter: "Then it's a case of beer... and a lesson that boy ain't gonna forget. And that gal too, if she's there."

Chapter 7 – The Omen

"Cold Cash! Cold Cash," Promise sang, still giddy from lying to Mrs. Kwong. She walked in the opposite direction—away from her uncle, his buddies, and Paradise Gardens. She stopped at the first bus stop she came to. Black blocky letters marked the bus routes. None of it made any sense: "Seventy-seven," "Ten," "Fifteen Express." The map with colored zigzag lines only made it worse.

LaKeisha Ann had said all Number Ten buses with yellow stripes went to Astroworld. Just be a woman and ask the bus driver what bus goes where, she had said. *They'll tell a woman anything she wants to know.*

"School buses are yellow," Promise thought. "And they're going to Astroworld today, so what Lakeisha Ann said must be true."

She noticed a bench near the stop. The backrest was shaped like a wooden cowboy. If you sat down, it looked like you wore an oversized ten-gallon hat. The bench advertised a car dealership that promised "Texas Sized Lincolns In Every Garage." The hat and its shady brim tempted Promise to sit—but her uncle might spot her and send her home.

She threw the flowers on the bench and stood behind the cowboy hat, peeping and sipping her drink. The soda burned her throat when she gulped, and some squirted from her nose. A purple splotch stained her dress.

Promise took the wet money from the sack and tried to clean herself, but the bills only smeared the stain wider. She worried for a moment about wearing a dirty dress to Astroworld. The thought of sneaking home to change crossed her mind, but LaKeisha Ann was sprawled on the porch. There was no way to get past her.

She took another sip. This time, the sweetness slid coolly down her throat. She forgot the stain and jammed the money in her breast pocket.

Promise watched LaKeisha Ann's arms sweep like a kitten chasing string. Even from a distance, she knew her friend was playing jacks.

"She got some nerve," Promise muttered. "That cheater, playing jacks on my porch."

Promise wanted to call out and fan LaKeisha's nose with the *cold cash* cooling her chest. She imagined rolling the cold soda can across LaKeisha Ann's face—flattening her nose and lips as it rolled toward her skinny neck.

It was LaKeisha Ann who once said on the playground that Promise's family ate nothing but beans. *"Bean cakes for breakfast, bean soup for lunch, and bean stew for supper."*

The name "Bean" had stuck for a while. All names did. Any name people threw at her clung like a sore. Didn't matter if it was her uncle calling her "Goose" or "Pee"—the names stayed until someone found a new one.

But today she was Promise Suzette Goodday, and she would remind anyone who forgot.

Her chest swelled with her *riches.* The shiny blocks of candy mixed with the money like jewels.

"Ho! Ho! Ho!" Promise said, mimicking Santa Claus. With a grand sweep of her arm, she pulled a candy from the sack and placed it on her tongue. The grape flavor filled her mouth with water.

She took a swig of soda, smacked her lips, and wiped her mouth with her sleeve—just like her uncle and his buddies. She laughed when the cold soda splashed her chin and slid down her neck.

She closed her eyes. In her mind, LaKeisha Ann stood before her in ragged clothes, hands outstretched.

Promise moved the candy to the side of her mouth and spat purple spit. LaKeisha Ann dropped to her knees and licked it up. The whole Jackson family crouched at Promise's feet, licking the spit like hogs. LaKeisha Ann's father jumped from his car to get his share. He slapped LaKeisha on the butt and made her move over.

Promise stood over them like a queen, laughing.

Her imagination ran like a kaleidoscope until a car backfired and startled her.

She sighed. There was no way to let LaKeisha Ann know how rich she was *and* still run off to Astroworld. LaKeisha was a tattletale. She'd get Promise in trouble with Mama or worse, Big Mama.

Presents! Promise thought. She'd bring everyone gifts. She pictured long hot dogs, gold chains, dolls, pretty sweaters—all displayed behind glass at Astroworld, just waiting for her to choose.

Cars gathered in front of her apartment. A long black car pulled up. A man in a black suit stepped out, tugged his sleeves, and stood by the door. Other cars lined up behind him.

People walked up the porch as if approaching a tomb. They paused at LaKeisha Ann and continued inside her family's half of the duplex.

A silver car nearly as long pulled to the curb. A dark-skinned man in a white shirt and greenish pants got out and pulled a checkered green-and-black coat from the back seat.

Then a stout woman pushed herself from the passenger side. She glanced up and down the street like she was lost—or scared. Her face glowed like tarnished gold.

Promise stuck out her lips. Her Aunt Susan and Uncle Stewart, with that wart on his forehead, always barged in like social workers—inspecting, judging.

Uncle Stewart complained about paying taxes to support "lazy niggers." Aunt Susan scolded Marsha like a schoolteacher.

Each carried a bag of groceries up the steps. Promise imagined Big Mama's crocodile tears of thanks. Her daughter—*the one she couldn't live with,* even though she had a four-bedroom home in Candle Light Trails and no kids.

Her mother, as usual, would stay behind the bedroom door with Nettie until the last minute, before emerging to meet insult with insult. Sometimes it ended with pulled hair—sister versus sister—while Big Mama and Uncle Stewart pleaded and refereed.

A loud clattering broke her thoughts. An old woman pushed a shopping cart full of cat food cans and rags straight toward her, as if Promise were invisible.

The woman wore a thick green-and-white skirt—a cross between a window awning and a burlap bag. Underneath: dirty khakis and fresh red-and-white Chuck Taylors.

A tattered Cardinals baseball cap rested sideways on her gray plats. She grabbed the bench, pulled herself around, and dropped onto it with a huff.

She fanned herself with the cap. A faint scent of pee drifted through the air.

She peered over the cowboy hat and stretched one eye wide. The other lid stayed shut, making her look like a Cyclops.

"Who you there, Little Bit?" she crowed.

"Promise!" she shouted, hoping to shut down any nickname attempt.

"Who you Promise?"

"Promise Goodday."

"Well good morning, Promise Goodday," the woman cackled.

"Hi," Promise said shyly. She studied the woman's weather-beaten face and jutting plat.

"Who are you?"

"Oh, they call me anything. But I think my mama named me Mandybell Harper-McGee. She was crazy about two men—one named Harper, one McGee. One was her daddy, one was mine. Is your mama crazy?"

Promise shook her head. She thought about Nettie but said nothing.

"You a good girl to go with that Goodday name?"

"I be good... almost."

"What you mean *almost*?"

Promise shrugged.

"What's that you got in your breast pocket?"

"Nothing," she said slowly.

"Aw, it's *something*. Something got you looking like you got three titties."

Heat rushed to Promise's face. The woman laughed as Promise dipped her head.

"I bet one of them tits is money. Don't worry, I don't want it." She shook a cat food can. "This here's money. I steal it outta Stop N Sack's and sell it cheap to some white woman for her cats. She say it's for her cats, but I think she eats it herself."

She looked Promise up and down, lingering on the purple stains.

"Give me one of them candies you eatin'."

"How you know I got candy?"

"Either you eatin' candy or death done turned your tongue purple."

Promise handed her a NowLater. The woman popped it in her mouth, unwrapped and all.

When she cackled, Promise saw she had only one tooth left—snuff-colored and leaning sideways.

"You a pistol, starin' at me like I ain't pretty. Where you headed all dressed up?"

Promise hesitated.

The woman stretched her eyes, waiting.

"Astroworld," Promise finally said.

"What's that?"

"It's a fun place."

"I went to a fun place once," the old woman said. "They stripped me buck naked and threw cold water on me. I ain't been back since." She cackled again. "You's a pistol," she said.

"Astroworld is for children to—"

"Who flowers is these?" the woman interrupted.

Promise looked at the roses in the woman's hands. She remembered the argument between her mother and Big Mama.

"Nobody's," she said softly.

"They mine now," the woman said, stripping off the newspaper. "I give you one if you help me pick up cans."

"I gotta go to Astroworld."

The old woman shrugged and rose. She picked scraps of newspaper from the grass and read them.

"Bad nigger!" she shouted and tossed one away. Then she smiled at a lingerie ad and tucked it inside a cat food can.

"Mash him with your foot!" she barked suddenly.

Promise froze.

"I said mash that nigger with your foot!"

Frightened, Promise stomped the crumpled paper into the soft earth.

"That devil-eye," the woman muttered.

"Was the Leaky Eye on that paper?" Promise asked.

The woman said nothing. She pulled her cap low and pushed her cart away.

"You do right, or right will do you," she called back.

That "do right" reminded Promise of the flowers... and Jonathan's funeral.

She called after the woman, but she kept going. Promise started to run after her—but a rumble made her turn.

A yellow-and-white city bus turned the corner.

On the porch, her mother spoke to LaKeisha Ann. LaKeisha jumped up and ran toward Kwong's Market.

The bus lumbered closer, yellow and white stripes like candy. Promise's heart leapt.

All that yellow must mean it's going to Astroworld.

She emptied the loose change into her hand and grabbed her soda. The bus rolled closer. In bold black letters: **10 Downtown**.

The doors whooshed open, and a rush of cold air brushed her shoulders.

Chapter 8 – Blind Man Driving the Bus

A woman with bulging shopping bags in each hand stood in the doorway.

Promise, eager to avoid LaKeisha Ann—who was walking down the sidewalk toward the bus stop—tried to squeeze by the bags.

"Gal, ain't you got no manners?"

Promise stepped back and let the woman pass, scowling as she did. She placed her foot on the step. The bus driver's finger stopped her.

"You can't bring an open can on the bus," he said, pointing at the purple soda can Promise held.

She stood on the bottom step, staring into the driver's brown face. Something was off. He wore dark shades, but under one lens, the flesh below his eye was noticeably lighter—like a half-moon had taken up residence on his cheek.

Promise stepped off to throw her soda in the trash. The bus lurched and huffed like it was about to pull away. Panic seized her. She cried out.

LaKeisha Ann loomed closer. She might have seen Promise struggling to board—if she hadn't been busy bouncing and catching a small red ball.

Promise thought: *If I miss this bus, I'll never get to Astroworld.*

The driver stomped the brakes, and the bus snorted like a donkey.

Pete yelled, "Come on, girl, I don't have all day!"

The doors closed behind Promise as she hurried on and dumped all her loose change into the coin box. The driver eyed the two quarters, one dime, blackened nickel, and five pennies.

"Where you going?" he asked.

"Astroworld."

Promise reached for her permission slip. The bus driver looked at it for a moment, then back at her. A smile flashed across his face—then vanished.

Promise squirmed. *Maybe I got on the wrong bus,* she thought. *Maybe LaKeisha Ann lied. Maybe all yellow-striped buses don't go to Astroworld.*

The driver touched his crotch and grinned. He tore off a green transfer slip and held it toward Promise. But as she reached for it, his hand dropped, and the slip fluttered toward the floor. He made a whirling gesture in the air, and her hand followed like a small bird chasing a drifting dandelion seed.

The bus began to move, and Promise stumbled into the driver.

"Man, I believe this chick is drunk," the driver chuckled to a man seated behind him.

He drove casually, as if Promise weren't even there. Her head spun. She grabbed the driver's sleeve to keep from falling. Tears filled her eyes.

The driver sighed when he saw her crying. He spoke in a softer tone.

"I'm just messin' with you. You're all right. Ol' Pete just being a dog. Your mama ever tell you about a dog?"

"No, sir," Promise replied, trying to steady herself.

"You got a dog?"

Promise shook her head.

"Well, I'm gonna be your dog. You can call me Spot, okay?"

Promise nodded, bewildered by the strange talk.

"All right then! You got yourself a dog. Now go sit down. And watch your step—your dog ain't housebroke."

The driver and his passenger burst out laughing as Promise stumbled down the aisle.

"Man," the passenger said, catching his breath, "you better not go diggin' for no bones in that yard. That dirt's too wet!"

"Shit, man," the driver said, "I ain't digging in nothing that fresh. That's more than jailbait—that's penitentiary bait."

They laughed harder. A woman sitting in a side-facing seat shook her head and smiled.

Promise dropped into an empty seat. The bus turned a corner, and Lyons Avenue appeared like a panorama through the large window. In one sweep, she saw Paradise Gardens, her uncle and his friends, and her school. LaKeisha Ann bounced her ball in front of Kwong's mural and stepped inside the store.

The corner where the War Boys waxed their cars and revved engines vanished as the bus crossed a busy avenue.

She'd ridden the bus before—with grownups.

Alone, she felt like she was hurtling toward the end of the world.

The feeling of being lost hit her. *What if I never make it back home?*

The bus picked up speed, dragging her deeper into the unknown.

The cord to signal a stop hung too high. She thought of running up front, begging the driver to let her off—to take her back. But she remembered his mocking laughter, his scolding.

The itchy tweed seat scratched the backs of her thighs.

A woman across the aisle noticed her.

"Relax, baby," she said kindly. "That man up there knows how to drive a bus—if he don't know nothing else."

Then she returned to the book in her lap.

Her calm voice reassured Promise, though it wasn't the bus driver's skills that bothered her. The woman's book cover, blazing in red and gold, caught Promise's attention. In the middle of a red heart, a couple kissed, arms wrapped tightly around each other. Promise thought of Sugar Face and Astroworld. Her shoulders relaxed. Maybe this woman was going to Astroworld, too. Her yellow blouse and shiny yellow pants certainly looked like something a person would wear to a fun place.

Promise glanced down at her own yellow shorts poking out from beneath the hem of her dress and wished she'd worn her yellow sneakers instead of the dirty white bunny slippers.

She noticed the high seatbacks and how they rose above people's heads like thrones. She looked at her own seat and smiled, feeling like a queen. Tucking her legs under her, she sat up taller to get a better view out the window and fished a Nowlater candy from her sack.

"If only that bus driver hadn't made me throw away my soda," she thought as the bus glided down the road.

The bus crossed a wide bayou, its banks lined with smooth, manicured grass. Then suddenly—like magic—mansions began appearing in the windows. Promise's small mouth fell open in awe. These houses looked like castles, frosted in gingerbread and buttercream. Lawns sparkled with fountains tossing water into the air. Some had sleek cars parked out front, like the one her uncle drove for Mr. Fritz. The "castles" nestled among tall, reaching trees that played with the sun.

Promise scanned for children playing, but saw none. She wondered if Mr. Fritz and his wife lived in one of these houses. Maybe the Leaky Eye couldn't get her out here, she thought. In her neighborhood, he slithered from shack to shack, disguised as a snake or a rat. But maybe in this place, he pretended to be a fluffy white cat. Promise imagined well-dressed women bending to pet him—and him suddenly turning into a raging black thing with claws.

These houses need children, Promise thought. Kids always saw the Leaky Eye and chased him away. Except Paula. He still got her and "ruint" her. Grown folks used that word like it meant something real bad. Maybe it was. Nobody had seen Paula since. It was like she was dead.

"Where you going, baby?" the woman in yellow asked, lowering her book and smiling.

"Astroworld," Promise answered.

"Astroworld? By yourself?"

"My school is going."

The woman looked around. "I don't see no school on here."

Promise sensed her plan might unravel. "I missed the bus earlier. They already there." She scooted to the edge of her seat and held out her permission slip.

The woman glanced at the paper and then at Promise's feet. She shrugged.

"You'll need to transfer. Did the bus driver give you a transfer?"

Promise showed her the green slip, with holes punched through numbers.

"Yeah, you'll need that to catch the number four, I think. The bus driver'll tell you."

Promise relaxed. Lakeisha Ann had said the same thing. She'd wait to ask the driver—maybe after his laughing buddy got off the bus.

"These sure are some pretty homes," the woman in yellow said before picking up her book again.

Promise thought so too. But the yards seemed empty without kids running around or folks out front laughing, talking, and drinking beer. She imagined filling those lawns with her friends and cheerful grown-ups. She'd even let one or two of those growling blues singers shout from behind the red and purple flowers near the porch. But the rest of the yard she'd save for boys—cute ones like Sugar Face who'd make her and the other girls squeal.

She remembered going to City Park with Mama, Uncle Bobo, and Lakeisha Ann. No "pretty houses" there, just grown-ups under trees eating barbecue and listening to blues howl from a stage. Those "my woman left me" and "that no-good dirty dog" ballads spiraled through the smoke from barbecue pits. That "whang dang doodle" poured from red and blue beer cans and made folks dance silly and shout out the love and pain bottled inside.

Big Mama always stayed home with Nettie on Juneteenth when the blues took over the park. She said she wouldn't go near that heathen music. Promise kind of agreed. The food, the soda water, the ice cream, and all the running around were fun—but those sweaty men and women growling on stage didn't seem "fly," as Lakeisha Ann would say.

"Girl, you wouldn't catch Sugar Face standing on stage growling at folks like that," Lakeisha Ann once said. "That's old folks' music."

"But Sugar Face 'sposed to be here today," Promise whined. "Uncle Bobo said he was. It's on this paper."

"Look, silly bitch, can't you read? It say here 'Sugar Beets and the Turnip Green Band.' That ain't no Sugar Face." Lakeisha Ann threw the flyer on the ground.

Promise picked it up. A pot-bellied man with fingers full of rings cradled his cheek and smiled up at her.

****

The houses shrank as the bus continued its journey. Three and four at a time filled the window with pastel blue, pink, and yellow facades. Patches of grass competed with old tires, tin cans, and the rusted bones of cars. Brown children ran across narrow yards and played in the ditches. Earth-colored men with forearms thick as stones spilled out of the houses onto porches.

The woman in yellow pulled the cord, and the bus slowed and stopped. Promise watched as a man ran up and kissed the woman the moment her feet hit the sidewalk. She tousled his hair while he playfully patted her on the rear.

Love, Promise thought.

Suddenly the bus hummed with life as Mexican women and children boarded, plopping noisily into the high seats. They brought the blues and yellows of the houses with them—in their puffed dresses and matching shoes. The women spoke loudly, half-singing as they scolded their children to behave.

Two girls around Promise's age, in puffy white and blue dresses, sat where the woman had sat across from her. Their duck-shaped mother sat behind them, speaking Spanish and reaching over to smooth their hair.

Promise eyed the girls' hair—it fell over their shoulders like dark silk scarves. She imagined cutting some off and pinning it to her own head. Promise closed her eyes, and she and Sugar Face were dancing all over Astroworld. She swung her hair, and it fell in soft waves across her shoulders. Gangs of boys ran up and tried to kiss her. They fought Sugar Face. One boy pulled a knife. Just as he aimed for Sugar Face's heart, Promise blew on her magic penny—and the boy fell dead.

The girls giggled, yanking Promise out of her daydream. The girl in pale blue stuck out her tongue first. Her sister followed. Their mother saw them, grabbed them both by the hair. They howled in pain.

Promise sat with her lips poked out. She remembered the Nowlaters. The crackling cellophane drew the girls' eyes. From the corner of her eye, Promise watched them watching her as she placed a piece of candy in her mouth. She pulled it out, examined it, then placed it back in her mouth—over and over—while their eyes tracked her every move until their mother cuffed their heads.

As the motor droned on, Promise grew restless. She craned her neck to see if the tall Astroworld tower was in sight. LaKeisha Ann had said you could see Africa from the tower. But all she saw was a water tower. She began thinking to herself:

Why the Bus Driver driving so slow? Maybe he can't see. That's why he's wearing dark shades. He's a blind man. Why they let a blind man drive a bus? And he's stupid too. He right to call himself a dog 'cause he sure look like one. Hurry up, blind man! Hurry up and drive this bus to Astroworld!

The bus stopped downtown and unloaded near Woolworth's. She watched the mother of the rude girls push them ahead of her. Promise looked around and wondered if she should get off too. The scent of buttered popcorn and a row of plastic dolls in plaid sundresses and grape-colored sandals beckoned from the Woolworth's window.

She thought of Sugar Face. *Sugar Face ain't at no Woolworth's. He's at Astroworld, waiting for his brown-skinned girl!* A warm feeling rushed through her. She felt grown when she called herself "girl." She popped another candy in her mouth and settled back into her "throne on wheels."

The bus pulled away from Woolworth's and made a left by a park. It leaned forward as it descended toward the tunnel. Promise hadn't noticed it coming. Suddenly—darkness slammed into the bus. The interior lights flickered, then flared brightly. The window turned into a dark mirror as the walls of the tunnel zipped past. She realized she hadn't combed her hair. And there was Jonathan—all in her eyes—looking like a frightened little girl.

She felt uneasy. Thought of home. Thought of Jonathan's funeral. She looked up at the cord that could stop the bus. *"Do right or right will do you,"* the old woman had shouted. A louder voice whispered now: *But what can you do now?* She felt sick in her stomach like she needed to go to the bathroom.

As suddenly as daylight disappeared, it returned. Promise sat back in her seat.

The sun, like a gold medallion, followed the bus as it rambled through the Bottoms. Abandoned warehouses and smokestacks pressed up against the backs of shacks, pushing them closer to the street. Bits of broken bottles glittered like emeralds and rubies on the narrow walks in front of the shotgun houses. Smoke and steam rose from the manholes.

Women in skimpy dresses darted into alleys. Some sat on porches, smoking cigarettes, watching the bus with narrowed eyes. Passengers inside the bus shook their heads and looked away.

A sign dangled by the front door of one of the empty houses: **CANDLELIGHT TRAILS: 15 MINUTES TO BLISSFUL LIVING**

Beneath the words were pictures of houses nestled in green hills with candlelit windows.

Those were the kinds of houses her Aunt Susan—her part namesake—called home. Promise had visited once.

There'd once been talk—just a whisper really—that her Aunt Susan might adopt her. After all, Marsha already had her hands full: a "feeble-minded" daughter, some wayward boys, and a no-good husband. So Promise had been sent—pressed up, dressed up—for what was supposed to be just a "weekend" with the aunt who had gray eyes, straight red hair, and a face the color of old school desks.

Rules were laid out like linens. Chores handed down like judgments. Uncle Stewart even built her a wooden box to stand on so she could reach the sink and wash dishes.

On the umpteenth time Promise asked when she was going back home, her question was answered with a slap to the face and a hissed reminder to *be grateful.* She was only six, but she remembered something Big Mama's minister had once said: *"It won't be water but fire next time."* All Promise knew about fire was that it hurt—and that it was hot.

So in her aunt's gleaming kitchen, she struck a match and dropped it in the trash can. The flames roared up and licked the walls as her aunt's husband hollered and aimed his red fire extinguisher. That fire earned her a ride back home.

Promise stuck her tongue out at the bus window as they passed a sign for Candlelight Trails.

The bus rolled forward and stopped in front of a large school building. Bold red letters on a sign read:

CITY COLLEGE AND VOCATIONAL SCHOOL.

A dozen women in dazzling white uniforms stood clumped together on the sidewalk.

"Angels," Promise whispered.

They boarded, chirping and clucking like birds in a wire cage, their necks turning toward the driver as if to peck at him.

"Hey, Funny Eyes," they hissed.

He gunned the motor, and the women stumbled into their seats, giggling. One plopped down next to Promise, smacking her gum.

They snickered and whispered among themselves. The driver kept checking the rearview mirror. One of the women stuck out her tongue.

"I wish he had passed us up like last time. I would've found out where he live and had my boyfriend beat his ass. Always looking at us with them funny eyes."

Promise looked up. The girl had ringlet curls and was pretty—until she frowned and cursed. She looked about the same age as LaKeisha Ann's older sister. Their grown-up talk made Promise want to lean in, tell them about her trip to Astroworld, and share secrets about boys like they were sisters.

She smiled at the girl beside her, but the girl turned her head and spoke to someone behind them.

"Chile, on Monday it's your turn to play with Mr. Pringle's ding-dong."

"Bitch, turn your ass around," the other girl snapped. "I ain't touching that ol' white man's dick."

The woman next to Promise laughed. "He can't do nothin'. He ain't got no balls. But if you don't, Miss Jones gonna give you an incomplete."

"I don't care if she do. I ain't touching that man."

"I bet if it was Fred laying there, you'd be glad to learn how to catheterize."

"Shit, Fred ain't lettin' me stick nothin' up his dick. Especially after I told him about that old man hollering."

"They say you gotta deal with that when you become a nurse."

The girl in back leaned over the seat and touched Promise's head with her long nails.

"Who that?" she asked, squinting at Promise's face.

"I'm going to Astroworld to see Sugar Face," Promise said, smiling proudly.

"You going to see Sugar Face?" The girls howled.

Promise turned away, cheeks burning.

"Who you on here with?" one of them asked.

The crooked smiles told Promise not to say she was alone. Girls like this one picked on smaller girls and took their money. She nodded toward the back of the bus.

The girl turned and spotted an old man in thick glasses blinking stupidly at the window.

"Well, I guess," she said. "I don't know what Sugar Face gonna do with you and gramps, but y'all go 'head on. Denise here got Mr. Pringle on her mind."

"Shit, I ought to transfer over to Court Reporting," Denise said beside Promise.

"Court Reporting? Bitch, you can't type. Remember Office Management? Before you finished typing your name, I had done typed half the damn page."

"Turn your little red ass around and think about Mr. Pringle's thang you held so sweet and gentle this morning," Denise fired back.

"And did you hear what Miss Jones told Betina? *'Make it hard so it'll be easy to stick the tube in.'*"

"That's stupid. How he supposed to get hard? He ain't got no nuts."

Another girl filed her nails and laughed. "And poor Betina was just massaging that thing. I started to tell her to blow on it."

"Ooh girl, you crazy!" the others howled.

"If Miss Jones had told her to, she would've done it. She would've flapped them fat lips of hers all over that dick. Looked like she was blowing a damn trumpet."

"Lord, have mercy."

"Betina do everything Miss Jones say. Got her uniform ironed, homework neat. Probably got her nose all up in Miss Jones' cootchie."

Laughter faded as the sky turned violet and thick raindrops splattered the windows. Denise stared out at the rain.

Promise craved a piece of candy—but was too afraid to unwrap the crackling cellophane and draw the sass-mouthed girls' attention back to her.

She needed noise. Quiet made her feel like people could hear her thoughts. At home, quiet meant Big Mama might catch her thinking about sugar water or sneaking into drawers she wasn't supposed to.

She scrunched her shoulders to hold her thoughts still. Her stomach growled.

Denise glanced at her, but before she could say anything, the girl behind them broke the silence.

"Lord, I'll be glad when they catch that 'Leaky Eye.'"

"You and me both," another said. "I heard he made one woman swallow after she sucked him."

"Lord! That filthy devil."

"Now he's starting to kill women."

"Ooh, girl, hush! I can't stand to think about it."

"Girl, a man is a terrible thing."

The talk of the Leaky Eye made Promise's skin crawl. She was afraid to look out the window. What if he was out there—riding in a car—looking up at her with those wet, runny eyes?

People called him a chameleon. LaKeisha Ann said that meant a lizard that could hide itself right under your nose. Some folks said the Leaky Eye was like that—changing into things. Dogs. Trees. Lizards.

Promise sank down in her seat.

****

The bus lumbered on.

Promise tried not to think of the Leaky Eye, perched like a black bird hidden in the trees, brushing the windows. The trees were thick, scraping against the glass like long, angry switches. She wondered if they were near a forest.

The girls were quiet now, half asleep. It felt safe to move. She raised up and peeked through the window. A break in the trees gave way to a glint of sunlight and a billboard. In big red letters, **ASTROWORLD** flashed like Christmas lights. Beneath it, a lit Ferris wheel twinkled, imitating motion. Next to it, a tall tower rose like a needle wearing a hat. A birthday cake hat—that's what LaKeisha Ann had called it.

Promise wondered how many stairs it would take to get to the top. Could she see Africa from up there? Could she reach up and pinch the man in the moon?

Her uncle was always talking about that "man in the moon."

"That nigger ain't got no more cash than the man in the moon."

"They ain't got no more sense than the man in the moon..."

She imagined what the moon people were like.

Mr. and Mrs. Moon kissing each other in their round moon houses while little moon children ran around naked in scaly skin.

Moon cars bumping into one another. Moon people climbing out to fight with moon guns. Moon dogs barking "woo! woo! woo!" with tails on their noses. Moon cats chasing moon rats until they turned into green cheese. A moon teacher spanking a moon boy for not doing his homework. Moon people with AIDS shitting purple cheese. Their moon Big Mamas cleaning them up and fussing about dying so young.

Did they have funerals on the moon? Did they come to Earth when they died?

LaKeisha Ann said the moon wasn't nothin' but a rock.

Promise wondered, *How can a rock shine?*

All that imagining made her sleepy. Her head bobbed like a puppet's, and soon her cheek was pressed against the cool glass, her eyes closed.

****

The young women left the bus just as noisily as they'd boarded, pulling the stop cord to get off at a convenience store for shelter from the rain. Pete ignored the bell at first, forcing them to yell and bang the windows. He finally stopped half a block past the sign. The women hopped off, shouting "fuck you!" and flashing middle fingers as they leapt over a wide puddle.

Pete slammed the doors and made sure the wheels kicked up a gusher of muddy water.

He turned down the road that led to the railyard. It was Saturday. No workmen waiting.

He flicked on the small radio resting on the dash.

Kind of Blue drifted from the speakers—Miles Davis.

Pete had thought the city was foolish for putting a bus route out here. Nobody rode it on Saturdays. But after a few weeks, he'd started to like the quiet. The solitude. The space to think. To talk to himself.

He was slipping, though. Getting careless. He hadn't even bothered to change out of his uniform earlier when he trailed the prostitute through that alley in the Fifth Ward. Usually, he chose places like cemeteries, warehouses, abandoned hospitals—those rubber mattresses made for decent cover. But this time? The house sat far back from the street, true. She hadn't screamed—didn't have time. But still...

She'd crawled through a busted window and leaned against a rusty box spring.

Hiked up her skirt.

Mouthed the words *"Ten dollars."*

He'd slammed his fist against her jaw.

Watched her face puff up like a mule's.

Twisted a handful of her hair and forced himself into her mouth.

When he finished and zipped up, she cursed him for not paying. "No-dick motherfucker."

That's when he felt it—the cartilage crunch in her throat, the bones soft under his hands.

He hadn't meant to kill her. He never meant to kill them.

Just wanted to teach a lesson.

He laid her body across the box spring. Curled her fingers around a broken bottle. Placed the other hand between her legs.

He thought about those "whores" who had just gotten off the bus. They needed to be taught a lesson.

Except one.

That girl who was always filing her nails.

He'd watched her in the rearview mirror. Caught her eyes—just for a second—before they dropped under her long lashes.

If she'd been alone, he might've stopped at the store. Let her run to safety. Maybe even offered the small fold-up umbrella he kept in his duffle. That would've opened a conversation. Maybe a phone number. Maybe she had a place of her own.

He imagined she did. She seemed like someone who thought a lot. That's what nail filing was—thinking.

She had her file. He had his hands.

What was she running from in her head?

Could they help each other?

He imagined lying between her blackberry nipples, her stroking his thick hair, coaxing his manhood to life—slow and gentle. No, Jackie, with her clock-watching and *"Get off me, you're making me tired"* routine.

The girl with the nail file would laugh. She'd guide him. Maybe even put her pink lace panties on his head like a crown while they made love.

When the babies came, there'd be no doubt they were his. Thick. Sturdy. Built like bulldogs—even the girls. Not some willowy-ass boy tall as a house.

Would the children have one gray eye and one brown?

Even if gray wasn't his natural eye color, could he pass it on? Would he want to? That eye was a gift from his uncle. And that wasn't no prize.

Pete sighed.

He wondered why he'd never gotten himself a real woman. The wife wasn't his idea. That was all because of *that boy*.

He'd had whores. But never a woman.

A real one. One who didn't judge him. One who didn't smell his shit and call him rotten.

Never found a place where he could go and get gifts of sweet-berried lips in a room quiet and warm as a womb.

He thought of his mother.

Hard as a jackhammer.

The last time he saw her, she had on men's clothes and a suitcase in hand, walking into the Greyhound station.

Never sent a letter before she died.

He sighed again. The bus was nearing the weedy spot where he parked at the end of the line.

Darkness settled over him.

He thought of the weight he carried.

The boy who wasn't his.

The woman who'd gone from soft cheerleader thighs to a shrill drill sergeant.

The mortgage was strapped to his back like a trunk.

The house that was supposed to be a shelter is now a burden.

Them sitting on his back like lions.

Some days it felt like he was carrying the damn bronze lions that stood at the entrance to Candlelight Trails.

What the fuck did he care about hills and woods?

Pete wiped his eyes and glanced at the rearview mirror.

At first, he thought someone had left a white sweater on the seat. Maybe the girl with the nail file.

Then he figured it was a pile of rags. Or maybe a doll.

"Niggers," he muttered.

But then a hand lifted. Rested against a cheek.

Promise.

She was still on the bus, sound asleep.

Pete pulled over and stared at her.

He smiled.

Kept driving.

Then glanced up at the mirror again.

"Old Coon Eyes," he chuckled to himself.

And tugged at his crotch.

Chapter 9 – War In His Heart

Voices sifted through Promise's dream. She stood in a large dimly lit room buzzing with voices. A dark blue coffin rested on a bier in the center. She peeked in. Big Mama's scowling head lay on satin pillows. Marsha, in a black silk robe, shouted from a pulpit. Uncle Bobo drove his boss' Lincoln through the wall like a ghost. Aunt Susan sat stiff and mean on the hood. The car disappeared down a long street. LaKeisha Ann came from behind and tried to kiss her. Promise pushed her away. LaKeisha Ann cried, her tears soaking her white dress.

A hand touched Promise's shoulder. Rain tapped the window like grains of sand. The sky was the color of gray cats. Her face was wet and sticky. She blinked at the bus driver's nametag. **PETE**. A gold star glinted beside it.

"Honey, I almost forgot about you," Pete said with a smile.

Promise sat up and looked out the window. Her eyes widened. Through tall weeds, trains twisted like a river. Tank cars crept over the tracks like pill bugs. Cows mooed in time with the whistles. Gondolas strained under sand and oyster shells. Boxcars clanged. Black logs lay in a ditch. A tower rose in the center of the yard, its black pointed roof like a witch's hat.

Promise bounced to the opposite window. Her shoulders slumped at the scattered low houses and a store flashing yellow lights: JACKS.

"This ain't Astroworld," she shrieked.

"No, baby, this is the end of the line," Pete said.

"But I thought this bus had yellow on it. It said Number Ten on the front."

"It's as yellow as I am brown," Pete said.

She looked for the women who'd been chattering—but now there was only rain. She slumped into her seat.

"Metro didn't tell me nothing 'bout Astroworld. They told ol' Pete to drive the Number Ten from Downtown to Fifth Ward, from Fifth Ward to River Oaks, from River Oaks to The Bottoms, and out to the Yard."

Promise looked at his eyes. He'd taken off his shades and held a bottle of eyedrops. One eye looked like a cat's, with a white circle. She couldn't tell if he was looking at her or through her.

"Did I pick you up from The Bottoms?" Pete asked.

"The bottom of what?" Promise asked, confused.

"Don't you and your sister hang out there?" Pete teased.

"I don't have a sister," Promise lied. In her mind, she never counted Nettie as anything but a big lumpy bag Big Mama fussed over.

"I could've sworn you was a Bottoms girl. Where'd I pick you up from?"

"I got on at Lyon's Avenue, I think."

"You think?"

Promise picked at her hair. She remembered walking down Lyon's, sitting on the porch with Uncle Bobo and his friends, the man with the long neck, the house where the Leaky Eye had killed someone, Kwong's Market, Sidney's blinking eyes. She remembered slipping away and catching the first bus she saw. But she wasn't sure if it was Bishop or Lee Street.

"I got on in Fifth Ward," she said quietly.

"Fifth Ward sure is the bottom," Pete laughed.

Promise looked down. She knew enough to know "bottom" meant something bad. She wished LaKeisha Ann was there. She'd know what to say to this funny-eyed man—make his jaws tremble, fists clench. But he wouldn't hit her. Men didn't hit girls. Not unless they wanted jail.

"You too pretty to be a Bottoms girl," Pete said, tugging at his crotch. Promise turned to the window.

"What's your name, honey?" he asked sweetly.

"Promise," she said, lowering her head. She touched her knees. They felt bony and familiar.

"Promise is a sweet name. The world lives on promises. Without you the world would die."

Everyone said her name meant something good, like it had magic.

"And I'm Pete. How about I get us a soda water?"

She remembered Mama's and Big Mama's warnings. She stood and placed her hands on her hips.

"I thought we couldn't bring soda water on the bus."

"That's when the bus is moving. I'm taking a break."

A cold grape soda would go good with her NowLaters. She remembered LaKeisha Ann saying the best lies had a little truth in them.

"No, sir, I don't want no soda water right now."

Pete smiled and winked. She turned her head.

"Sit down, honey. Astroworld's not too far. Those trains over there—taking stuff to Astroworld."

"For real?" she asked.

"For real."

"They got cows at Astroworld?" she asked, listening to the mooing.

Pete ignored her and motioned for her to sit. She did. He sat next to her, stretched his leg, flexed his foot.

"A real pretty girl rode this bus last week. Pretty like you. She had pigtails and sand-colored skin. You ever been to the beach?"

Promise thought of Galveston—gray water, brown sand, wiry grass. She went once with Jonathan. She expected ships and whales, but all she saw was dancing men in a big playpen. People threw money at them. Big Mama had fussed at Jonathan for taking her "around a bunch of sissies."

"Sand is ugly," Promise said.

Pete looked over. She was just a shadow in the window.

"You're thinking of Galveston. I'm talking Corpus Christi. You know what that means?"

She shook her head.

"Body of Christ," Pete said smugly. "The sands are white until the sun turns them copper. Like that girl's skin. She had teeth shiny as pearls."

Promise thought of her lucky penny. "She looked like a penny?" she asked.

"Naw," Pete laughed. "Her skin was brown...sweet, sweet brown. You know what pearls are?"

She thought of Jonathan in Big Mama's wig and church beads, strutting around.

"Yeah, I know what pearls are," she said.

"Yeah?" he asked, raising an eyebrow.

"I mean, yes sir."

"That's more like it. Pete don't like his women sassy. The girl I'm talking about was nice and polite."

"Did she go to Astroworld?" Promise asked.

"Yes, she did," Pete lied. "Cute boys played with her hair. Bought her candy."

"I like NowLaters," Promise said, holding up her half-pack. "Grape."

"That's nice," Pete said, slightly annoyed. "Don't you want to hear how they kissed her and showed her their muscles?"

Promise stared out the window. The sky was darker now. She saw her reflection—no long hair, no shiny brown skin. Her bangs flipped like a cap. A tuft stuck out by her left ear.

"My hair ain't long and I'm the color of dooky," she said softly.

"What did you say?" Pete leaned closer.

"I said I'm ugly."

Pete smiled. "You're the color of what?"

"Dooky?" she said. She didn't know if it was a bad word. But what else could she say?

"Honey, who told you that?"

"Big Mama."

"And what color is Big Mama?"

"She's black as the ace of spades."

Pete's face twitched. His chest rose like he might cry. Then he howled and slapped his knees. Promise jumped.

Pete laughed until he wheezed. His howls echoed through the empty bus. Promise looked at the floor. A dirty penny lay next to a wad of gum.

If only she had her lucky penny. She'd whisper a prayer and turn him into a frog.

Pete's laughter faded into hiccups. His smile dulled to somberness, as if he'd remembered his troubles. Eyes wet, he stared at Promise—from her white dress stained purple to her skinny legs and bunny slippers. He rubbed his face and held his temples as if squeezing something out. Then he got up and paced.

"I'm going to make a man out of you," Pete heard his uncle say.

Pete shivered in the cold room. His uncle had made him strip. Miles Davis' "Summertime" drifted from the funeral home's speaker as Lazarus Chesterfield prepared a little girl's body for viewing. She'd been hit by a car. Her body was mostly intact, except for a jutting arm bone and a rib poking from her side. Her right cheek was scraped, but otherwise she looked asleep, like she might wake up and reach for her dolls.

As his uncle repaired the girl's face with rouge and powder, he fondled himself—and Pete. Pete watched her blood flow from a tube in her neck into a toilet, where it turned the water plum purple. Lazarus came inside the girl's pink panties, then sewed the incision closed, dressed her in a white shroud with a purple bodice, and gently placed her in the coffin.

"Get dressed, boy. I've had enough of your punkish ways," his uncle said as he left.

Pete looked at Promise in her purple-stained dress. He thought of the young woman he'd killed the other day.

"But this is a little girl," a voice whispered.

"I'm going to make a man out of you," his uncle's voice answered.

The voices fought, a whining in Pete's head growing louder—like an embalming machine. Until he couldn't take it anymore. He looked at Promise and went to work.

"Don't listen to your Big Mama," he said softly. "You're a pretty girl. See my eyes?"

Promise looked up into one gray and one brown eye.

"These eyes make everything beautiful. Over there," Pete pointed toward the rail yard, "I see rainbows. Candy forests. Boys and girls in houses made of peppermint. Chocolate milk rivers. See?"

Promise strained to see.

"Only a fool can't," Pete said. "You're not a fool, right?" Promise shook her head.

"I see a girl drinking from the river. Her dress is up—her panties showing. That's a bad girl. You're a good girl, right?"

He moved closer. His breath smelled of coffee. Promise thought of Big Mama.

"I don't see nothing but men and trains," she said.

Pete pressed close to her, pointing.

"You don't see that pretty girl on her knees? A boy swimming in lemonade? Boy, put your clothes on!" he called out to the imaginary scene.

Promise's eyes followed his thick finger. She shut her eyes tight, trying to see. A clown flashed in her mind, but she didn't know if it came from Pete or long ago. She opened her eyes. Trains. Mud. A dog drinking from a ditch.

She didn't want to be called a fool. She tried pretending. But in the end, she shook her head and burst into tears.

"I wish I could give you my eyes," Pete said. "Then you'd see everything."

He leaned back in his seat.

Promise sniffled and wiped her face.

Pete's voice broke the silence. "Round two."

"You ever seen a naked boy?"

Promise shook her head.

"That's too bad. Guess you ain't fly."

"Sugar Face is fly," she said. "He—"

"Who's that?" Pete interrupted.

"He's a singer. I'm going to see him at Astroworld. I'm going to marry him."

Pete smiled. "Then you gotta see him naked. That's what husbands and wives do, see each other naked."

Promise stared out the window. She remembered playing husband and wife with Lakeisha Ann. It had been raining. Big Mama was asleep in front of *All My Children*. What started as a tea party turned into something else. Lakeisha Ann had stripped to her underwear and pretended to shower.

"I saw a naked girl," Promise said quietly.

Pete chuckled. "Baby, a girl can't be your husband."

"We were just playing."

"Was she naked all the way?"

"She kept her underwear on."

"Did you?"

"No. I was cooking dinner."

Pete rubbed himself. "Did you get in the bed?"

"She got mad and went home."

"What for?"

"I don't know."

Pete stared out the window. A dog walked by and peed on some crossties.

"A husband's a man. You have to see him naked. Don't you know that?"

Promise shrugged, watching the dog.

"I saw my brother," she said.

"Is he younger?"

"He's big. Like you. But not old."

Pete smiled. "How'd you see him naked?"

"He was sick. Big Mama had to clean him."

"What was wrong?"

"He had the A's. He's dead now."

"A's... Oh. AIDS. When did he die?"

"When I got home from school. He threw up green stuff."

Pete thought of embalming fluids. Green meant rot.

"You got other brothers?"

"They all dead. That's why I want to go to Astroworld. I'm sick of funerals."

Pete looked away. "I went to a lot of funerals as a boy."

"All your brothers died too?"

"My uncle was an undertaker. I helped with bodies."

Promise's eyes grew wide. "Was you scared?"

Pete shook his head. "The dead don't hurt nobody. It's the living you gotta watch."

"The dead do hurt people. In a movie, I seen a zombie tear a woman's head off."

Pete looked at her, then out the window. A war churned inside him. His eyes watered. He faced her again.

"Did you see everything?"

"What everything? In the *Zombie* movie?"

"Your brother—his dick. Was it long and thin? Or fat like a bullet popsicle?"

Promise thought of the thick chocolate popsicles she and Lakeisha Ann liked. Paula refused to eat them, saying they looked nasty.

"I bet you touched it. When no one was looking. Didn't you? Answer me."

Promise fidgeted. She wanted Lakeisha Ann there. She thought of her magic penny and whispered to it far away in her cigar box.

"Why you askin' me that?" she said, looking into Pete's mismatched eyes.

He dropped his head. Her question knocked him off balance. He regrouped.

"I'm sorry," he said gently. "I didn't mean nothing. My little brother's sick too. Mama has to clean him. Sometimes I just look at him and cry. Even my eyes can't make him better."

He smiled softly. "You're a sweet girl. Helping your grandmother. God will bless you. You believe that?"

Promise shrugged. Why would God love her? Lakeisha Ann's daddy said God didn't love anything Black. Promise folded her arms and shut Pete out.

"The Lord protects sweet little girls from the Leaky Eye." The words surprised Pete. It felt strange using the name others had given him.

Promise looked at Pete like he breathed fire. She turned toward the window to check for the man with the runny eyes. Pete's own dripping face made her tremble.

"You seen the Leaky Eye?" she asked.

"No Leaky Eye's getting on this bus to bother a sweet girl like you," Pete said. He pulled out a handkerchief and wiped his face, then used an eye-wash. A clear tear ran down his cheek. He placed an arm on the seatback behind Promise. Though he didn't touch her, the heat from his arm warmed her neck.

Her defiance wilted. She slumped forward, boneless.

A voice in her head said run. But Pete's leg pressed against hers. She didn't dare move.

"Yes, the Lord loves sweet little girls. Now, baby, tell me how your Big Mama cleans your brother."

"She washes his face and chest..."

"But what about down there?" Pete interrupted. "People with AIDS always mess themselves."

"She takes off his diaper."

"Does she make him spread his legs?"

Promise hesitated. Pete touched her shoulder.

"Yes."

"Yes what?"

"Yes, sir."

"Yes sir, what?"

"I don't want to see it no more."

"See what, baby?"

"His thing."

Pete smiled. "Pete wants you to see it." He touched her cheek.

Promise spotted something poking through the dark opening of Pete's trousers. It looked like a finger. Then it coiled, red-tipped like a snake. She screamed.

Pete clamped his hand over her mouth until she quieted.

He moved her hand to his lap.

She tried to pull away. He pressed her hand harder.

"My little bitch," he whispered. "Look at me."

His eyes sparkled with sadness. Promise cried for her mother, but Pete stopped her.

"Come here, little whore." He leaned into her, stomach and chest pressing down. The bus windows fogged. She searched for sunlight but found only his sour breath, like rotting trash. His tongue nibbled her ear. She screamed. He yanked her dress and stuffed her mouth, gagging her.

His tongue swept her lips. His teeth gnawed her neck and shoulders. He grunted, calling Jesus's name as if in pain. Fingers tore at her underwear. He entered her.

"That don't hurt. Say it. That don't hurt."

She thought it was Sugar Face whispering. Through tears and pain, she muttered the words.

Pete moaned and thrust. She bit his shirt. He didn't flinch. His rhythm grew wild.

She pressed into him, hoping it would hurt less, that somewhere on his body there might be a soft place. There wasn't.

She closed her eyes and saw Jonathan in his coffin. In her mind, he raised a knife in hand. He plunged the blade into Pete's back. Pete grunted and collapsed on top of her.

****

Promise opened her eyes. They burned as if soap had been poured into them. She blinked. No Jonathan. Something heavy crushed her. She couldn't breathe. She pushed against Pete. He didn't move. His face turned away, as if asleep. The minty sweat of his hair stung her nose. Panicked, she beat his chest. He shifted slightly—just enough for her lungs to open.

A train whistle blew in unison with her scream.

Pete bolted upright, glanced out the window, then at Promise, gasping. He zipped up, stared at her raised dress and the panties dangling from her ankle. Her overturned bunny slipper was filthy. He stood, brushed off his pants, and walked to the front of the bus.

He stood still, arms crossed, head bowed. His mind raced like a rat in a trap.

Too many eyes. Got to finish the route. Too many eyes. People would see the bus creeping down a quiet street. They'd remember. "I saw a bus, then I smelled something three days later." He glanced back at Promise. *She's simple. I can keep her quiet.*

Promise watched him. Watched his back rise and fall. She reached for her panties. A stab of pain made her wince. It felt like she'd been split in two. She moved slowly, pulling them up. The pain eased. She saw the neon lights blinking at Jack's. Maybe someone in there could help.

Pete fumbled at the dashboard. His hand slid to the front of his pants. She stood, smoothed her dress, and stepped toward the doors.

Pete spun around.

"You lousy bitch! You whore! How dare you get on my bus and turn tricks!"

He tore off his belt. It whipped the air around her, cracked like gunshots. She ran to the back. Pete followed. The belt whooshed past her ear.

"I can't believe this," he barked, holding the belt to her face. "Doing the nasty with that boy! Can't be more than eight. You got a mama?"

Promise stared. What boy?

"Don't look at me, you little whore!"

She ducked. Pete loomed over her.

"I should call my Supervisor. Maybe the Police. You move, I'll tie you up." He walked back to the front.

Promise stood frozen. "Lord have mercy," he'd said. Just like Big Mama. She kept her head down.

I ain't did nothin'. Why's he saying them bad names? What I do? I ain't seen no boy on this bus.

Crackling. Pete speaking into the radio:

"Uh huh. Yeah. A prostitute. That's right. Should I call the Police? Okay. I'll ask her."

He returned.

"What's your name? Full name, woman!"

"Prom... Promise..."

"Promise what?"

"Promise Suzette Goodday." Her voice broke like hiccups.

"Bet you're lying. Whores always lie. That your real name?"

She nodded.

"What was that boy's name?"

She stared at the floor.

"It was Sugar Face, wasn't it?"

No answer.

Pete laughed and went back to the mike. She heard her name spat like snuff. She cried. He came back and shook her.

"My boss said don't call the cops. But your name's going in a computer. Do anything wrong again, and the Police'll come. You hear me?"

Promise nodded.

"Even if your teacher sends you to the principal, the Police'll come."

Tears and snot soaked her dress and slippers. Her head jerked.

"Shut up that crying. Look at me."

She raised her face. Pete was a blur—no mouth, no eyes. Just a white shirt and a finger in her face.

"You understand me?"

She nodded.

"Good. Now sit behind me. Don't move, don't talk, don't get off till I say."

He jabbed a finger in her jaw, held it until it was slick with tears.

"If you mess with me, I'll tell your Mama what you and Sugar Face were doing. You want that?"

Promise shook her head.

"What's your Mama's name?"

Promise pictured her mother on the porch—arms folded, belt in hand. "Mary," she lied.

Pete smirked. "Mary'd blast to the moon if she knew what her daughter did. And your old granny'd tear your ass up, wouldn't she?"

Promise stayed silent.

"Answer me!"

"Yes, sir."

"Make you get naked and whip that ass, wouldn't she?"

Promise broke down. Pete laughed and took his seat. He switched out the white transfer slips for red ones, punched holes, letting the chad fall like confetti. He fanned them in the A/C breeze, drummed the steering wheel, and looked at her in the mirror.

He reached into a metal box and pulled brown paper towels, embossed with a winged bus logo.

"Wipe your face. You're a grown woman now." He pointed at her.

"And don't tell your Mama what you did. They'll put her in jail too. They do that for bad girls."

Pete dropped his finger, flipped a switch, and the bus shook. He gunned the motor. The bus slid past the rail yard toward the freeway.

Chapter 10 – Home Bound

The bus crept past the trains. It rolled under a high scaffolding of iron beams. For a second, Promise thought it might be a rollercoaster. Then she saw lights blinking from the thing as it raised its arms and let the bus pass.

She sighed as the bus rumbled across the bridge. She had dabbed her eyes, but her nose was full of snot, and she sniffled loudly.

The bus driver caught her in his wide rearview mirror and sneered.

"You better dry them tears, or I'll have the police lock you in the crazy house. You know what the crazy house is, don't you?"

A vision crept into Promise's mind—men and women with wrists bound, walking, mumbling, biting each other.

She sniffled. The bus driver sighed and massaged his crotch. His voice dropped into a low radio hum.

"They take whores like you and put them in a room full of wild boys with big things between their legs. And they stick them in you and make you have babies with horns. Horns that stick you between the legs when you birth them. That's your punishment. You gotta have a baby every day. If not, they throw you in a hot oven. So dry up them tears."

Pete checked his watch.

"Shit," he muttered. "I'm late."

He gunned the engine. The bus lurched like a bull, racing off. He left dozens stranded at stops. Raised fists and curses followed.

When traffic or red lights forced him to stop, he picked up passengers quickly, then sent the bus snorting forward again.

"I'm late, I'm late," he repeated to anyone who dared question his reckless driving.

"Had problems at the other end. Almost had to call the police. Lord, some of these children pretend to be innocent, but they'll do anything a grown person will do."

The world blurred—like she was underwater. Promise's eyes welled up again. She knew the driver was talking about her, feeding lies to passengers who began to look and whisper.

Hot stares burned her cheeks. Even white women, who usually smiled at dark little girls like her, now sat in cold silence.

"She's a runaway... stole a woman's purse... cuttin' up with a boy... Little prostitute... whispered nasty things for a quarter... Child of the devil..."

Pete spat lie after lie.

"Child of the devil."

The words echoed in her ears. Not from Pete now. From Big Mama.

In a white frock under yellow sanctuary lights, Big Mama hovered, pointing a skinny black finger. Behind her stood the Church Mothers, clad in holy white, their fingers like tree branches jabbing her cheeks and eyes.

Even Nettie stood among them, her white smock smeared with grape jelly, pointing and grunting.

"Jezebel... Lot's wife... the whore at the well... the whore who was about to be stoned—

But Jesus saves! Jesus saves!"

The preacher circled her, face red, voice rising. Promise sat in the "sinner's chair," trembling with every beat of the drum and vibration of the organ.

"Keep your dress down!" the Church Mothers shrieked.

"But my dress wasn't raised," Promise whispered.

"Mary didn't raise hers either. But the Lord's holy spirit caressed her soul one night, and she conceived without sin!"

"But *you*—you're a whore, my child. You enticed the devil. And he spilled his seed into your body!"

The preacher turned from her, waving toward the congregation. Faces wet with tears twisted in rapture.

Promise had seen the "purges" before—people collapsing, foaming at the mouth, sins spilling out in frothy vomit. Fingers pointed to the cross, then to the sinner, then back to the cross. A Jesus painted mid-ascent, launched skyward by unseen rockets.

Marsha had stopped sending Promise to church when the nightmares and crying spells started. But this time, there would be no escape. The purging awaited her.

The bus felt submerged underwater. People's mouths moved like fish. Her head swam. She closed her eyes, but the rickety "sinner's chair" waited like an electric chair.

It *was* the electric chair—from Huntsville's death chamber. Straps still intact. Sinners sometimes strapped in for their purge, bodies jerking as if currents sliced through them.

She heard the Bishop Overseer call her name... and Big Mama's.

The sermon would begin:

"Oh Sister Sharon, how you suffered—caring for your grandson Jonathan while Lucifer tormented him. And you, Promise... you wouldn't even go to his funeral. He was your last brother. But you wanted to go to Astroworld!"

"The devil put that thought in you. Yes, the devil works through little children. Through beasts of the earth and fowls of the air. He spills his nasty seed onto our legs, arms, mouths, lungs, and ears—bringing sickness. But worse, he spills into our hearts, into our souls, and makes our children rise up against us."

"He causes parents to slay children, and children to murder parents! That demon is busy, I say! Busy! Get thee behind me, oh Satan!"

****

Promise shivered as if freezing. She opened her eyes. Pete stood over her, shaking her thigh roughly.

"You gotta get off my bus. You back in your neighborhood. See? There's where you caught the bus." Pete pointed at the bench with the cowboy hat sign. The old woman who had taken her flowers sat there, watching.

Promise stared out the window. The street and buildings looked unfamiliar. It had rained, but now the sun glossed everything in gold. She tried to stand. A searing pain between her legs forced her back into the seat. She clutched her lap.

Pete bent low and whispered, "Police," in her ear.

Promise stood on wobbly legs.

"Go on," Pete coaxed. "Get off the bus. You holding up people. And listen to me—"

Promise turned back. His finger hovered near her face like a weapon.

"We got your name down at Metro. Don't you ever catch this bus again—or any bus. If the police see you, they'll throw you in jail or the crazy house. You hear me?"

Promise nodded and stepped gingerly toward the doors. Each step felt like safety pins snapping open inside her. She held her crotch like she had to pee. As soon as her feet touched the sidewalk, Pete slammed the doors. The bus hissed and groaned away.

"I'm dead," Promise whispered. She imagined her mama on the porch with a switch in hand. How long would they beat her? A whole month?

She thought of the whipping after Kwong's store. She hadn't even stolen anything. But Mrs. Kwong told Marsha and Big Mama she was part of the ring of girls. Paula had only snatched some Tootsie Rolls. But Promise was the bad one.

Marsha beat her first. Then Big Mama. Then Uncle Bobo with his cap. They'd beat her till she was pissy. Even Nettie got in a lick. They'd threatened to press her thieving hands to the stove.

She remembered how quiet it was on the LaKeisha Ann side of the duplex—just screeches of laughter. Promise wondered if she could slip away and hide with the Greens forever.

As she started home, heads turned. Eyes followed her limp.

She passed the bench. The old woman stared at her, suspicious. She opened her mouth but froze when she saw the blood on Promise's bunny slippers. She handed Promise two white roses from the six she'd taken. They had withered and browned at the edges. Promise mumbled "thanks" and walked on. The woman raised her cap, like a salute.

The rain hadn't cleansed her block. It dulled everything. The grass smelled like cabbage. Trash swirled in the wind, bits of paper sticking to her ankles. Ants had built a bed in the sidewalk crack. Some crawled into her slippers and stung her, but she didn't react.

She saw her reflection in a puddle.

A bird's nest sat on her head.

Why not a crown?

If she wore a crown, she could save herself. Her bodyguards, dressed in silver, would snatch the straps from Mama and Big Mama. Her magic man would bring Jonathan back to life. Her neighborhood would become Astroworld. Kids wouldn't get whippings—unless she gave the okay.

And bus drivers...

She froze. A needle stabbed between her legs. She shook the thought away.

If only she wore a crown.

She started to cry.

Through tears, she saw fingers pointing. Mouths moving—"Who?"

She imagined they had all seen what Pete said she did. The nasty thing.

Still trembling, she walked toward her house. Ants stung her legs. She cried harder. She tried to think of a story—something to save her.

But Mama and Big Mama didn't believe in pirates or monsters.

Maybe Jonah and the whale? But where would a whale come from? The nearest water was a bayou, and it barely held minnows.

She regretted everything.

I ought to went to Jonathan's funeral. He was a good brother. I wonder if they buried him already... All locked up with flowers and dirt all over him.

Flowers... Why didn't I bring Mama the flowers? I'm a bad girl. I didn't mean to be bad. I just wanted to go to Astroworld for a little while. I was gonna come back and get the flowers, Jesus. Yes I was. I was coming back. Don't let Mama be too mad at me.

She looked at the roses in her hand. Darker now. But they gave her hope. Maybe this would prove she tried to be good.

Then she saw the car. Lights on top. Parked in front of her house.

She dropped to her knees.

Pete had lied.

She imagined two cops reading from a book of sins. Her mother crying. Big Mama yelling, "Lock her up and throw away the key!"

Promise started to scream.

"I ain't did nothing, Mama! I don't wanna go to no jail! Please, Mama, don't let them take me. Daddy! Daddy! Please! I'll be good!"

A crowd gathered.

LaKeisha Ann ran into the house. Promise's mother came rushing out like the house was on fire. Uncle Bobo followed.

His arms scooped her from the sidewalk.

A policeman approached. Blood and urine ran down her leg. One slipper was gone.

"I'll be good," Promise whispered over and over into her mother's chest and her uncle's arms.

"It's okay, baby. It's okay," Marsha whispered.

When the officer stepped forward, Promise saw his patch and nameplate.

She fainted.

Marsha carried her back inside, pressed tight to her chest. She could feel Promise's heart pounding. She needed to feel it—so her own wouldn't stop. She couldn't bury two children.

Big Mama came out onto the porch, arms crossed.

Then she saw Marsha carrying her granddaughter like a corpse.

She fell to her knees.

"Lord Jesus, come by here!"

Chapter 11 – The Devil

When Pete pulled up, his son was outside, dribbling and shooting a basketball. Pete sipped his beer, watching Shadrach's long arms stretch upward and disappear into the limbs of the tree as he made the basket.

The boy paused when he noticed Pete standing there. He said nothing, just went up for another shot. Pete watched the loose shorts rise, brush the boy's thighs, and fall back to his knees.

In a flash, Pete felt two things at once — a sharp hate for Shadrach, and his own loins tightening, blood rushing south.

He hocked and spat. Shadrach missed the shot.

"Your mama gone yet?" Pete called.

"They gonna take a later flight," Shadrach said. "Her and Dr. Cook got a School Board meeting first."

"I bet," Pete spat again.

Shadrach's eyes dropped to the paper bag Pete was holding. Pete followed his gaze, noticing the bottom was wet. He lifted the bag in both arms to keep the cans from falling through.

He grinned, tipping one can in a mock toast. "It's gonna be me and you this weekend. Man to man. A man needs to get away from womenfolk sometimes. Too much trouble."

Shadrach said nothing, turned, and shot again. A siren wailed in the distance. The ball hit the rim and bounced away.

When he chased it toward his mother's flowers, he saw Pete open the front door and step inside. Shadrach let out a breath, dribbled, and went up for another shot.

****

Pete entered the house and locked the door. "Make that nigger knock like a peddler if he wants in," he muttered.

Jackie's bags were lined up by the door, smallest in front, largest in back. *Poppa Bear, Mama Bear, Baby Bear,* he thought. *That bitch must be going for a week with all these bags.*

He heard water running upstairs. His eyes started to burn. He didn't remember seeing Jackie's car outside. *Damned nigger must've left the shower running,* he cursed, starting up the stairs.

The water stopped. He froze, listening. A hair dryer whined, then died.

Blond hair swung between slender shoulders as a nude girl bounced from the bathroom into his son's room. The door clicked shut.

****

Pete stood outside Shadrach's door, listening to shuffling on the other side. Music started.

He set the bag on the floor, popped open another beer, and took a long swallow. He tried the doorknob. Locked.

He moved down the hall and looked out over the driveway. Shadrach was still outside, shooting baskets. When the boy looked toward the window, Pete ducked behind the curtain.

His eyes landed on the little highboy chest in the hall. He opened the top drawer, found a small screwdriver.

At the door again, he listened. Music played — then a loud commercial. He slid the screwdriver into the hole, turned. The knob gave, and the door opened.

****

Ashley sat on the bed in her panties, back to the door, brushing her hair. Her shoulders rolled to the beat of the music.

On the bed beside her: tan shorts, a white bra, a striped top.

She lifted the brush in the air, then whirled around. Blue eyes blazed. Her mouth twisted in sudden pain.

Pete crouched and sprang like a frog.

****

The girl lay in a heap at his feet.

From outside, his son banged on the front door. Pete didn't move. Sweat poured down his face.

Shadrach's footsteps thudded through the gravel pathway toward the back. Now pounding on the rear door.

Pete knew he had seconds before the boy climbed through the kitchen window. He tried to shove Ashley's body under the bed — one leg stuck out.

He stepped around her, bumping her ankle, thinking about the knives in the kitchen... and greeting his son with one at his throat.

The phone rang, jangling his nerves.

He panicked. His foot kicked the bag of beer, cans rolling and clattering.

Pete shot out the front door, jumped into his car, and roared down the road.

Chapter 12 – That Night

"...he found his nobody."

It was after two a.m., and Shadrach couldn't sleep. He was cocooned in his Grandmother Mae Vera's brass bed in her spare room. The pink chenille bedspread smelled of cedar and weighed heavy across his bony shoulders.

An old wind-up clock ticked too loudly, the sound hurting his head. Angry voices seeped through the walls. Now and again, the wallpaper seemed to flutter, bruised by the condemnations.

"Lord, the horror that poor child went through."

"They had a made-up confession right there for him to sign. Tried every trick in the book."

"I knew Pete wasn't any good."

"He never wanted nothing."

"I hope they catch that nigger."

"All he would do when he came around here was look mad and spit."

"I always thought he looked like some kind of mongrel, all burnt around the eyes."

"Why did Jackie get mixed up with him in the first place?"

"She always had a weakness for the wounded."

"I hope and pray to God that boy ain't his. Don't look like him no way."

Shadrach rolled over and put a pillow over his ear. A sharp pain stabbed his rectum where a cop had kicked him. The spasm eased, leaving a dull ache in his hips. He shut his eyes. Memories trickled back to him—all red.

****

The noise of his father's car played over and over in his head. It had squealed as if in pain as it tore out of the driveway. The sound made him miss his jump shot. He was aware he had to piss.

One more shot, he kept telling himself. *One more shot before I take a piss.*

Normally, he'd have gone to the side of the house, pulled out, and sprayed his mother's flowers. But she'd gotten after him about such "niggerish" behavior.

"What if the neighbor looks out her window? Only trash uses the bathroom outside like dogs."

He missed another shot, grabbed his crotch, and headed for the front door. Locked.

He ran to the back door—locked too. He remembered Pete had gone inside, and he thought Ashley was still there. Or maybe she'd showered and left.

****

The Interrogation Begins

"You thought she was still there?" The cop's mouth was small—just a gash above his chin—but his eyes were sharp.

"Yes, sir. I didn't know for sure."

"A white... a girl came over to your house to take a shower; you stayed outside and shot baskets, and you didn't give a damn if she was there or not?"

"I cared if she was there," he stammered.

"Well, if you cared, you must have known if she was there or not. You're not making any sense, boy."

"How many times did you knock on the door?"

"I don't know, three or four."

"Did you call his name?" "

I don't think so."

"Three or four times you knocked because you had to piss, but you went back to shooting baskets? Doesn't make sense. Did you piss outside?"

"No, sir, the neighbor might see me."

Over and over, they drilled him until the truth didn't make sense. Still, he hung on to it as best he could.

****

He'd heard Pete start his car and roar off. No, he hadn't run to the front yard to see what was going on. Pete always peeled out like that in the old Lincoln.

A few more shots at the hoop. Then, probably minutes later, he tried the back door again—still locked. Front door, locked.

Down the street, he'd seen the smoky haze left by the Lincoln. He climbed through the kitchen window.

Inside, he danced his way to the powder room near the living room, yanked his shorts down, and barely got himself out before his water started to flow.

Relieved, he shook himself, then checked the seat for splashes. That bathroom was reserved for guests. He took toilet tissue and wiped the bowl so his mother wouldn't fuss.

He flushed and went to the kitchen to wash his hands.

****

"Why didn't you wash them in the bathroom?" the cop with the small mouth asked.

"I didn't want to get water all over the sink."

"And so then you went upstairs."

"Yes, sir."

"You said a while ago you went to the refrigerator."

"I went toward the refrigerator until I saw Ashley's books on the counter."

"Those books made you remember Ashley?"

The bald-headed cop looked at him funny. "A pretty girl upstairs in your house taking a shower, and it took seeing her books to make you remember her?"

"I knew she was up there."

"You said a while ago you didn't know if she was up there or not. You said you didn't care."

"Were you two drinking?"

"Who bought the beer?"

"Nobody bought beer, sir."

"Beer just walked in the house and fell all over the floor, I guess," the small-mouth cop sneered.

****

On and on, the two of them circled him, making him double back on himself. The room was low, the fluorescent lights humming like insects.

They slapped tables, slammed telephone books. They made him strip, stand wide-legged, arms high in an X, turn in slow circles like some fool in a cruel dance.

They looked at his genitals.

"When was the last time you jerked off, boy?"

"Sir?"

"Spanked your monkey, goddammit!"

"I don't know, sir."

The small-mouth cop chuckled. They probed about the scar on his knee. A doctor came in, examined him, and shrugged. "Couldn't have happened today."

Sweat poured from Shadrach's face as the doctor twisted his penis, dabbed a swab inside the opening, turned his underwear inside out. The doctor left. The two white cops banged fists on the desk and started again.

****

A black detective walked in. The others stepped back. He lit a cigarette, took a puff, and sneered.

"What you sweating for, nigger? How can you be hot? You're naked as midnight, Spook..."

The black detective leaned in.

"I tell you why you're sweating. You're one of those young punks who think you're the shit. You're one of the few jigs up there in Candlelight Trails, and all of a sudden you're a privileged character.

Well, you ain't shit, and that girl didn't want to give you no pussy. Ain't that how it went down, Brother? She didn't want to give your jungle bunny ass no pussy. So you said you were going to get yours.

How dare she deny me?

So you wrestled with her. You wanted some of that white pussy. I know how you feel, Brother. I fucked a few when I was fucking around up north at school. White pussy is good. It yields like butter.

You wanted them long white legs wrapped around your black ass. But she said no. So you wrestled and choked her."

****

Shadrach shook his head. Snot and tears dripped from his chin.

"That's how these white bastards in the DA's office are gonna play it for the jury. And you know what, Brother? Ain't none of your peers gonna be on that jury. Not one spook like me or you.

If they do let a nigga on the jury, it's gonna be some coon-ass preacher sitting there frowning at you like he got a dick up his ass."

The cop sat on a stool, faced Shadrach, and sighed. He picked up Shadrach's underwear and threw it at him.

"Put some clothes on, Brother."

Shadrach flinched, grabbed his shorts, and pulled them on. The black cop rolled closer on the stool.

"Okay, here's how it went down. You two got to wrestling on the bed and it got out of hand. You'd had a couple of beers, you were feeling good. All you wanted was some pussy.

You didn't mean for all that other shit to happen. It was just an accident, wasn't it, Brother? You didn't mean to kill her. You can tell me. I'll stand up in court with you, if you just tell the truth."

****

Shadrach heard himself blurt out, "I thought she was playing hide and seek."

The black cop slammed his fist down. "Aw, nigger, don't start that shit again."

"If you were outside playing basketball, how could you be playing hide and seek?"

"I saw her under the bed, and I thought she was playing hide and seek."

"Was that y'all's thing—run around naked and play hide and seek?"

"We didn't have a thing."

"Your story is full of shit, man."

****

That's what Shadrach remembered—the foul odor, the brown mess on her backside when he pulled her partly from under the bed.

That's why he'd run outside and vomited. He'd started running down the street just as his mother drove up.

****

Jackie Arrives in waiting room.

****

"Tell me why you started running after your father's car after it was long gone?"

"I don't know. I just did."

"You just did? But he was gone. You had time to piss and play with your meat. Then you thought about Ashley, and you wanted to have sex with her again."

"We never did nothing."

"She just liked to come over to your house and get naked and take showers?"

"No, she came over that day because the water was off at her house. She wanted to take a shower before work."

"The water was off? What do you mean?"

"Something was wrong with their bathroom."

"Where did she work?"

"McDonald's.

"She ever come to your house before?"

"Lots of times."

"She take showers any other time?"

"No."

"Was she ever alone in your room?"

"Sometimes... we studied."

"With the door closed?"

"The door was open. My mother made me keep the door open."

"So, nobody was home when you got there. Here was your chance to get with a girl, but instead, you gave her a towel from the linen closet and went outside and shot baskets, leaving a pretty girl naked in your house."

"Yes, sir."

"Shadrach, are you a cocksucker?"

"No, sir."

"Yes, you are. You're a cocksucker. You like boys, don't you?"

"No, sir, I don't."

"That's the only thing that could make sense. What kind of young brother would stay outside shooting baskets while a girl was running around naked in his house and no parents around? Does that make sense to you?

When was the last time you had some pussy?"

Shadrach hung his head. There was a secret he should tell them, but he couldn't pull it from the place in his head where he kept it—his secret and her secret.

It had been an accident, the discovery. Varsity practice had run late, same for the cheerleaders. Ashley had her father's car and said they could go to the mall afterward.

He'd turned the corner first, just as Ashley and the other girl pulled their lips apart. He'd distracted his teammates by tossing the basketball their way.

After she dropped the girl off and they were on their way home, she told him how grateful she was for what he'd done. He was grateful, too. His own crushes on teammates poured from him like water.

Their secrets became a bond. He could not tell this secret of secrets to the cops. So, he hung his head.

****

"Answer me!" the black cop pounded the table. Shadrach jumped.

A uniformed policeman entered carrying a black plastic bag. He turned it upside down, spilling women's panties across the table.

The detective picked up a pair with his pen and held them in front of Shadrach's face.

"You want to tell us about these?"

Shadrach shook his head.

"Oh, so you don't want to talk about these?

"I don't know about them."

"We found them in your house. Some in your room, tucked under your mattress. How did they get there?"

He shrugged.

"Did the tooth fairy bring them?"

No answer.

"I said did the fucking tooth fairy bring them!"

The cop slammed the wall next to him. Shadrach began to cry.

****

It went on and on, the cops drilling like Marines, him swearing he was telling the truth.

Then—a knock on the glass. One cop peeked out. The others stiffened as a high-ranking officer walked in.

"Give him his goddamn clothes. He's got a lawyer. You three, step outside."

****

While Shadrach dressed, voices rose in the hall. "This is not no fucking Adrian Johnson!" the cop barked, invoking the name of the Black boy they'd sent to the chair years ago on flimsy evidence.*

They took him to another room. His mother sat trembling next to a bald man in glasses.

When they saw each other, mother and son rushed into each other's arms, holding like they'd both come back from the dead.

****

"At first I thought she was playing some kind of game of hide and seek," Shadrach told his mother as the lawyer scribbled notes.

When he finished, they were ushered into the hall to wait while the lawyer, detectives, and DA conferred.

Shadrach laid his head on his mother's shoulder. Tears wet both their cheeks.

****

A news story flashed on TV: a little dark-skinned girl grinning, showing every tooth. Her mother's face was twisted in grief as she pleaded for her daughter's safe return. She clutched the photo in one hand and three withered flowers in the other.

Jackie prayed for the girl and her mother, her own voice breaking:

"Jesus, Heavenly Father, please, please, let that child be safe. And Lord, bring peace to my soul and my child's soul."

****

Her peace had been shattered hours earlier when she'd driven up Tender Vine Drive and seen her son running down the street in a soiled T-shirt, basketball shorts hanging off his hip.

Her first thought: the neighbors. What must they be thinking?

"What's got into that nigger?" she asked aloud, the way a white neighbor might.

She honked the horn. He kept running. She turned into a driveway, backed out, and pursued, tapping the horn softly, though eyes still followed—eyes that saw a big gray Buick chasing a boy like prey.

She drove ahead, got out, and grabbed his shoulders.

"He did something to Ashley! He did something to Ashley!"

Vomit stained his shirt. She pushed him away, then caught him again and shoved him into the passenger seat.

Out of sight of the staring eyes, she grilled him.

"Who did what to Ashley?"

"He did. He did, and she's dead."

"Who?" she screamed.

"Daddy."

Jackie knew it was serious. Shadrach only called Pete *Daddy* when he was terrified. She floored it.

****

The next thing she remembered: kneeling over the white girl and shaking her, even knowing it was no use.

The body was soiled, the back of her thighs streaked with feces. Jackie screamed at her son. He covered his ears like a child.

"What happened?"

"I don't know, Mama! I don't know!"

"Nigger, what happened in my house?"

Darkness swelled in her head. She slapped him. He fell back, his foot kicking Ashley's side, the body jerking as if in reaction.

Banging on the front door. In seconds, the house was full of cops.

They seized her son. She tried to pull him back but was shoved away. They hauled her to the kitchen, him in handcuffs. Ugly words spat in her face.

Ashley's body came downstairs, wrapped in swaddling sheets, small as a doll. They stopped long enough to grab her books off the counter, then yanked Shadrach toward the patrol car.

Neighbors stood thick and white as statues. The cops began tearing the house apart, room by room.

****

"That bastard! That bastard!"

Shadrach opened his eyes. A new voice, fresh with anger.

"How is the boy?"

"He's resting. Doctor said to keep him in bed a few days."

"And Jackie—do you think she's going to make it?"

"Honey, Jackie is dead to the world right now. Took two Valium and a shot from the doctor to calm her down."

"That nigger ought to get the needle," the voice said.

Chapter 13 – End of the Line

Pete had been driving for miles in the same circle. His eyes burned like fire. He hadn't slept. The cops were after him. He felt like a rat in a maze.

He needed to steal a car. He needed to eat. He needed to shit. But first he needed to ditch this piece of junk. Stealing license plates would only get him so far.

The radio kept spitting out the make, model, and color of his car: *1976 Lincoln Continental. Dark blue. License plate number FGH 775.* Right car, wrong plates.

The Lincoln was a hand-me-down from his family's mortuary business, now run by his brother. Its blue-black shell blended into the night, but dawn was coming.

A rat needed a place to hole up in daylight. Pete kept to dark, rutted roads, avoiding lighted boulevards. He didn't know where he was going. *Where does a hunted man go?*

Wild Kingdom flashed through his head—an ape fleeing the hot, gaping jaws of lions. He laughed at the image of the ape's blue and red ass, even imagined painting his own and running down the street naked.

A helicopter buzzed overhead. Sweat dotted his forehead. He was delirious with fear. The chopper veered off, and he exhaled.

He flicked on the radio. Every station carried his name.

"Pete Chesterfield... forty-four-year-old Metro bus driver... suspected in dozens of attacks on women..."

A store owner claimed to have seen him kissing a girl on the bus.

"That one-eyed lying son of a bitch," Pete muttered.

They warned he was armed and dangerous. *Armed with what?* he thought. A tire iron in the trunk?

The repetition of his name gave him a strange chill. "I'm famous," he told himself, right before flashing red lights ahead made him swerve down a side street.

The next station cut from his story to a sultry malt liquor ad. Another station's Spanish announcer rolled his name like a song over strumming guitars.

Up ahead, a small whitish dog wandered into the road. Pete hated dogs. Even now, rage flared. He gunned the Lincoln. A yelp, a scream, then silence.

He got out and walked back. The tangle of fur and blood reminded him of a wreck victim his uncle had once pulled from a car—skin soot-colored, nose half gone, brains leaking through nappy hair.

"Look at it, boy. Death is an ugly son of a bitch."

Pete stared at the animal. "Look at death," he said aloud.

A whimper caught his ear. Across the sidewalk stood a white woman in a yellow housecoat, short blonde hair sticking up, an empty leash dangling at her side. Knees pale as potatoes. Her eyes—blue sapphires—sparkled with fear and rage.

Somewhere far off, a siren wailed. The heat from her body seemed to warm his belly. The siren grew louder.

"You lucky bitch," Pete told her, turning back to his car. "You know I'm famous, don't you?" he shouted before slamming the door.

He drifted past the Bus Barn, headlights off. A few fellow drivers in white shirts and black pants stood under fluorescent lights, like big moths. Rows of buses sat like patient elephants. One bus stood alone, wrapped in yellow police tape. Evidence, Pete figured. He drove on.

The Lincoln's engine dimmed, sputtered, and died. The temperature needle sat far past "H."

"End of the road, nigger," he muttered.

He climbed out, following a ditch toward distant steel girders. *Maybe the docks,* he thought. *A boat to Jamaica... or Africa.*

He'd never seen Africa, but in his mind it was a mass of black skin glistening in the sun—faces blending into one, men and women indistinguishable under close-cropped hair. No one could pick him out there.

He listened for water. Only frogs answered. The ditch felt like a grave.

The muck sucked at his hands and knees. The Bible story of Christ healing a blind man with mud came to him. Maybe it could fix his eyes... or his heart.

He smeared mud into his eyes, sat, then rinsed them in a puddle. The stinging was gone.

And then she was there—Ashley. Drunk, he'd only wanted to kiss her. She'd kneed him, nearly crushed his balls. His hands found her throat. A knock at the front door. A foul odor. Her panties full of shit.

Faces of other women crowded in—nude, twisted, stained. He screamed at them to go. They vanished, leaving only the siren in the distance.

A Ferris wheel rose over the road. He wondered where he was. He'd never ridden a Ferris wheel. Never taken Shadrach to a carnival. Now here he was.

Car doors slammed by his abandoned Lincoln. Lights spilled around it like on a dead beast. Pete buried his white shirt in the ditch, crawled through a culvert to the park's skeletal rides.

The Ferris wheel loomed, half its seats gone, metal littering the ground like bones.

Hounds bayed. Pete climbed, settling high above the ground. From there, he saw the police with dogs sniffing his bumper. The chopper's light swept the ditch.

They'd find his shirt soon. He took off his belt, looped it around a beam. The leather smelled fresh. He struggled with the knot, then jumped, trying to choke himself. His feet kept hitting the platform.

The searchlight locked on his face. "Sir, put your hands in the air!" came the sharp voice from above.

Pete reached into his pocket, pulled out his silver ticket punch, and aimed it like a gun. Officers dove for cover.

A ping by his ear. Then fire tore through his throat. More stings. He fell to his knees. The punch clattered away.

By the time the cops climbed up with their flashlights, his neck was stretched like a chicken's. Gray matter from his bulging eyes streaked his face. His pants had fallen around his knees. Far off in the distance, the new Astroworld sign flashed a dull yellow in the cloudy sky.

Chapter 14 – The Next Day

The sun found an opening in the green graveyard canopy and blazed down on Promise, standing rigid, clutching her mother's hand. A limp white rose brushed her knee.

Her short black velvet dress, with its oversized white bow just above her hips, squeezed her ribs. Her hair was oiled into a ponytail. Big Mama had approved the thick white stockings and black patent leather flats with their own white bows.

Earlier that morning, staring into the mirror, Promise had thought she looked like a huge fly—bows like wings fastened to her body. For a moment she imagined climbing onto the bed, leaping, and flying straight out the window. But the house had been too busy—too many eyes poking into her doorway, too many hands touching her face as if feeling for cracks.

Her most persistent guard was Big Mama, who'd insisted Promise sleep beside her. All night, hands and voices had probed her: "Who did this to you, baby? Who? Who?"

At first, Promise only shrugged and cried. But Pete's warning—*They will take your mother away if you tell*—rang in her head, sharp as his rage-filled stare. She was a bad girl. She had to keep the secret.

It was the policewoman who finally drew it out. When the family and male officers had given up, she came in alone—yellow pantsuit, like the woman on the bus. She wrapped Promise, lost inside an adult hospital gown, into her arms. The woman's stroking hands softened the hard knot inside Promise, and the story spilled out in jerks and sobs. By the time she finished, her voice was flat, as if reciting words from her second-grade spelling list.

Afterward, the policewoman left to speak with Promise's family. Promise stood at the window, seeing only her own reflection against the night. In the darkness, she thought she saw a girl falling from a window. Arms lifted her from the floor, and she woke in someone's hold.

****

The graveyard heat pressed into her dress. She turned into her mother's side for shade. Across Jonathan's bronze coffin, Bishop Overseer Elder Ella Brazille's voice rose and fell:

"The sins of the father follow the child, but the Lord is redemption. This brother, Jonathan Goodday, through God's grace, is as sin-free as a newborn babe. I was told that he cried out on his deathbed, 'Lord Jesus, save me!' Then he closed his eyes for this his final rest. Well..."

She dabbed her face with a handkerchief, smoothed tufts of hair under her white scarf, then raised an index finger to the sky.

"Well, all our Jesus asks of us is a little act of faith. We are not saved by works alone. Our redemption comes in believing in Him. The Lord cleanses... Redemption! Redemption cleanses... cleanses..."

Her voice echoed off tombstones and through the tall pines.

Promise shut her eyes and saw, behind them, a giant front-loading washing machine. Tiny dark-skinned people wrapped in white cloth bobbed in the suds. *Maybe this is how God washes away sins*, she thought—giant hands scooping washing powder from a blue box, sprinkling it over the dirty and the mud-caked, then drowning them in a rain like a hundred thunderstorms.

When she opened her eyes, Jonathan's coffin was open. His dark head rested on a white pillow. Sunlight blurred his features, making his face look greased with Vaseline.

Her mother squeezed her hand. Promise stepped forward and placed the white rose on Jonathan's chest. A gust lifted the flowers around the coffin, but her rose stayed, caught between his folded hands.

She touched his fingers. They were stiff, unyielding.

"Make it all right, Jonathan! Make them stop talking to me! Make it all right like you used to!"

She tried to pry his fingers apart, but they were locked.

"Please, please come back, Jonathan! Please come back!"

Hands pulled her away from the coffin.

Some Years Later-Her Voice

Chapter 15 – I Am Lost

It had been years since Jonathan's funeral, years since I was the little girl in black patent leather clutching a white rose.

Now I was fifteen, and whatever softness I'd had back then was long gone. In my house, love was a rumor, and survival meant keeping your mouth shut and your eyes open.

I am lost.

I wish this bitch would shut up. All she do is crow all day—
"Uhh Buuudd! Bud! Uuhh Buudd!"

When Mama goes to work, I shut Big Mama up. A couple pops on her ass with a wet towel usually does it. When that don't work, the rag goes over her nose and mouth for a few seconds. Sometimes longer. I'm surprised I ain't killed her yet. Some days, I wouldn't care if I did.

Ain't nothing for me to love. I've screwed plenty, but there ain't never been no real love behind it—just a whole lot of "love talk" whispered in my ear. I call it dick talk. Every boy I've ever smelled thinks his dick is more important than his heart or his brain. Always quick to unzip, pull it out, let it hang, maybe bounce it a little—waiting for me to smile and lick my lips.

Mama calls it a root. Tree roots start in the ground. I wonder what part of the body this man-root comes from.

"Baby, your pussy is special because I love you... Suppose I get shot and you ain't give me no pussy, then what?... If you don't, I'll turn into a punk... If I got pussy from you, I could let my sister alone... Every time we fuck a white man dies... One little piece ain't gonna make you pregnant—we got to do it five or six times in an hour before you have a baby, and then it's only a one in nine chance..."

Jesus, the lies I've heard. One college boy told me every time he saw me his heart filled up, and that made his dick fill up, and he had to pour his heart into me. That line got him three pieces of free pussy. My heart was starting to fill up at the sight of his brown neck, but after the third time he pulled up his pants and said, "See ya."

"See ya... see ya... later... I'll be back in a minute... I woulda come back, but the police picked me up... I had to go to the store for my mama, then I went out of town... I became a Black Muslim... My mama died... You too good for me... If you fixed your hair different... You wear too much lipstick... You don't—I don't know what it is, but you just don't!"

The excuses boys use for getting out of pussy are just as bogus as the ones they use to get in it. But I'd still rather hear a reason than just "see ya."

One day, riding the bus home from the mall, something told me to take the For Free sign off my pussy and put a For Sale sign on my big sister Nettie's. That voice told me no love in the world was gonna get me out of Mama's house and away from emptying Big Mama's bedpan. Love juice going the wrong way, splashing all over your eggs—that would just get you pregnant and keep you trapped here forever.

Most times on the bus, the voice says crazy things—train whistles and "All aboard!" or cows mooing, or people speaking Chinese with cat voices. When I was little and vomiting at the sight of a bus, Mama took me to a woman psychologogist—I still can't say the word—who told me to take a deep breath, count to ten, and let it out when I got close to buses. That's what I usually do. But the voice about taking the Free sign off my pussy made too much sense to block out.

I thought about my friend Lakeisha Ann, eighteen with three kids, her dress hanging off her like a rag, hair uncombed, room smelling like shit and puke. Naw. I'm going to college. And as long as Nettie stays mute, I'll get there.

One thing I do know—men will fuck anything. Mama says men will fuck dogs, cats, even their own mamas. They've fucked this world and wanna go to space to fuck other worlds. I don't have to take Mama's beer talk to heart. I see it myself—men picking up nasty crackhead prostitutes with dried pee on their legs and gravel in their hair.

I'm fifteen. I've got time to save money for college. And in a way, it was a blessing Nettie was born the way she is. Can't talk, don't see or hear too good, kind of cross-eyed but with big titties. She's twenty, but acts six.

After Jonathan—my last brother—died, Mama kind of lost her mind. She cut all Nettie's hair off. Never said why, but folks said she wanted a boy to replace the sons she'd lost. She couldn't have more kids and was too poor to adopt. With Daddy in jail most of the time, and me still throwing up at buses and men in uniforms, our house was no kind of home.

Mama started dressing Nettie in jeans and T-shirts, made her train for the Special Olympics. Uncle Bobo tried to teach her basketball, but all Nettie could do was throw the ball at the ground like she was busting an egg. Running worked better—Mama would stand at one end of the park with candy and make Nettie sprint to her. The faster she ran, the more candy she got. Nettie got pretty good until race day, when she saw Mama standing halfway down the track. She cut across every lane to get her candy and lost the race.

Eventually, Mama gave up trying to make Nettie a boy. Nettie's tits told her God had other plans. I took over and bought her cheap stockings, a couple dresses from Woolworth's, and a box of Kotex.

The morning I "became a woman" was something else. Big Mama lectured about keeping my dress down and nasty boys wanting to get under it. Mama, when she was in a good mood, said a boyfriend was nice to have—just make sure he was good looking, strong, and in school. In a bad mood, she reminded me I wasn't a virgin and ought to "naturally" like boys. I knew what she meant. Could've been that morning I ran off to Astroworld, or when she caught me kissing Felicia from my English class. The rain makes me do strange things.

Mama bought me mini dresses and short skirts. Big Mama screamed. Truth was, I would've felt more comfortable in Big Mama's "old lady" dresses. You can't run or skip in a tight leather skirt, and you've got to keep your legs crossed all the time.

The big blow-up came one morning when Big Mama told Mama,

"The change of life has made you a fool. 'Cause you can't get pregnant, you tryin' to wish a baby up on your child."

Before Big Mama could close her mouth, Mama was calling her every kind of liar and bitch. The walls trembled. What saved it was me.

On the bus, the voice told me if I started taking a birth control pill every morning, it would bring peace between them. I brought the permission slip home from the school nurse. Big Mama and Mama stared at it, then Mama grabbed a pen, signed it, and stalked off. The fussing stopped. So did Mama buying me clothes. Didn't matter—I didn't need her no more. Soon, me and Nettie were in the "money for pussy" business.

We got into this money thing by accident. I had Nettie by the hand, and we were coming from Ol' Lady Kwong's store. Ol' Man Kwong had been shot and killed a few years back, and Mrs. Kwong had renamed the place Lady Kwong's. She'd put curtains over the burglar bars and even hung a little chandelier over the cosmetic case where she sold Avon. The store smelled better now.

Anyway, we left Kwong's. Nettie wore a flowered dress, and I still had her by the hand when a Mexican in a truck started following us. His eyes were the color of tea, like someone had splashed hot sauce in them. He waved money at me. But I never liked being around anybody who could say something in a language I didn't understand. Somebody might be telling you they're gonna kill you, and you'd just stand there grinning like a chess cat. And Mexican men—at least the ones I'd met—always smelled like they'd been outdoors all their lives.

I thought about walking up to his truck, leaning in like the prostitutes I'd seen, and snatching the money. But Nettie might slow my getaway. I grabbed her by the neck of her dress to hurry her along. That cheap thing ripped like tissue paper, and suddenly Nettie's titties were all out. I didn't know what to do. I couldn't just let her walk down the street like that. Panicked, I pushed her toward the Mexican's truck. He opened the door, and we jumped in.

Nettie sat between me and the Mexican. He drove around, nearly wrecking twice from staring at her. When we passed my high school, I remembered I wanted to go on a Home Economics field trip to a place where they made underwear. I needed money. I glanced at the Mexican—his eyes were bugged out, and the way he kept squeezing his hands between his legs told me he wanted some real bad. So I tugged Nettie's dress open a little more. His tongue slid between his teeth like a lizard's. He steered the truck toward the woods behind my school.

"Money god damn," I shouted. "I need some money goddammit!"

My cursing woke the Mexican up. He sputtered something in Spanish and held out some wrinkled-up money in front of Nettie's nose. My hand swooped in and snatched it. Two ten-dollar bills. They smelled like dirt, but I put them in my bosom anyway—what little bosom I had.

The Mexican got out of his truck and walked around to the back. He fixed up some old carpet scraps to make a pallet in the truck bed. It looked like a dog bed.

I started to take Nettie and run out of the woods, but part of me wanted to see what Nettie would do when she was having sex. With her being slow, would she know what to do? When he stuck his thing in her, would she grunt like a wild animal or take it like a woman?

The only thing Nettie knew about sex was when she rubbed herself between her legs. Big Mama tried to cure her of that habit—swore up and down me and Mama had something to do with Nettie gapping her legs in the middle of the room while we were watching television. Didn't matter if Uncle Bobo was there either.

She'd rub herself like she was on fire. Big Mama stuck Nettie's fingers to the stove whenever Nettie "acted ugly" like that. But that didn't stop her from doing the "feel good" thing—just drove it behind closed doors like any other girl. Still, I knew Nettie had never been with a boy or a man.

We kept her around the house like a pet. She never went anywhere alone and never stayed in the house by herself.

I pulled Nettie up into the truck bed and made her lie down. I raised her dress and pulled down her panties. It was hot—so hot the grass crunched between the toes of my sandals.

The Mexican pulled down his pants. He leaned over Nettie and started kissing her. He ran his tongue over her tits and grunted something in Spanish. His ass twitched, moving round and round.

She must've liked his tongue on her tits and his thing slapping the top of her pussy, because she started humming in her throat. But when he tried to stick himself in her, Nettie bucked and yelped like a dog.

I held her hand like people do when a woman's having a baby. I stroked her arm, rubbed her tits myself, and that calmed her down. She cooed and rocked her body to the Mexican's rhythm like she was a woman who knew what to do.

Everything was fine until he started grunting loud and squeezing her breasts too hard. Nettie began fighting him. I held her shoulders down until his breathing eased up.

He rolled off her and started snoring. I helped Nettie pull her dress down and get into her panties. I found an old safety pin and some tape in the truck and fixed the front of her dress.

We stood there a moment, looking at the Mexican as he slept—pants still around his ankles, snoring so hard his body shook. His little thing between his legs looked like a baby bird. Nettie stared at him with her mouth open, looking so dumb I wanted to slap her.

"Bitch, you just had sex for the first time and all you can do is look stupid!"

Nettie just stared. What's the use? I told myself maybe it's good she don't know what's going on—she'll never be hurt.

I pulled his shoes off and took his pants. In his pockets I found more dirty money, which I slipped into my bosom. I rolled the pants tight, meaning to throw them into the weeds.

But then the smell of dirt and sweat hit my nose. I remembered the same smell in my daddy's clothes, how it felt good the few times I hugged him. I looked at the Mexican lying there half naked, oily, and brown. A funny feeling came over me, like I was in love with him or something.

I touched his balls. He snorted and brushed my hand away. I sighed, rolled up his pants, and put them in my sack.

When we got home, Mama was gone to work and Big Mama was asleep—chemo makes her weak and sleepy all the time. I counted the Mexican's money: ninety dollars.

I hid most of it, washed the man's pants, and stored them in Jonathan's old dresser. I bought Nettie a big Hershey bar and gave her a birth control pill.

And that's how this money business got started. Now I got close to six thousand dollars and two plastic garbage sacks full of men's pants and drawers.

I don't know what it is about me, but every time I sneak a boy in to see Nettie, I steal his drawers. Or if we're out in the woods with an old drunk for Nettie, I steal his pants.

Mama says she wishes there was a man in this house. I think about my garbage sacks full of drawers and say to myself, "It's plenty of men in this house, woman."

Sometimes, when there's no business, I put on a pair of boy drawers and stick a banana or something down the front. I walk around the house, grabbing myself like men and boys do on the street.

When I do that, I feel powerful—like I could fight anything. Red drawers are my favorite. On days I don't have to dress for gym, I wear the red ones to school. I sit in class, gap my legs a little, and boys swarm around me like flies.

That's one way I get customers for me and Nettie. Boys don't have much money—five dollars gets them all the pussy they want, but it ain't me, it's my sister.

Sometimes they only got three dollars. I tell them, "If that's all you got, that's all you got. Page me later and bring some of your old drawers for charity."

When Mama goes to her night job, here they come through the back window like roaches—grinning, frisky, and carrying drawers.

I show them Nettie, laying on the bed in the short pink gown and fishnet stockings I bought her. They look at her crossed eyes and some of the dance goes out of them—until Nettie sticks out her lips, turns on her side, and rubs her thigh. I taught her that.

One time, I had four or five basketball boys in here. They had twenty dollars between them. One was so horny he couldn't wait his turn. He walked around like a frisky dog, sweating, clutching his crotch.

"Damn hurry up!" he kept shouting at his friends, their asses pumping between Nettie's thighs.

He started looking at me funny, and I got scared he might rape me. So I told him I had another girl saved for special boys. I led him into Big Mama's room. It was dark.

I pulled down her covers, raised her gown a little. She hadn't pooped on herself, thank God—just lay there with her eyes twinkling.

"Who is this?" the boy asked.

"She's good. She's real good," I said, touching his back. That loosened him up. He pulled off his pants and got into Big Mama's bed.

Just as he rolled on top of her, she squawked, "Buuud! Uhh Buuud!"

That boy jumped like he'd been shot in the ass—nearly broke himself in two getting out the window. That's how I got the drawers with green shamrocks. I call them my lucky drawers.

Not that they bring me luck, but shamrocks ought to be lucky.

"Buu-uud! Uh Buu-uud! Where you at, nigguh?"

Shit. There goes Big Mama again, calling her husband dead for over fifty years, like he's just around the corner.

I'm a snap this towel on that old woman's ass.

Chapter 16 - A Little Bit Later

Lord, my trials and tribulations. Nettie acting like she don't like boys and men no more. I had to slap her the other night 'cause she didn't want to go down on a guy. Shit, that was fifty dollars I was about to lose. I'll be glad when I finish high school and go to college. If I raise prices and teach Nettie some more tricks to do with her tongue, I might have fifteen thousand in cold cash by the time I'm eighteen.

Maybe by then I'll find real love and can burn this sack full of drawers.

I know hearing all of this you wonder how I'm ever goin' to get in anybody's college. But I do good in school. Straight A's and haven't ever been to the Principal's office to be disciplined. I'm scared to do anything bad in school. I'm scared to set foot in the Principal's office.

It ain't because my Mama going to whip me if I do. She couldn't care less with her drinking Bull malt liquor a six-pack at a time some days. I'm just scared that something's going to leap out of the black cloud that I'm always seeing out the corner of my eye. And this somethin's going to press its thick body against me and keep pressing and pressing until I'm dead.

I see the shadow real clear when I'm on a bus. All this time I've been scared it's in a dark corner of a principal's office or under a desk.

The principal of my high school is a nice white woman with light blue eyes named Mrs. Wicks. Her husband was the principal of my elementary school. She always have nice things to say to me, but her eyes stay on me all the time like she's got secrets on me. And the better I do in school, the more she watches me.

Miss Brown, my Homeroom teacher, sent me to Mrs. Wicks' office one day. Because I'm a good student, I get to be kind of like a secretary for all of my teachers. Miss Brown asked me to carry the

Absentee List to the Principal's office. I did it with dread like I always do.

I think they ought to make the bad kids carry things to the office. That's their second home anyway.

So, I was walking along the hallway hoping it would grow longer and longer. I passed exit doors and started to duck out of them. But I thought to myself that would make me get in trouble. Maybe even involve the Police—who would keep on asking me questions and pulling the thing in the shadows closer to me until I'm leading them to the hiding place for my money and all them drawers and pants.

Everything in uniform scares me. Even the school band makes me shake. A school psychologist—damn I hate that word—is working on that.

Anyway, I get to Mrs. Wicks' office and hand her the list. She smiles at me and asks me if I've read over the literature on the pre-S.A.T. test. I nodded my head yes. She said she expected nothing short of two hundred from me. I smiled and she smiled.

She then told me to hold on while she checked the names against the master list in her computer. She touched a button and green words filled up the screen. They were the names of everybody in my Homeroom class and where they were supposed to be at first period.

I don't think Mrs. Wicks ever got to the end of the list. I saw my name rolling by on the screen and there was HOE next to my name. I remember screaming, "That man!" And that was it for me.

When I woke up again I was on the Nurse's couch with ice on my forehead.

When I was able to walk, Mrs. Wicks took me into her office and explained to me that HOE was her short way of saying Home Economics and nobody had ever called her office and said I was a "whore" or any of the other ugly words that I screamed out.

She patted my arm and said I was the best student in the school and asked me what man has been calling me those names. I shrugged my shoulders and clamped my jaws shut.

Mrs. Wicks seems to watch me more and more. Seems like I'm in her office being secretary more than her own secretary is. I think she's tryin' to pry stuff out of me. Maybe her husband told her something about me. Or, I wonder if she knows about me getting boys for my sister.

Sometimes when I'm counting my money, I look up and see her eyes winking at me like daytime stars. I even imagine myself being called to her office and when I get there, she got my big bags of drawers on her desk. And she's got some spread out on the desk with all my money dumped out in the middle of them and her eyes locked on me.

But what boy would tell where he gettin' some secret pussy from? They like it too much, throwin' their whole skinny trembling hips into Nettie like they ain't goin to never get no more in their life.

I shifted my sacks of drawers and money to a different hiding place right under Big Mama's bed. Mama don't like to hang around in that room too much. And she's more than happy I volunteer to sweep and mop the floor.

When my broom touches them sacks of money under Big Mama's bed, I wonder what that HOE next to my name really means.

Chapter 17 - Big Mama

Dear Lord Jesus And you wonder why I'm a praying Woman,

My little granddaughter thought I was being mean and hateful because I didn't want her to go to Astroworld—well we was burying her last brother. But I knows something else about them carnivals. I don't care if folks say Astroworld is bigger than a carnival 'cause it has roller coasters that can go higher than some buildings downtown, and you can call it any kind of "world" you want to, I still say it's a carnival. Carnivals are crooked places full of the devil's reality. And that reality is evil and full of games and unreal people. People in and around carnivals come from the edge of hell—elephant man, skeleton man, bearded women, and creatures who are both men and women in the same body. This child she didn't make it to Astroworld. But her undoing was trying to get to that carnival. She met up with the devil and he took from her, her girlhood and done made her a ruint woman. My daughter Marsha, she sad right now all inside. She's a woman burdened with dead sons, a raped daughter, an idiot child, and a no good husband.

I love my daughter, but I think that man of hers—that man they goin to bring to his son's funeral all chained up like a wild hog, he brought a lot of grief to this family. I don't know where my daughter met him. I suspect he kind of attached himself to her like some kind of puppy, stray tomcat, or something. Marsha was always picking up strays when she was a child. Most times they drifted off and attached themselves to other people, or got killed. I wished that had happened to Suliman. Wish he had got himself attached to another woman or got himself killed. He did get another woman once. Marsha went over to that whore's house and beat him out of there. Rode his back and beat his ass like he was some kind of horse. After that, the only thing that keeps him separate from Marsha is prison.

Suliman steals anything that ain't nailed down. He up there in Midway now for sassin me and violating his parole by getting hisself throwed in jail. All I did was voice my opinion about Jonathan. Nobody tol' him to start cussin' and throwin' stuff around. If he hadn't been a thief, he wouldn't have been in trouble the first place. And can steal some of the most stupidest stuff. Lord, have mercy. Walked into a store and ran out with a whole counter full of lipsticks.

"Suliman, what you goin' to do with a tray full of lipsticks," Marsha asked him.

"Sell 'em I guess," he answered like a fool. Well, he had stepped on one of the lipsticks, and the police followed his red footprints right on up here to my daughter's house. Cops smeared some hot pink lipstick around his mouth before they lead him out. Talk about an example of manhood for your boys—going out with your mouth looking like a sissy's or a baboon's ass.

This last time he got caught stealing tombstones. Now he didn't go into no cemetery and take the stones. He stole them from Bishop's shop around the corner. Bishop carves tombstones for a living. Got a lot of marble and granite in his yard.

Now if you gonna steal a tombstone, it looks like to me you'd have sense to steal a blank one. What crooked undertaker can use a tombstone that's already got a "Mrs. Alvie Rae Jones 1936 – 1986" written between a set of praying hands? Well the boy got caught. They tried to make it a federal case 'cause Mrs. Alvie Rae Jones was a retired postal worker. Luckily his two- bit lawyer had enough sense to fight that. I could go on and on about Suliman. My Mama once said there was people who could steal death from the dead. Suliman is a prime example.

Another way Suliman is bad news for my daughter, is all these poison children he gave her. Somethin wrong with ever last one on them.

Nettie is retarded. Promise is strange. Poochie was hardheaded as a mule. If you told him to go left, he went right to spite you. Bobo was just unlucky like he was born to cross paths with black cats. And now this Jonathan boy got full of AIDS and died. I often wondered how that boy got to be a sissy. He was a lovable boy, nice looking, could make you laugh. Women loved him like bees love flowers.

I told Suliman one time, the time that got him in jail once before—I said, "Suliman, if you gonna steal something, why don't you steal somebody's manhood and give it to your son. Well that got the house tore up and brought the police up in here, where they found a bunch of women shoes Suliman had stole. My daughter didn't let me come to her house for two whole months until her lights got cut off and I paid the bill.

My first husband Bud, who I married when I was fifteen, was an altogether different kind of man. He was twenty-five. A good man. Maybe too good for me. We snuck off and got married here in Texas where nobody knowed us. I dressed up in some big clothes and lied about my age. Came back home and I was a married lady. Had the paper to prove it. Didn't get no whippin'. Bud was a hard worker. Plus he got a little check from when he got shot up in in the second war. His left foot swelled up a lot because of that. Other than that he was all man. We started a little farm out from DeQuincy Louisiana where we grew some of the best sweet potatoes all around. I cleaned house in Lake Charles for a rich white family. We had it going okay. Okay for colored people in those days.

When I was seventeen, the fair came to Sulphur Louisiana. Sulphur was where I was born and sure didn't want to return to, not even to sell sweet potatoes. I ain't never been too crazy about a lot of lights and glittery things. Just makes you dizzy and foolish. But Bud said it would be a good way to sell a lot of sweets at a better price than they offered at the farmer's market. Plus, have some fun too. Bud loved his sweets. Used to put the candy from the sweets on my nipples. Even after he learned another man had had the pleasure of my nipples he still loved them. Any other man would have killed me, but not Bud. Licked these big old thangs like candy right along side that gal Susan who weren't his. He forgave me of my lies about Susan taking after somebody on my Grandpas side. I confessed out of spite and to knock some of that goodness off Bud. I at least deserved a beating for getting myself pregnant with that Bible salesman's baby. Other niggers would have cut their women, but not Bud. He sulked for a day when I rammed the truth into his chest with my fingers. By night he was brushing up against me. All was forgiven.

Anyhow Bud and me, (Susan was toddling and his child Lena was in my belly) set up our sweet potatoes under an ol' tall scrawny pine. I had me a fly swatter for flies and any hands that tried to pilfer a potato. We might a been doing okay, but a whole lot of folks around us wasn't. The war and the depression had Louisiana by the neck. I made a big sign for the potatoes out of croaker sack that said "sweets fifteen cent a peck." Did my best to draw a nickel and a dime on the sign. Even if you couldn't read or write, you ought to knowed what a dime and a nickel look like.

Around four that evening the sun was slipping behind the pines and the whites was coming out from hidin' from the heat. We knew our time on the rides was up. We gathered around each other's tables sampling cakes, pies—Sister Berry and her big pot of chitlin stew didn't attract nothing but flies, bless her heart. A few poor Cajuns came by me and Bud's table. Claim they didn't have but a dime. We sold 'em sweets anyway. That's the kind of man Bud was. Everybody seemed happy. The air cracked with backslappin' and cackling.

A nicely dressed white couple sidled up to our table. He nodded polite. I knew who he was right away. That keen nose had slid between my legs and called out my name. I ducked my head down and turned Susan's face to my thighs. His woman smiled at first, but when she saw Susan squirming and got a good look at that sandy hair and them freckles and thin nose, her face turned red as a beet. She rolled her eyes at her husband the Bible seller. He didn't pay no attention to nothing. Just asked how much was the potatoes. You know when you got a sign up and people still ask, it means either they can't read or they want to bargain. Well Bud said very firmly and politely fifteen cents a peck.

"Fine lookin taters, don't you think, Dorothy?" Dorothy looked at the sweet potatoes like she was lookin at turds.

"I sure would like some to go with my supper."

"You sure love you some nigger taters, Jim Lee. Nigger taters ain't the only thing you love." How much you pay for nigger whores?"

Dorothy took some change out of her pinched up purse and throwed it on the table. Jim lee looked at her and looked at me. His mouth hung open like it was a fly trap. I don't think Bud heard everything she said because some children had got to squawking over a bear being led around on a chain. So he thought her anger was over the price of the potatoes. Bud picked up the nickel and saw that it was a nickel. But the other coin was a steel penny. Now it was three things that Bud didn't tolerate. It was turnips, liars, and cheats. He said turnips only fit for cheats and liars bound for hell. He tol' the woman very politely that it was only six cents on the table. She opened her mouth and spit on the table next to the money. Bud looked at her, which was his first mistake, then knocked her money off the table. He upset some of the potatoes and one fell on her foot. She turned her ugly face up toward God's heaven and went to screamin' as loud as she could.

"A nigger hit me! A nigger hit me!"

Her husband tried to "now Dorothy" her down and move her away from the table. But she wasn't having it.

"You gone let a nigger and his bitch git away with hittin' your wife?" And she bawled again. Mouth as black and rotten as death. The air around us stopped. The sun seem like it came up again from behind the pines and got scorching hot. It felt like fire was all over me. I thought my bowels was going to run off. I clutched Susan close like I

wanted to put her back in where she came from. Ol' sheriff come runnin'. Didn't ask no questions. Knocked me off our platform and sent Susan sprawling. Him and some more men dragged Bud off.

I don't need to go into all that other mess. It don't do no good to try and put yourself in people's shoes. I heard a woman talkin' one time about she wished she knowed what the last minutes was like for her daughter who got killed by the Leaky Eye rapist. Maybe that works for some folks. But I don't see where that would do me any good. I loved my husband with all of my heart, but my body is my body and his body is his body. My soul is my soul and his soul is his. I can't feel no pain for him and nobody else, no more than he and anybody can feel pain for me.

What I saw hanging from that pole high up where the flag had flew next to the Ferris wheel wasn't Bud anymore. Wasn't Bud at all. Just a tattered thing with no hands and one shoe on his foot that always swelled. Them carnival folks roasted and ate our sweets, while Bud looked like a big ol' mess hangin' above them. They gave the hulls to that bear. I ain't had no use for sweet potatoes no more. And no more use for carnivals. If I pass by a carnival or amusement park, it makes me sick.

I'm goin on in the front room now. Goin to take that little woman child to my bosom and try to hug some love into her. She think I don't love her, but I do. If only Suliman wasn't her daddy, she wouldn't have come up with no crazy idea like she had this morning. I don't know if she'll ever be able to have children. Doctor said she all tore up down there. Probably a good thing for her not to have children. I believe she going to be tore up in her mind from now on.

Well, the old lady is gone. Me, Bobo, and Nettie is all that's left of her poison grand children. Aunt Susan lost her baby. So Big Mama lost her chance to coo over a big red grandbaby. She had nothing but us poison dark spots. Well this letter is going where it should, in the trash pile to be burned. Or I could tuck it in her casket. It can burn up with her in hell. Thinking about that.

Rust Hills

Chapter 18 – Shadrach Chesterfield

I play basketball for the Birmingham, Alabama Blitzers. Smallest team in the Continental League. I had a short run with the Miami Heat, but being Pete Chesterfield's son ruined that. At least I wasn't named Pete Jr., but "Shadrach Chesterfield" still got me stares—like people wondered if I kept a piece of my father in my pocket.

When I was a kid, I'd hear him and my mother fighting behind their bedroom door. It always ended with him chanting, *"Mama's baby, Daddy's maybe."* One day, after all the mess with him came out, I asked Mama if Pete was really my daddy. I prayed she'd say no—that I belonged to anybody but him. A hobo would've been fine. But she said yes, and I cried for days.

Pete's face was everywhere—TV, newspapers. He was dead, but I was left to fight for him. If I didn't fight, it felt like I was saying I was proud he was my father. If I did fight, it felt like I was defending him. I wish Mama had lied. Every drink I took, every needle I pushed in my arm, came from carrying his name.

I made it to the NBA out of a tiny Georgia college, kept my drinking quiet long enough to dominate the court and get drafted second round. But with the Heat, every game brought some loudmouth in the stands, some whisper on the bench. I wasn't good enough for management to overlook me leaping into the crowd to shut somebody up. The heroin didn't help.

A therapist during one rehab suggested I visit the girl Pete raped. Said she'd been committed for killing her child. I didn't see the point. Mama once tried visiting one of Pete's victims, Paula—she slammed the door in her face. But the therapist kept pushing.

I drove to Rust Hills with my boyfriend at the time. Mama thought my being gay was the root of all my troubles, but that wasn't it. Men tried to love me, to protect me from myself. The more they loved me, the lower I sank.

Rust Hills looked like something out of a painting. The doctor in charge knew why I was there and asked if I was sure. I shrugged. They brought Promise in, led by a huge Black guard. She sat across from me, staring at the floor. A sign above her said "Confront and Be Cured." We sat and I decided to let her speak first...take the lead.

"Where's Lakeisha Ann?" she asked.

I frowned. "Who's that?"

She slammed the table, shrieked.

"All right in there?" the guard called from outside.

She stuck her tongue out at the wall. "What you come out here for, Pete Chesterfield?"

"I'm Shadrach Chesterfield."

"My Lord! And Shadrach, Meshach, and Abednego stepped out of the fiery furnace, not a hair singed. Big Mama would've liked your name. She didn't like mine much. You don't look like that frog Pete."

"I came to apologize... for Pete Chesterfield."

"Who?"

"The man who hurt you."

"Nigga, that is your father!"

The words hit me hard.

"He didn't hurt nothing," she went on. "He did what he did. I'm the one who hurt something. I hurt my child. He's dead. I'm not. I was a fool. I let the rain ruin me. The rain was just the rain, but I made it more. Don't turn him into the rain. Let him just be your father. Forget his ass. You got long arms—what you use 'em for?"

"I play basketball."

"My husband uses his arms to reach up women's twats."

I stared. She grinned. "Always had an ugly tongue. Used to shout cuss words at home when the radio was up loud so nobody heard. Let me see your arms."

She yanked up my sleeve, traced the needle marks. Looked me in the eye.

"You's a fool."

She called for the guard, and that was it. I thought it was a waste. But a year later, on my knees about to suck a man for drug money, her voice came back—*You's a fool.*

From that moment, I let Leaky Eye go. Pete Chesterfield was just my father. That's all he'd ever be. I didn't have to carry his bags. We spend too much time letting what happened to us consume us.

I hope Promise is doing well.

Chapter 19—Love Letters

Red syrup
   flows freely
   from the Christ child.
   Merry Christmas
   and
   God bless the
   holy hole
   Mama opened
   in your head.

Early

Dear LaKeisha Ann:

I feel as if I've been in a valley of silence for a long time. Yesterday morning I found myself lying in the palm of a gigantic hand and being lifted up. I saw myself rising up to meet a brown skinny girl who had wings. The girl had a face like my dead brother Jonathan's. I realized then I was going to meet myself. I heard myself thinking. The voices in my head were loud as the engines of one hundred roaring buses. Pictures tumbled in front of my eyes. You were in one of the pictures—black and skinny limbed.

I'm in some kind of a Hospital. I'm sure you read the papers and saw my pictures all covered with red. The red is supposed to be blood. But I was cooking that day the picture was taken, so I'm sure the so-called "blood" is food coloring.

I think I have missed two years. My tongue is so thick it fills my mouth and blocks my speech. I see nothing but shadows. I'm a bird in a cage and am very aware of the cage. You should see some of the other birds here who are oblivious to the cage. They walk in circles until the attendants herd them to the dinner hall. After dinner, the birds walk some more. They're in constant motion until they're strapped to their cots at night. Even then, some of them move their legs as if walking until they finally fall asleep.

Evidently, I was not a walker. I was a sitter. My ass is as flat as a chair. Dr. Bacon the psychiatrist here told me that nothing reached me. Not the ice baths, electric shocks, nothing. But I'll tell you what woke me out of darkness and that was some man's fingers up my snatch. Those fingers traveled through my womb and tugged at my vocal cords. The fingers propped open my eyes. Someone inside me screamed for two solid days at monsters.

Child, the visions were something else. A small boy in a gold suit lay in a casket. His head was bashed in. Blood gushed like a spring from his ear. Headless singers in blood red robes swayed back and forth as if caught in a spell. A man with legs thin as broomsticks slept in the middle of a big bed. His penis was erect and large as a long barrelled pistol. A white woman offered me strawberries from her breasts. I bit into one and it was rotten and bitter. But yet I yearned for more. I was lured by the redness. And then there were buses. They were driven by drivers who bled from holes in their temples. They drove toward me at high speeds as if they were trying to crush me. But the buses went through me as if I were air. The woman inside me screamed as if death was coming at her. And there was not a Christ anywhere to save me. Not a christ anywhere to save me from this torment. But I'm so much better now.

Please come and visit me. They say this place is called Rust Hills. The trees are orange and red. The grass is green as seaweed. I'm sure from an airplane, this place looks like a nice salad. It's in a valley. I can see cows beyond the fence. The cows have more life than the zombies inside the fence. The staff has stamped their motto everywhere: "Confront and cure." "Confront and cure" on the walls, on the dishes, on the bottom of your glass after you've drank your milk.

A man did come and see me yesterday. He called himself my husband. He acted as if he hadn't seen me in a hundred years. He grabbed my hands and kissed them all over. I guess my silence had locked him out too. I offered him myself. But he said no.

Now what kind of husband is that? I'm standing on the table with my gown hiked over my ass and he says no. But maybe I didn't smell very good as a wife. However the man with the far reaching fingers didn't mind my smell.

Dr. Bacon, the woman who runs this place thought it would be good for me to write you. They want me to remember things—go back in time and come up to the day I was found covered with the red stuff. It's about something called confront and be cured. What can you do? I don't know. I heard that you do have an education now.

Perhaps the plan is to surround me with an educated triad—you, Dr. Bacon, and the man who calls himself my husband.

I hope I have your correct address. I know we had some differences. Our lives went different ways after I graduated. If and when you do come, don't take the bus. The belly of the bus like the belly of the whale, is full of shit. As women and as my friend we'll smell bad together if we have to.

Love,

Promise

PS. Bring my child too.

Dear Charlie:

After a long and bitter sleep, I've finally arrived at the plantation Rust Hills. The white Mistress greeted me motherly or perhaps motherfuckerly. I can't imagine that the syrup that oozed from her was sweet. It must be a poisonous sticky trap. You know the old saying about trapping flies with honey.

She says she's a Doctor. I'm not sure if she's a twat doctor like you. But I think she likes twats. She's very touchy feely with us girls. Well what else is there to touch. I don't think there are any men here, except for the head nigger in charge. And he's a soft fat old boy with big hammy hands. all that is missing is a red handkerchief for his black moon head and he would be "Topsy." I call him Big Fingers.

His job is to oversee us. He oversees us as we wash in the shower, as we shit and piss. Overseeing us as we eat, as we leave the dining hall with our gowns lifted to make sure we aren't stealing a breadstick or donut. Always a little switch in his hands to "tan" our legs to herd us along through the maze of room and roomlets.

Dr. Bacon rarely visits the slave quarters. She prefers to avoid the glaring piss and shit of our habitats. I've only seen her in her blue office painted the same color as her eyes. I wonder if the walls are really blue or if the things I'm seeing are bathed in the reflection from her eyes? Our gowns look blue. Our little booties look blue. So I don't know what's going on. I fear Dr. Bacon. Her blue eyed serenity is too luring. She's pulling me into her to drown me in her pools. I know this. I think I'll stake my life on her head nigger. His eyes are plain and black like some old coon's.

Well this is where you've put me. And I shall be here. Be kind to our son.

Love,
your wife Promise

Dear Charlie:

Why do I keep seeing our son as a corpse? His head lies on a tiny satin pillow. Why is he wearing a hat? I'm ready for answers. Am I not a good Mother?

Regards,
Promise

Dear Charlie:

How could I kill a child? I taught them how to clap their hands to songs about birds and cats. I helped them to create giants bugs from egg cartons, to spell out words. Words like I LOVE YOU MOMMY YOU ARE THE BEST MOMMY IN THE WHOLE WIDE WORLD. I taught them to stick their hands in paint and draw turkeys with little fingers for feathers. Husband, I loved our child. Please, Please come and get me. Stop this awful charade. If it's another woman, I'll let you go. But don't tell these lies on me. Don't keep me from my own flesh and blood!

Love,

Promise

PS Tell thar Dr. Bacon woman to stop lying on me. I ain't killed nobody. Fuck her confront and be cured bullshit.

Dear Charlie:

Oh well, I guess I'm a beast. Dr. Bacon showed me pictures from when they took me to jail. In one photo I'm handcuffed and bathed in blood. The other shows a small body wrapped in a rubber sheet. Who wraps their child in a rubber sheet in the summer? Can something so small have bled so much? Forgive me.

Your Wife

Dear Charlie

You doctor's are a bunch of butchers. Who cut up and ate our child? Who did this? Got his heart on a scale like it's a knot of stew meat. Where is the top of his skull? I can't see his eyes. They've pull off his face. Listen I know I did our boy wrong. But I didn't do this much wrong. No wonder you wouldn't let me come to the funeral. Or was it a barbecue. You guys are beasts from hell. If you come back here, I'll kill you! I swear to god I will, you butcher.

Hatefully,

Promise Goodday

PS I've gone back to Goodday. I won't dare wear your name Silvers.

Dear LaKeisha Ann:

Girl, how come you haven't been out here to see me? I miss you. Ten years is a long time. I want us to see each other alive in the flesh, not in death. How are your babies? Well, they're not babies anymore I guess. Which one has made you a grandma, LaTrisha or LaMargaret? Your Mama sure love to put "La" in front of names. Just imagine if she had had boys—LaDavid, LaJohn, LaMichael LaAnthony. That would be a mess.

If you are a Grandma, I hope you're a cool grandma and not trying to act all holy and shit like my Big Mama used to act. But I can't imagine you telling your daughters and granddaughters shit like "keep your dress tail down." You still kind of young. They probably tell you to keep your dress down. I know how it is to be near the end of these thirties. Something makes you want to keep your dress raised up to your neck. Girl, I want it so bad sometimes my pussy trembles. But unlike you out there in the free world who can get any any ol' fine brown negro they want, child, all I got is Big Fingers who is some kind of attendant here. They won't even let me and my husband Charlie have a conjugal visit.

You know he hasn't divorced me. I killed our baby and he says he loves me. And you know, I know he does. The boy can get all the pussy he wants. He stays up to his elbows and nose in pussy. White pussy, brown pussy, black pussy, yellow pussy, sick pussy, well pussy, hairy pussy, bald pussy, and he still says he loves me. Wants me to hurry up and get well so I can come home. What home? Shit, he's sick for wanting a bitch like me. And believe me I doubt if I'll ever love a man. I like dick. But a man is just a means to an end. What end? I'm not sure. Money, security, a child? Or maybe it gives you your reason to be in this world. Welcome to the club of "couples." Chapters in every city from Atlanta to Zurich. Do "couples" things like set up your own little hut and fill it full of furniture and babies. Then one dies and leaves the other to bury it. So maybe that's the value in having a man, to insure yourself of having an ordinary life. But who wants ordinary? Spend your whole life massaging an ego so you can be ordinary? I think not. Just give me the dick. A mechanical man with a dick suits me. Okay, sometimes arms are nice to have wrapped around you.

I do need me some arms. I want your arms, your daughters arms, and my Momma's arms. I want us all to be girls, laugh, pour tea, and lock men out of our lives—if only for a moment one Sunday evening. Come see me soon. But Do Not Come If It's Raining!

DO NOT! DO NOT! DO NOT!

love,
Your friend,
Promise

Dear LaKeisha Ann:

Oh, child! Green, green, green. At first the scheme of things here was all blue. Then I assume voices revealed to Dr. Bacon that green is better for a nuthouse. So now everything in this place is green, green like the puke that ran out of Jonathan when he died. I don't blame you for not coming to visit. You couldn't find me anyway. My green gown blends me in with the puke colored walls. And the puke colored walls blend in with the green vegetable mush they feed us here. All of this green dissolves into green shit we shit into the green water in the green toilets. Then the green flies dance in this shit.

So you see, girl, you cannot see me because I'm blended in to the green. But if you see a green fly crawling on your pink silk curtains, don't kill it. You see it might be carrying parts of me on its feet. And I'm not ready to die yet.

Love,
Promise

Dear Mr. Shadrach Chesterfield:

It was so useless for you to visit me—coming to apologize for your Father. What is there to forgive? He was my first lover. I was the whore that seduced him. That day on the bus when it parked at the end of its route and while the rain beat the windows like a couple of mad niggers with sticks, I went up to that man that you want me to forgive and I sat on his lap. Storm clouds were in his eyes. They were silver and gray like the sky outside that bus. He tried to push my whorish ass away, but I clung to his arm like a starving bitch clings to a precious piece of carion. I pressed my small hand to his crotch and made his root thick and hard. He shook his head and tears rolled down his cheeks as I unzipped his pants. He could not fight me off. I paralyzed him with shame and passion.

I got down on my tough knees. Baby, I made your daddy buck like a wild horse. I licked until that man, your daddy said he loved me with all of his heart. We became lovers. Every evening after school I'd get on his bus and sit so he could see me in that big rearview mirror. I wouldn't wear panties. By the time the bus emptied and we got to the end of the line, he would be trembling as if he'd been sitting on electrical wires. He'd dash toward me, lift me high in the air and impale me on his cock. He'd cling to me as if I were a lifeline that kept him from drowning in the raging sea.

You have bastard half brothers and sisters walking around the streets of Houston thanks to your daddy and me. So don't ever come back here crying your vinegar tears and apologizing. Perhaps the real source of your tears is that you regret you never got a chance to love your daddy like I did.

Sincerely,

Mrs. Promise S. Goodday-Chesterfield-Silvers

PS. and keep your sleeve rolled down. I don't believe for one minute your Daddy had anything to do with those needle marks in your arm.

To: Mister Pete Chesterfield
Dear Sir:

I know your watery gray eyes are forever closed and have been closed for a long time. But I feel somehow this letter will reach you. Your son came to visit me one day. His visit unsettled me. He was like vinegar—very pure and clean, but he funked up the place. So I'm between guilt and anger. What am I, angry or guilty? I don't know. I know that I hurt. Maybe this hurt grows from the bitter root of my anger.

Poor you. You are dead and can't hurt. Aren't you blessed? Your coffin is tarnished. The satin lining is tattered. And you have rotted into shit colored bones. But you don't hurt!

Some nights I love you. I remember your fingers and eyes and I love you. And there are nights when I boil you in the cauldron of my hate. Your skin puffs, blisters, and separates from your bones as you cook in the roiling waters.

But to sum up my feelings and in the spirit of forgiveness, I think of you as ... Oh God ... as a . . . a black son ... Shit! It's raining again. The rain torments my soul like the worms torment your body. But you don't feel a damn thing. I feel. I hurt.

?????

Promise

Dear Big Mama:

A voice asked me over and over, "Do you love Jesus? Do you love Jesus? Do you have the Holy Ghost?" Well I don't know if I love Jesus or not. I mean it is peculiar to me how a bunch of old nappy headed black women is supposed to love this white man with eyes the color of a blue computer screen and hair like you take a mop and dip it in oil. It's very peculiar to me. And this Jesus induced orgasm you old women have, you call it the Holy Ghost, but I call it a shame. So what's with you Big Mama? You going to marry Jesus? Going to have a gold baby by Jesus? Or was that bible salesman your Jesus? You worshipped your Susan. Gave her that white sounding name. And she ain't ever let you stay in her house. Didn't hardly come to see you when you was sick. But her daddy hanging on a cross, you just love and love. You loved him while you hated your daughter, the nigga she shacked up with, and her children. Your religion was a weapon. a dagger made of sugar that was sweet when you licked it and deadly when you used it against me and your daughter. From the safety of your God's bosom you called me an imp and your own daughter a whore.

I applauded the little red imp when, when God's back was turned, he threw cancer upon your bosom. My regret is that the stroke that twisted you, made you childlike and innocent. I could not make you remember how you made us suffer. You were wracked in pain and didn't know why. Well maybe the vision of your first husband constantly in your face was enough punishment. I know you heard him scream as the flame's hot teeth ate and chewed huge chunks of that boy's flesh. He should have been your first love—a boy who you loved with your heart. A boy you let kiss you everywhere. Did that boy become your Jesus? I mean they both suffered. Maybe that's why all you old black women love him so. He reminds you of your own men, and he don't knock you upside the head with his hammy fist. Well love on, old lady.

But I tell you one thing, If I ever get to Heaven and if Jesus is driving a bus, I'll make him wish he had hung on that cross a little longer. Do I love Jesus? We'll see.

Bye,

Promise

Dear Aunt Susan:

How is life in Candlelight Trails? Still quiet and sleepy? I bet. I saw on the news the other day on the TV while I was typing Doctor Bacon's reports, that it was discovered that Candlelight Hills was built over some kind of place where they dumped medical and chemical waste from hospitals in the 50s and 60s. Gave you clowns bad water. And you thought the "Leaky Eye" was the cause of your sleepless nights. Couldn't believe that you lived two streets over from that beast. I wonder why he never raped you? He sure got me. Maybe he didn't like your skin color. Most of his bitches were black or brown, except for that white girl he killed, right in your neighborhood just two streets over from you. You dammed fool. Slapping me for not wanting to be out there. Like that there place was some kind of better life. I was clairvoyant then, like I am now. I knew that place wasn't no good. But you slapped me and called me ungrateful. What was I supposed to be grateful for? So what, I struck a grateful match and tried to set your grateful house on fire? You bitch! I can't believe the Leaky Eye never made you suck his cock. Or did he and you never told anybody? Well kiss Uncle Stewart on that big tumor that grows from his forehead. Now you know why it's there. There are secret tumors in you too. Five near your ass and pussy. A big one about to slap the shit out of your brains.

Love

Promise

PS

Is your Daddy selling bibles in hell?

Dear LaKeisha Ann

While Big Fingers was beating me the other day, he called me an evil bitch. I had shit on the floor of my cell and when he came in to bring my supper or play with my twat—I'm sure he came in to play with my twat – but he had to clean the floor instead. In isolation we are always naked and chained. All the pretty girls in here get put in isolation for the smallest infraction. I'm not pretty, but my pussy looks like a huge black plum. It used to drive Charlie wild when he ate it. Clanging your spoon against your plate too loud gets you—isolation. Laughing at the TV when its off, because you thinking about something funny—isolation. Chewing gum too fast—isolation. Well anyway when he came in grinning and carrying a hot dog in his nasty hands, I took a turd and slammed it in his face. Well that lit him up. He upchucked his morning breakfast. When he caught his breath he pulled off his belt and beat me over every inch of my body. It felt like volts of electricity. After a moment I stopped screaming and was numb as a pillar of salt. I was stoic. He beat me still until he was exhausted and he started crying. Then he called me an evil bitch. I had an epiphany. The day I tried to go to Astroworld instead of Jonathan's funeral, I had no feelings. I had that same numbness from Big Fingers beating. My mother's cries didn't move me. Big Mama's admonishments were like stale air. So maybe I am an evil bitch. Some folks think evil is all hissing and biting or cutting a man's guts out. That's passion. Maybe evil is numbness in the midst of everyone's tears. Maybe it's being unable to feel your pain or theirs. I could not be moved. I'm evil.

Love

The Queen of Evil

PS When Big Fingers saw he could do no more beating, he said he would tie me to a tree outside when the next big rainstorm came. Now he has my attention. He knows what rainstorms do to me. It would be like if a jew went to visit a concentration camp. Everything comes back.

I gotta steal some candy from the pharmacy so I can be put in isolation again. I won't let Big Fingers win. No naked in the rain.

Dear Lakeisha Ann:

Hey, girl, what are you doing right now? Listen at me sounding as if we are on the telephone. I just got through watching some kind of political debate on the TV. What a way to spend a Friday night—watching a man and a woman both with as much personality as biscuits talking about how they would ensure world peace. Neither one of them mentioned lobotomy or castration. Well that's my proposal—docilize the masses. After the debate, the host came on and said the usual spiel, "We would like to take this opportunity . . ." and the word "opportunity leaped out at me. I began to think about it. And it seems to me that the pursuit of opportunity is what rules the world. Civilizations have rose up, died, and gone to hell in the pursuit of the opportunity to grab land, bitches, or both.

A woman meets a man and sees opportunity for a movie and a cheap bottle of perfume. (He sees a quick fuck.) If you're real lucky, your "opportunity" might set you up with a million in mutual funds, a multi-layered house on River Oaks Boulevard, and platinum charge cards.

If you're a simple woman, then a chicken dinner and twenty dollars is enough opportunity for you.

Opportunity. All a little girl wanted was the opportunity to go to Astroworld. She relied on a man to drive her. She did not want to be made afraid of the rain.

The rain. Lord have mercy. She did not want the rain to make her bash her doll into the side of a silver bus. All she wanted to do was go to Astroworld.

Love,

Promise

PS. Pray for me and kiss that grand baby.

Dear LaKeisha Ann:

I am getting better. I wrote this poem during one of the group sessions. For those of us who don't like to talk Dr. Bacon prescribes writing. I wrote a poem about a little boy I saw in a magazine. He was hugging his mama's legs. The words above the picture said "Slender Pants Pantyhose are made to stand up to Little Boys."

I thought it was cute. I wrote this:

Little Lost child
floating around up there
in the heavenly air.
You got no more Mama
to leave you
and make you cry.
You died too little
to learn what makes
the heart so brittle.

Dr. Bacon said it was a good poem. She asked me if the little boy in the ad reminded me of my son Chester? I told her hell no! Then she said if I wanted to go home I have to acknowledge what I did to my child. "Remember, Promise, confront and be cured."

Home? Girl, what is that? I've never been home. I've been housed. Isn't a home supposed to make you happy? I don't remember any four walls of happiness. Oh there is fun from time to time in any house. But right on the heels of happiness is that snake of bitterness. Christmas morning it's Santa Claus and tinsel. Christmas night, a brother dead. Fourth of July, it's barbecue in the park. That night Daddy going to jail.

So home sure ain't no carrot on a stick for a Doctor to dangle in front of me and make me answer questions the way she wants me to or make me acknowlwdge anything. But deep down I know that writing about the pictures I see does make me feel better. I can talk to those people in the picture and they talk to me. And Dr. Bacon does not have to know the secrets pictures whisper to me.

Frankly, I think she needs to shit out some demons. I heard she screws around with Big Fingers. I guess she likes that black dick.

Love,

Promise

PS If they really wanted to show how tough pantyhose are, they'd show a man trying to yank them off some bitch and not being able to. And they'd show the bitch hanging him by the neck then putting on those panting hose and switching her ass off to earn some bacon in corporate America. Now those are tough pantystockings!

Dear LaKeisha Ann:

What kind of beast is the Big Fingers thing. Is it woman or manwo? Bulging stomach but soft curved shoulders. Biceps like hams and paws. Mouth small and round as an asshole. Eyes black as a switchblade handle. Hair in pus filled knots on his chin. What is it? This girl Nancy say he has evolved way too far or nor far enough. He could be a woman. I mean his fingers know my snatch better than my own fingers. They don't fumble. My Charlie the pussy Doctor, fumbled and was very clinical with me. But this thing gets to the heart of the matter as he strokes me. And in my moaning I forget about the purple wounds on my ass that he has inflicted. Damn he's good.

Love,
Promise

Dear LaKeisha Ann:

Lord, lord, if I were a beast, I would rip Big Fingers's heart out and eat it. You would think this man was on a period the way he swells and bellows toward the end of the month.

He sent another girl to the infirmary. He beat Collette because she forgot how to spell her name. She wrote "'Let'" on her medicine sign-out sheet. She didn't really forget how to spell her name, but you know how it is to be seventeen. You wake up one morning and decide that you want a new name. Big Fingers told her to write "Collette Smith" on the form. She insisted on 'Let. His blistering coaxial cable did not make her change her mind.

If she dies, I hope death does not rob her of her spirit. I will buy her a tombstone and have "LET" chiseled into its granite face.

Love,
Promise
PS. What's new with you, girl?

Dear LaKeisha Ann:

Child, we had a bad storm here yesterday. The rain battered the windows like a shower of fists—mens' fists. I screamed at the men. Girl, I screamed at them and cursed their Mamas. They started up the bus to drown out my screams. But, baby, I out-screamed their buses. finally they sent in Big Mama to point her finger at me. I came close to biting her finger off at the root, and sucking her until all that was left of her was bitter and dry. But I didn't bite Big Mama.

After the rain, I woke up in shackles. I think Big Fingers shackles us girls just so he can get a chance to touch our pussies. When you come out here, I'm going to introduce you to Big Fingers in case you're in the market for a husband.

kiss them grandbabies.

Love,

Promise

Dear LaKeisha Ann,

I can understand why you haven't visited. I was snotty to you when we got grown. Even before we got grown. All those children you started hatching for the War Boys. I didn't invite you to my wedding because I thought you wouldn't fit in. I didn't fit in either, me a black fly dressed in white in the middle of Charlie's high yellow sisters. My mama had to be there and Uncle Bobo stood up sober long enough to walk me down the aisle. Afterward he almost fell in the wedding cake. I should have invited you to share that day that was happy. I don't blame you for not wanting to come out here where it's black and evil all day and all night. Forgive me.

Love,
Promise

Dear LaKeisha Ann:

They have tricks here with ropes that would make an ass out of any cowboy. I dream all the time of pretzels, nooses, and electrical cords.

But there are some things they've gotten all wrong. There's this girl here who has a habit of cutting her wrists and other parts of her body. One Day some God somewhere filled Big Fingers and his cronies with the wisdom of how to break this child's habit. They stripped the girl naked and made her count every cut on her body. I think the number came out to be sixty-seven. They flipped her over on her stomach, and tied her to an examining table. They beat her with a frayed ironing cord—making her count until she got to sixty-seven. Her ass looked like a map to hell. The next day she cut her legs. She got another ass whipping. She cut her chest. Another ass whipping. Then she takes a curtain hook to her face. Big Fingers and his cronies are stumped. There's not a place left on her ass or back to whip. But oh! The top of her head! When they get through with her, her hair looks like Christ's crown of thorns. Suddenly she's happy.

Nancy is her name. She's the one who thinks Big Fingers is a creature from evolution. She walks around in her hospital frock all salved up. (Big Fingers tell Dr. Bacon that Nancy's wounds are from her breaking glass and rolling around in it) Nancy is a very intelligent white girl and rich. Her Daddy owns a huge chicken farm, but she hates him. She was on the road to becoming a forensic Psychologist or something like that. But her road forked. She said she was standing next to the poultry in Safeway and suddenly she started screaming. Her mind told her that all of those chickens wrapped in plastic were the bodies of babies. She bought chickens and buried them in her back yard. She said she wound up in Rust Hills when she tried to solicit Priests to do funeral masses for her "babies." She won't eat chicken even now. And she also has a fear of coat hangers.

We've had lots of long talks, but she won't talk about coat hangers. She said this assylum is more therapeutic for the likes of Big Fingers than it is for the inmates. She said the real reason why assylums, jails, hospitals, and schools exist is to allow folks like Big Fingers to have a place to go and vent their pent-up rages—beat and torture those that have no voices, no rights.

She said Big Finger's cruelty toward women comes from the suffering he experienced from a cruel Mother or some matriarchal figure. Nancy said this was probably a woman who laid into him with beatings and covert seductions. When Big Fingers reached adolesence the woman probably became more amorous and abusive. Abusive to cover her guilt for being amorous. And amorous to cover her guilt for being abusive. Nancy said Dr. Bacon is a Mother figure in Big Finger's eyes. That's why he grovels at her feet, and personally serves her coffee. Doctor Bacon is very buxom and maternal. Nancy thinks Big Fingers is a latent homosexual. She said when he paws us girls it's an act of agression.

Well Nancy has beautiful big brown eyes like a puppy's, and she kisses very sweetly, but I don't swallow all of her theories. I know Big Fingers too. I have felt the warmth and tenderness of those fingers. I have kissed and sucked them. In my darkest hour in a padded cell all I had to comfort me was those four chocolate Twinkie colored fingers. Sometimes the fingers are brutal. But brutality is better than isolation. I told Nancy to go to hell.

Love,

Promise

PS. When you come, bring me a pair of extra extra large panties. No girl, I haven't gained weight. I'll explain later.

Dear Nettie:

I know you're out there floating in pieces of yourself above the earth. But I do wish you would come down here and show Della and Stella all the stuff I taught you about loving men. They are kind of stubborn and resistant at times to sucking on a man's "root" as Mama call it. You see their "good" mind flashes back at them and they remember when they were school teachers and proper women who never stooped so low. Sometimes I steal their medicine so they can stay in their crazy state and do what I tell them to do. But I can't do that all the time. They need you, who never knew no right and wrong, you who never had normalcy to fall back on—you need to visit them in their dreams and sprinkle them with your innocense. Make them docile lambs like you were, Big Sister. You gave your body naturally. No one ever told you about keeping your dress down, because no one assumed you had the sense to lift it or anyone would lift for you. So you never had any pangs of guilt that caused you to lock up your pussy because you were afraid of turning into a whore. I used to watch you with the boys and men. You used to rock so gently and coo. Coo and rock. You could slow down the most trembly nervous jittery boy and make him rock easy with you. And you did it because it felt good. You got so you didn't give a damn whether I bought you a Hershey bar or gave you a quarter. You was a woman because it felt good.

Whisper your magic to Stella and Della Big Sister. Take away their stubborness.

Love,

Your sister Promise

PS. Forgive Mama for not having you buried. I was out of the loop when all of that stuff happened. And Big Mama who loved you the most was resting at the bosom of Jesus. Having your brain and body studied by medical scientists is not the worse thing that can happen. You're dead. When they got finished they burned you up. But I don't know what they did with the ashes. You're not Nettie no more. You're anonymous. Well you are Nettie to me.

Dear Lakeisha Ann:

I saw in a last years copy of Rap Soul Magazine, that Sugar Face got ten years for killing his teen lover boy. Girl who would have thought that? We was crazy about Sugar Face when we was young. You think he liked boys back then? Maybe it was something that happened to him after he got older. All of our pussies got too old to lust after him and he was too old for any young pussies to lust after him. I saw his last concert on TV when I was pregnant with Chester. He looked pitiful. Trying to hide that big ol' belly behind some high waist pants and a sash. Then had a doo rag on to try and hide the cowlicks in his head. He looked like a big ol Pirate. All he needed was a parrot on his shoulders. Just to think, I wanted to go to Astroworld and see him. Could have lost my life. Well I did lose something. Age makes men's asses bigger and flattens ours. The panties full of dollars is getting fatter. That's all that matters. Got these heifers working overtime.

Love

Promise

PS If you have an old Sugar Face Poster send it to me. My uncle Bobo with his lying self never brought me one. Still lying and saying he going to bring it. I don't see how he's going to get one. There ain't no place he can steal one from now.

Dear Lakeisha Ann:

Nancy died last week. She took an axe and hacked off her leg for no reason and bled to death. Well I suppose there was a reason in her own mind.

I heard her screaming. I tip-toed to her room and watched the blood rush from her knee. It poured out of her and spread as if someone was unrolling a red velvet carpet. She whimpered and twitched, and then was still. The axe stayed wedged in her fists as if it had taken root in her palm. The leg looked like a piece of a doll. It was a shapely leg, very curved. It deserved gilded slippers on its foot, not paper house shoes and thick cotton hospital booties. I wrapped the leg in a sheet and tipped out before Big Fingers and crew arrived. I hid it in the freezer underneath boxes of government chicken livers until the hoopla died down. And a hoop it was. The place swarmed with suited men and women. They searched our rooms and closets. They sent a dog in to smell for that leg. He smelled around my room and then went for the kitchen. But the day before was mopping day and Big Fingers had had us girls scrub the floor with Bo Peep ammonia. The dog's nose hit that fresh ammonia and he backed up like he smelled a bear. Mother fuckers looked all over for that leg, except the freezer underneath boxes of chicken livers. Dr. Bacon had to lie down with a glass of scotch a few nights.

I love Nancy's leg. I sneak it out and dress it stockings and women's shoes that I find in Big Fingers' locker. Don't ask me to explain that. I just make Nancy's leg as fine as I can. It deserves that.

Love,

Promise

PS These bitches are still trying to figure it all out. One shoe, one leg—one shoe, one leg all going and gone.

Dear LaKeisha Ann:

I'm bored. I dream of nothing but body parts: Nancy's leg, my drooping breasts, other women's breasts. I wish we didn't have these open showers. Our bodies are so ugly. The schoolgirls we once knew are nestled in fat. Stomachs stick out. Backs are hunched. All that we have left from our girl days are our fingernails. You dab a little red on the tips and polish them until they look like a ruby crowns. They're there when needed to scratch an itch or keep time to a rhythm when you feel groovy. Suddenly one day you look at your finger and there's this ugly gray tumor growing underneath your finger's ruby crown. In fact it's pushing the crown away and taking over the whole head of the finger. The finger takes over your whole train of thought. It's a new baby. You poke it, suck it, wrap it in pure white gauze. Your finger becomes a mystic man in a turban. You ask it questions like why is a baboons ass like the rainbow. Then ol' Doc gets involved with you and your finger. Here comes his needle. You hold your breath. Your lungs tighten like drums. You scream like it's the first time you got fucked. Here comes, through a hole in your finger, nine months of yellow corruption, black thoughts of murder and suicide, and some little child with his head bashed in. When you're drained you feel good. You hum a little tune and stroke the Doc's latex hands. You look at your finger turbanned and mystical and healing. You fall in love with it all over again.

Love,

Promise

PS

congrats on your third grandchild. Your daughter is pumping them out like you did.

Dear My God:

They say you are so all-knowing. But if you know of this place, Rust Hills Hospital, why haven't you sent one of your fireballs down to destroy it? Or is this the hell you've created for us sinners to be eternally damned to suffer? Well we do suffer as the wonderful staff reduces us to the lowest common denominator—a bunch of eating, shittin, and pissing robots. On paper, this place is a model of innovation. Syrupy group encounter leaders open their mouths and vomit sweet salve, (*"Now Promise, what is the poor little girl thinking as she bangs her doll on the table?"* I look at the doll with the painted on blue eyes and yellow rubber hair. I bang the doll on the table. One cheek crushes in and pokes the other cheek out. The doll looks like it's going to spit out a jowl full of snuff. I say to the doll, *"Bitch I ought to have aborted you!"*) But it's not what the encounter leaders want to hear. Their pens forget how to write. Then there's the "rap sessions" where we are supposed to "rap". I look around at the bunch of rocking grunting morons. I decide that I'd prefer to rock than rap also. I never say what they want me to say. They run this place like a jail sometimes. They give you demerits for not showing angst and remorse. They want cups full of tears. I give them spit.

They even crush our drugs in sweet malts. Doctor Bacon soothes away our sticky burrs with a pat of her hand on our troubled heads. Even Big Fingers gets into the act when he's on the day shift. You should see him smiling as he scrapes shit off the walls in the isolation room.

"Make it sound like Heaven," Dr. Bacon says. And by God I do. When I finish typing the reports, you'd swear we live in gingerbread houses and swim in lemonade rivers.

The experimental drugs**
Lythum and *howl-doll* does
not induce hallucinations
of terror. But rather its

effects produce in the
prescribed, a pentacostal ectasy
or Jesus joy that I've seen
in the old girls from my
Big Mama's church. This
joy is the source of their
writhing and guttural
utterances.

Doctor Bacon stands ready with her inky red editing pen to put things in more clinical terms. She crosses out my "Jesus joy" and "old girls." The report I'm typing looks like welts on white skin.

But Lord, the stinging truth comes out at night. The electric cords whistle shrill songs as they crack skin. The calm pink covers are yanked off the wash tubs of crushed ice water. Cold steam rises off the water like ghosts. The lights wink from the volts of electricity running amok in the shock therapy room. Too much Hydravaliumcyon is administered. Your children, Lord, double over with cramps. Burning shit runs down their legs. Your boy Big Fingers and his minions stand in front of us like you yourself God might stand, and recount sins of previous hours. This is their version of "Confront and be cured." A poor girl whipped for throwing turds against the wall. The shock is applied to a woman who can't keep her hands off her snatch. Her hairs crackle. The old rich white woman, who swears her Mother is Scarlett O'Hara, and who let's slip a "nigger" or two when she addresses the orderlies—boy you should see her false teeth dance right out of her mouth after her ice water bath. And for being stubborn and not wanting to take your medicine in the sweet malt—well you get your meds through a greased rubber hose down your throat followed by a nice warm glass of piss to settle your nerves.

Lord, I wonder how do you keep Dr. Bacon so innocent? Or do you send nightmares her way when she's asleep in her little cottage far away from the main drag here? The next morning in her blue walled office, I type and the bitch smiles like a saint. I guess a good woman is an ignorant one. Am I ignorant for writing to you, God? Do you already know this? Did you know it before I even wrote it? Did you know I would write this letter before I even came into this world and before Rust Hills Hospital was ever hued out of the lava from hell? Answer me, God! Or are you too busy with my Big Mama and Jonathan who are in battle over the coveted spot known as the bosom of Jesus?

Regards,
Promise
PS Confront and be cured, God.

Dear Lakeisha Ann:

They administer the Electro therapy in a chair like the sinner's chair in Big Mama's church. This woman here, Edith, she gets it often. Well Edith needs to calm down. She just scream at nothing for no reason. I don't think she killed on purpose all those children. I don't think she did that on purpose at all. I read her case when my eyes is clear enough to read. It's a matter of conflicting opinions. Her lawyer said she forgot to apply the parking brake. The DA said she sent the school bus rolling into the fire on purpose. She was always arguing with the parents because she was late all the time. And a parent had cussed her out that morning. But whatever the reason a whole school bus full of children blew up in a large fire that was blazing up by the side of the rode early one morning. Now it wasn't one of them big school buses where the normal children ride. It was a smaller one full of little folks with just a bit more sense than us in Rust Hills. Edith got out to look at the fire and when she looked back the bus was rolling towards her. Well what could a hundred and ten pound woman do against 5 tons? We can't do nothing against Big Fingers. He don't weigh five tons, but still, we gotta take what he dish out. Well Edith ben crazy since that day all them children got burned up. But her smart lawyer said she was crazy before that day. That's why she stopped the bus to look at the fire in the first place. The jury must have believed his side of things and Edith been here since. She could have got the needle. And you probably thinking folks ought to be patting her lawyer on the head and saying Good Boy. But her lawyer was a fool for getting Edith sent to this place. Once a month when old Edith gets to squawking at the walls and throwing her shit at them, they strap her in the sinner's Chair here and give her some electric juice. Poor Edith be just a zigzagging in that chair like she on fire. She raise her ass off it and her legs be gapped like she getting some good dick. But ain't no dick to get around here. Unless you count long hard vegetables. Afterwhile Big

Fingers stop looking at his watch and wag his finger. Old baldy who works under him pushes a button. Edith collapse in the chair. All her demons run out of her in a trail of yellow piss down her legs. She's calm again for a little while.

I seen the same thing happen in Big Mama's church. When the Elders, saints, and the organ player get through with whatever sinner in the Sinners Chair, He or she be all slumped over in the chair, with their tongues hanging out and all their sins running out like snow white froth from their mouths. There is science in everything. Well be good. Come see me again. If I can I will sneak Edith in the Electro Chair and you can see for yourself.

Love

Promise

Dear Big Mama:

When your breasts sprouted ulcers that looked like dark flower buds, Mama should have sent you to this hospital. The staff here is all smiley and kind during the day. They pat your hands and tousle your hair. They whisper gentle "no-nos" at you if you smear turds over yourself. I know on your last days you craved a gentle hand. Mine was a wasp. It stung your ass and face.

At night they bring out the razor straps of jolting electricity. And this electricity that tints the world blue is what would have cured you of your cancer. It can turn your ass inside out. I'll bet you've never seen a blue banana or a blue sun. And yes, old lady, the moon is really blue when you're under the calm electric spell. They have Big Fingers here too. He's so kind. One finger at a time in your snatch until your womb wraps around his hand and he feels good inside you like you're growing a baby. Been a long time since you've had that having a baby feel, hasn't it old girl?

Well I must go. I hear the outer door whispering softly. Big Fingers is coming with his velvety gloved hands and a tube of warm vaseline.

Bye,
Promise

Dear LaKeisha Ann:

You finally made it. I was sure glad to see you the other day. You were salve to my wounds. What happened to the little skinny neck girl that used to be you?

You sure have a pretty grandbaby. And you have perked up so. The last time I saw you, you were dragging around in your Mama's house smelling like baby vomit. But the other day you came through here like a storm wind—washed and styled my hair, squawked about the funk in here, got me all cleaned up, and brought me that nice pie too. Child, your tongue can start fires. Always could. Big Fingers whose nostrils blare and whose throat trumpets, tiptoed quietly around you and waxed the chair you sat on. You were so so proper, *"Could not you people practice at least the very minimal of hygenic standards that kennels practice?"* Words, girl! Your words!

Getting an education sure did you good. An education didn't do me much good. It opened some doors for me. It got me a Doctor for a husband and put me in with the High Society women. But don't buy into that High society bullshit. They just a bunch of fragile folks in cashmere drawers and diamonds. The men don't give a damn about their wives tea parties, recitals, and Theatre board duties. It's all appearance for the sake of appearances. The poor wives, who might even be Doctors or high powered lawyers themselves, get their asses whipped just as quick as a street whore in a ten-cent halter top can. And talk about lonely and love starved? I had one neighbor who was to the point of being malnourished. She would wait until the garbage collectors were right in front of her door then go flying down her driveway in a flimsy low-cut nightgown dragging her trash behind her. Some of my neighbors said she should have jumped in that trash bag. But I understood that woman and even masturbated at the vision of her and the high school boy who sneaked through her vines at three in the afternoon. Nobody knew about that but me. Her husband like to have caught her one day. I was sunning by our pool and the boy come tearing through the vines into my yard dropping one shoe and dragging his drawers and pants behind him. Still had the condom on his dick. He could have finished with me what he started with her. But I too was trying to be a proper lady. I simply showed him the garage and told him to get dressed.

This place is full of women like my ex-neighbor. Of course a woman must be crazy for having sex with underage boys, so in order to get the statutory rape charge dismissed she agrees to seek help. Rust Hills has a day program for them. The rest of us are hard core cases and we gotta stay overnight. Ah, you've abandoned your baby? You refuse to feed it? You refuse to cook? Well you are crazy. Rust Hills will fix you up right nice. And it don't be nothing wrong with some of these women. You can see that yourself. They just get tired and want to rest for a minute. Sometimes your hands just can't wipe another shitty ass or fry another strip of bacon. You got to rest. I'm not sure why I'm here. All I remember is one day it was raining and I got tired. I was cooking a lot of food and I just got tired. And here I am, husbandless and childless.

Girl, you use that education to help people. Don't join the league of empty unfulfilled women in crazy houses like me. Rest yourself sometimes.

Love,
your friend Promise

Dear LaKeisha Ann:

How was your Christmas? I'm sure it was better than mine. Fools are in charge here. First there's red all over the place. Any fool should know that you don't use a lot of red in a nuthouse. I mean it's red lights blinking and twinkling all over. The pale green Christmas tree is strangled in strings of tiny red lights. It looks like it's got some kind of fever. It's certainly no burning bush for any Moses.

And talk about fights? What would you expect when you give out nightstick-sized candy canes to us mentally challenged folks? The walls are wet with blood. Oh well, the motto is "confront and be cured." And there has sure been a lot of confronting.

We didn't have a Christmas Pageant this year. With Nancy gone away, there was no Joseph. Ann and Collette are out of the picture, so no wise men. Ruth pulled the legs and arms out of all her dolls, so we wouldn't have had a baby Jesus either.

But families did come and visit. Almost everyone is sporting new robes and big pink hairy house shoes that look as big as beavers. I wanted a diamond necklace and black lace panties. Charlie bought me a terry cloth robe, without pockets, as they don't allow us to have garments with pockets in them. My poor hands. They literally scream, NO PLACE TO BE SOMEBODY! (Smile).

Well I must stop. The noise of so many candy canes going thwack! upside so many skulls is giving me a headache.

Love,

Promise

PS. You wouldn't happen to have a spare pair of black lace panties would you?

My Dear LaKeisha Ann:

I don't know what it was. I don't know if it was Big Fingers massaging my titties last night or you visiting with your grandchild, but Lord, I woke up missing my child this morning. How I miss him! I see him as a baby and that's what I miss. I see his little baby fist grabbing my nipple and those baby lips sucking. I miss the toothless chortling and his eyes lighting up when I put my face next to his. I miss his room of clowns and smiling bears. Do you think we do our children a disservice by painting smiles on bears? A bear is a beast that can kill us and eat us. And yet we shield our children from this reality by painting smiles on bears. But then again very few of our children are ever hurt by bears. Maybe mommies ought to be drawn with shark teeth and have "Mr. Yuck" stickers plastered on their faces.

I said in my letter the other day that I never had the feeling of home. But my little Chester—that was my little piece of happy home. Me, Charlie, and my baby, that was love. But lord, the dark clouds wouldn't let me see that. The rain kept a heavy veil in front of my eyes. If it wasn't for the rain, I would have seen that ray of sun—Charlie, Chester, and me in our nice home on the street that was wide and curved like a river bend. The rain, that awful gray veil kept me from seeing my happiness. Pray for me, LaKeisha Ann. Pray that the rain goes away from me.

Love,
your Promise

Dear Father: (The invisible One)

I know you're out there somewhere in the world. I hope you're not behind bars. I miss you though you've done a poor job of being a daddy lately. Well you did a poor job altogether. Big Mama said all you gave Mama was a bunch of afflicted children. They're all dead except me. Don't lie to your other women about how you took your daughter to Astroworld or the mall. Like all men, I know you're going to try and invent some truth, but don't go there, Father. To give you credit, you were not cruel. My back is not marked by crisscrossing scars from any whipping you gave me. Your finger never slipped the wrong way up my thigh. Yet my most biggest memory I have of you outside of handcuffs, is your cock. I saw it by accident that day when you walked out of the bathroom naked and singing to Mama. It was long and black. It swung side to side like it was keeping time to wind chimes. So there you are Daddy, cock and handcuffs.

I tried to find you in that black silk robe you wore. I used to caress it all the time when you were in jail. Even that got snatched away when Big Mama burned it with Jonathon's soiled linen. I guess I don't blame you for leaving the last time. You left on your own free will to go live with another woman. Mama didn't fight you. I heard she had fought like a tiger when women tried to take you. But I guess that was before I was born. Mama just got deeper in the bottle. She was trying to find her soul, or maybe she thought if she drank enough, that one day, there you'd be in the foam of her malt liquor all sudsy and white.

The girls here at the hospital where I am—well some are here because they got too much from their daddies. Too much beatings. Too much cock. They remember like elephants all parts of their daddies. Even the tiniest details like a knotty corn on his little toe, or the knuckle was sharper on the left hand, a knot on the right shoulder. And there were hands that smelled like motor oil and crotch and plaid pants that made you dizzy when you stared at them hanging over the shower curtain rod, (You did have a nice robe.) Yes girls remember things.

You should have been the one to drive me crazy. It should have been you taking my girl thing and turning it into a woman thing. Instead it was a stranger. You're the one I need to love/hate. Not the big goon who works here and is taking up all of your slack with his own funky fingers. It should not have been some pot-bellied bus driver, Daddy!

I _____ you. Can't call it love. Can't call it hate. I just whatever you and will try to keep you in my memory somehow.

?????

Promise

Dear LaKeisha Ann:

Been on a crying jag since my last letter to you. In my dreams I see you in a black frock and high white collar. You walk solemnly behind a girl carrying a large gold cross. The girl looks like you when you were a girl. She wears red high heels under her white smock. You wear red high heels too. Then when you get to the altar you vanish.

A Priest comes here a couple of times a year. He sprinkles water at us and offers us some dried crackers and grape juice. Everybody goes and gets the treat whether they're Catholic or not. Then they set him up in one of the rooms and with a hanging bed sheet draped in front of him. We're supposed to confess stuff. Some just sit and stare at the sheet like they're watching television until Holy Father rings his little bell and says, "Go and sin no more," as Big Fingers leads them off and another one comes into the room.

Big Mama never cared much for the Catholic religion even if it was all around her down in Louisiana. She said didn't nobody go to Catholic Church but a bunch of high yellow cajuns who couldn't even spell latin let alone understand it. Besides you needed the holy ghost not some holy father to get a seat next to Jesus. But you my girl, are my priestess. My heart has been troubled by the lies I've heard about me. And something else is gnawing at me. The more medication I take, the more the fog lifts. The more the fog lifts, the guiltier I feel. The guiltier I feel, the more medication I need. I'm like a dog perpetually licking her cunt—can't get enough and feel bad 'cause I'm getting too much. So don't ring any damned bell until I'm through.

First of all I did not microwave my child as the lies in the paper stated. I didn't eat him either. I was not some exotic bitch doing stuff like that. My day began with the rain. The sun didn't come up. The rain just washed out of heaven. I got up and fixed Charlie his breakfast. He ate and went off to his clinic to lord over his patients, leaving me to drown. Well I shouldn't say that. Charlie is a good man.

He found time to love me between appointments. And I tried to be a good wife and keep up the nice home we lived in. I loved my child and did all of the right I could.

And I tried to bury the past. I bought nice headstones for my Grandmother and my dead Brothers. I kept Mama in a nice apartment and gave her extra money to stretch her pension. I told the guy at Bob's Liquor store to put in two cases of beer in Mama's refrigerator every two weeks so she didn't have to bother me much. I did all right except for rainy days.

Rainy days always made me take baths three or four times a day. To me the rain is grimy and filthy. The smell of rain reminds me of an unwashed man. If the rain stays on the ground too long and don't dry up, I feel like I want to throw up. My temper rises on rainy days. If it's raining outside, the least slight and I was ready to roar. This brings me to why my baby is dead.

I kept me thinking about Charlie at his office gazing down at cunts. Why he had to go in on Saturday morning I don't know. If you ever marry, Lakeisha, don't marry a gynecologist. What man wouldn't get ideas seeing a bunch of women laying on their backs all spread eagle like that. Marry a veterinarian. It's easier to compete with a four legged cow than a two legged one. Anyway I shook all them ugly thoughts of Charlie and his patients out of my head and made my obligatory phone call to Mama before she got too drunk for the day. I held the phone and peeled sweet potatoes while she rambled and cried about the boys she birthed a long time ago. As we talked, the sky turned oyster gray. I wanted to hurry and get off the phone with Mama. I felt my skin crawl and I knew I was going to turn into a bad Daughter and call Mama a bitch or some other ugly name. Thank God her doorbell rang and she got off the phone with me. When I slammed the phone down, Little Chester woke up. He ran into the room and demanded a cookie and some juice. We were out of cookies. I offered pudding and jello. But he screamed he wanted cookies. I tried to reason with him. I had a sweet potato pie in the oven. He had even licked the batter bowl. But a damned peanut butter cookie was on his mind. Tried to make him watch a muppet show I had recorded. I picked him up and tried to hush him. I sang, danced around the kitchen, cooed, and cajoled all I could. But I guess the rain clattering down and knocking acorns to the roof was just too much noise to calm either of us. And suddenly the little radio with the electrical short blared out some music. When I went over to turn it down, the News announced that they had just buried the Leaky Eye rapist. And all that time I thought he was rotting in the ground in some cemetery or garbage heap. Why they let his ass stay on this earth cooling inside some morgue for twenty-something years, I'll never figure it out. The county said it was an "oversight." How can you forget about a beast like that? Do you remember how scared we were of the Leaky Eye? All them stories about some acid that came out of his eyes and burned you and how he made you lick it when he did nasty things to you. Well the truth is none of that was true. He had one good eye and one bad eye. Wasn't no acid in his eyes that day I met him on the bus. Nothing but milky colored tears. Children will believe anything.

So that day I am thinking the beast has been burning up in hell and the radio is just announcing his burial. A tremble went through my heart. I had Chester in my arms and was nuzzling my chin in his hair and holding him as if I was protecting him from something. He had calmed down. I stood in front of the window looking out over our front lawn. Well there is a bus stop in front of our house. I didn't want it there. And why the city exercised its right of eminent domain for such a small piece of our property, I don't know. And Charlie who is sometimes a coward was afraid the city could take our whole property, so he gave up the fight and made me give it up too. And so these buses—these goddamn awful belching buses stop in front of our house and spit out its cargo of maids and cooks for the houses around us. I had a maid who came in twice a week. But I insisted she have her own car. So anyway this bus was just sitting there in front of the house. Sitting there like some kind of beast in front of my beautiful home—disturbing my peace, the sanctity of my life.

I picked up Chester by his heels and had him upside down. At first he giggled and I started to swing him round and round. His squeals turned to crying. But I went round and round with him until I was dizzy. When the world stopped turning I was out in the rain cursing the bus. "**Get out of my life, mother fucker!**" I heard myself yelling. The bus driver sat on his perch in front of the bus. His hand rested on the giant steering wheel and he looked indignant at me like I was a crazy woman. The two or three scraggly passengers peered down at me with worried looks on their faces. I beat on the doors of the bus and kicked its big ugly tires. And finally it belched like a beast and lumbered away from my life.

I ran back into the house with Chester. I shouted to the walls my victory cry over the bus. I felt light and school girlish in my legs, hips and arms. I was in a dance. I raised up Chester to kiss him, but something red dripped from him into my eyes and blinded me. My child's blood blinded me. His head was all soft red jelly. I didn't know that I was beating the bus with my own child. That filthy beast stole my baby from me. Lord, have mercy on me. I didn't know what I was doing. I swear to you LaKeisha Ann, sitting on the throne in front of me robed and all goddess like, that I never meant any harm to my child. Dr. Bacon called it an unfortunate convergence of events that led to a PTSD event. Big Fingers said I was lying and killed my child, so I could wind up at Rust Hills with him. He says that and rubs my titties and I believe him.

Love,
Promise

Dear LaKeisha Ann:

The news we get here is very strange. Is it true that King Nicodemus of Macademia wants to buy the Astrodome and Astroworld? I understand he wants to raze the entire complex, dig out a hole, fill it with water, and build the world's largest man-made frog there. Of course the frog would contain in its belly a dog racing track, a casino, restaurants, movie theatres, a midrise apartment complex, and a small hospital. Please send me any news clippings you might have on this.

I think this "king" was once an inmate here. Jennie Rutgers used to collect frogs, paint pictures of them, and make them from aluminum cans. She wore pants all the time and also a turban to hide her bald head. She had breast cancer and the radiation took all of her hair. I wonder how she got so rich? She always did say she was a king though. Rich as pie!

Love,

Promise

Dear LaKeisha Ann:

How dare you, bitch, call me a delicate flower. And whispering to that woman you brought with you. The stench of your breath as you whispered about me made me retch. But I suffered through your rot as I have suffered through the rot of my life. You call me delicate, but don't forget I persevered through the stench of death from a dying brother and an old Grandmother. And why did I have to endure my brothers death? Because your AIDS filled welfare office working Daddy fucked him in the ass. Fucked and fucked him so, until his ass resembled rotted cauliflower. I saw it. I wiped green shit that seeped from his ass and from holes in his neck. And you call me a delicate flower. You a bitch who never did nothing but spit bastard daughters out from your glory hole. Bitch, I have walked with the devil. I am a survivor. I'm not like your crazy mammy who walked around the neighborhood butt naked. I've kept my pride. Despite my difficulty I've kept my pride.

Fuck you,

Promise

PS. And when you visit me again, don't whisper. It drives me nuts.

Dear LaKeisha Ann:

Out of the depths of my despair came light. The light was purple. The rays of the sun was the color of my grape NowLater candy. I stuck out my tongue to catch the sweetness, but a hornet stung me. The purple faded to cobalt blue. The cobalt faded to sky blue then to white. The light chased away the despair. I saw only white. She was a goddess. Her nectar the color of raspberry syrup was as sweet as honey. This nectar sustained me. Nancy was a good girl.

I wanted to keep her leg, but the stench brought Big Fingers and he pried it away from me. Of course he left half his guts on the floor. Every heave he took doubled him over as if Nancy was kicking him in his belly. I cheered her.

Love,

Promise

Dear LaKeisha Ann:

Criss cross criss cross criss cross criss cross criss cross criss cross—child, my arms sure did hurt me. All day and all night my arms were just criss-crossed in front of me. I sat in my shit and piss until I thought I was smelling good. I kept my sanity though. I kept my sanity. I said criss-cross over and over until the bell sung sweet church music and Big Fingers and the Doctor untied me.

Love,
Promise

Dear Mama:

I hope you're not too drunk to read this and remember who I am. It soon will be Mother's Day and I'm your only living child. Don't go to Jonathan's grave. Don't go to Poochie's grave. And Nettie ain't got no grave for you to visit. I know Nettie disappointed you that day in the Retarded Olympics. But you still could have had her a funeral when she died, instead of "*so kindly*" donating her body to science. I'm sure her legs are somebody's walking cane walk and her skull props open the door to some medical student's apartment.

But you have another daughter. Don't throw me away. Come and see me. I was good to you when I was able to be. But now I can't even be good to me—as far as buying stuff and having money.

You know what's sweet about Mother's Day? It's not defined by race or the "goodness" of a woman holding the title of "Mother." There is no "white" Mother's Day or "Black" Mother's Day. A whore can squat down on the sidewalk with her legs gapped, let her baby fall out of her womb, take a pen knife and cut the cord, leave her bloody child in the path of footsteps, go on about her business, and still qualify for the title of Mother. Not Mother of the year of course, but still "Mother."

Mothers! Sweet cookie baking things or scowling scolders, Aristocratic Mothers, Seductive mothers in little black panties, Steel colored hair-wrapped-in-a-bun-matriarchs, Mothers going shoe-less so the young-uns can eat, Mother taking a fist to the eye from a brute to keep the roof over her brood, Drunken Mothers, Murdering Mothers—all to be honored on Mothers Day.

Mother, I looked but Hallmark doesn't carry our cards. **Yours** in the shape of a beer bottle. You open it, it reads:

DEAR MOTHER, HERES DRINKING TO YOU.
love,
your Daughter Promise.

My card: Picture a woman behind bars baking cookies. I open it, it reads:

THANK YOU, MOMMY FOR SENDING ME TO HEAVEN. IT BEATS SCHOOL I GUESS.

Love,

Chester

My baby never got a chance to go to school, ride a bike by himself, or ride some girl. Never never Never.

So anyway woman, Happy Mother's Day. Come and see me.

Your Daughter,

Promise

Dear Woman:

How could you lose so many sons? So so many. It's like you had some kind of abortion after you gave birth to them. What kind of a woman are you?

Perplexed,
Promise

Dear Dr. Charlie Silvers:
Cholley Cholley Cholley
Good Golly Golly —It's
Cholley Cholley Cholley

My song I wrote to you. Remember that? It fit the high yellow naive little sonny boy type that I thought you were. A nerd—that's what the ebony and mahogany Alphas called you and those like you who didn't move to the african drum beating in your blood. You scurried around like white boys, looking whiter than them in your lab coat. You high-fived the other white boys in celebration of our school's Polo team victory. *Polo*, I thought to myself. The Alphas had to take off their shades in disbelief. They tried to stare you and those white boys into oblivion. But your saving grace was that you stared back with a look that said, I can like Polo if I want to. Your nostrils flared. The nigga rose up in you. The Alphas put back on their shades. That day in the Student center I fell in love with you.

I'm thinking about you today. I'm thinking you're a pretty red nigga. Doctor Silvers? So what? You're a nigga first. My pretty red nigga. And I know you've got another woman. It's in those gray eyes that light on me for two seconds when you think I'm not looking. I see the other woman in the new muscles you've grown in the gym and in your new clothes—I thought you hated purple. I smell her in your cologne. It's a neat concoction of sweat, rose petals, and menses. I like the fragrance.

But Charlie, you're my red nigga. Don't divorce me. I know I'm not much to look at. Practically bald headed and swollen faced. However I am a wife. Your wife. You've stuck by me for so long. You gave me such a pretty name and now you want to take it away. I know that little Chester isn't alive to be the glue that holds us together. But my love ... can't love be enough? Can't love . . . Shit. It's futile to beg. Some cunt with hair has put a bug in your ear and a rope on your heart. What can I do except sing:

Cholley Cholley Cholley
Golly Golly I love you.
Love,
Promise Silvers
PS I will confront and be cured.

Dear LaKeisha Ann:

You ask me why I named my Baby Chester? You say it's not a pretty name. But Chester is better than Metro, which is what I started to name him before he was born. Metro Silvers. Wouldn't that have been something? Charlie talked me out of that one.

When I saw my baby's gray eyes, something silver like a halo appeared in front of me for a few seconds. There was a name etched in this halo. I turned to the nurse who stood by my bed with a fat clipboard. I whispered and the nurse wrote. She wrote for a long time. Then she handed me the paper. She had written in red "Chester." I studied the paper and wondered whose name was that. Then I remembered. Everything turned silver and I fainted. When I awoke i felt troubled, but Charlie was smiling. He said he had an Uncle named Chester. So I let it go. Maybe if I had named him something else, he would be living today. Who knows.

Love,
Promise

Dear Chester:

Your Mother is so sorry, so sorry she has cut short your days of walking on the warm green grass. I've denied you a chance to grow up and make babies that would have put grand in front of my name. Imagine me—Grand Mother Promise instead of Old Promise molting in an insane asylum.

Your seed would have been the spitting image of you and Charlie—sand colored and slate-eyed. Lord, that white blood from Charlie's side was going to flow like a river through you and fertilize your seed. But Your Mama dammed your river with her act of nullification. Yes that's what it was, an act of nullification.

Please forgive me. Forgive Mister Pete Chesterfield for making your Mother hate the rain. And forgive the rain, my child. The rain was innocent on that day of your nullification.

Love,

your Mother

Dear Chester:

One day you will thank me for saving you. Yes, saving you. Any Mother worth her salt will try and save her child. How lucky you are to have carried to God your gift of bright-eyed innocense. I know God gets so tired of old sour-faced prunes that are eaten up with the cynicism of crushed dreams. I saved you from cynicism. You tasted the candy and cake batter of life. The day you died, you had licked a spoon of sweet potato pie batter. The coroner's inventory of your stomach at my trial still echos in my head. An astute judge would have seen that I was a good mother and let me go free. I had fed you applesauce, cereal, milk, a piece of mashed up donut, and the spoon lickings from sweet potato pie. But judges are judges. God sees the truth and all sides of a rhombus at once. He knows life is hard. He read your cards and saw the heartbreak and pain you were destined to suffer. Those are the things that squeeze us, line our faces, and make us lose our hair. I saved you from that.

May you forever chase butterflies with the sun gently blowing it's warm breath on your face.

Love,

Your Mama

PS Well I've confronted. It took your daddy mentioning divorce.

Dear LaKeisha Ann:

They don't do much cooking here as you probably figured out the first day you visited. In a way this is good, for I'm sure the nourishment would be full of poison. Most of our food comes to us in a big blue truck driven by a soulful black sweet daddy that I've started to notice. His big muscles lift the crates of foil covered tins and wheel them into the kitchen.

Lately I've been on the verge of starvation. I feel hunger in my thighs. They yearn to have a fullness between them. I fill my belly, but that doesn't satisfy my thighs. When I eat candied yams, the brown body of the truck driver stands before me. He is a statue made out of brown sugar. He dissolves into the yellow yams and turns them orange.

Maybe you'll get to see him if you visit me in the morning time. He's not squishy squashy like Big Fingers. And nope he wouldn't make a good husband. Wears shades at seven in the morning. Shirt makes a wide open V from his navel to his chest. But now if you want to touch a piece of jazz and pull it to your bosom . . .

Love,
Promise

Dear LaKeisha Ann:

The nigga who drives the AMCO truck winks at me. Takes off his shades, winks, and shows me his teeth. I'm falling in love with teeth. They're small teeth like a baby's. When I think of those teeth, my bosom aches. At night I welcome Big Fingers. I close my eyes and Big Fingers's hand grows into a shadow. The shadow shows me his baby teeth. I undulate my hips and the shadow pours into me all love. Sweet sweet love.

Love,

Promise

Dear LaKeisha Ann:

The pantry is a strange place for love. It's full of rat traps. The shelves are dusty with flour and swollen silver skinless cans. But it was quiet, effiecient, and cheap. I hiked my shift up to my belly and placed my hands on my knees. The AMCO truck driver drilled into me like I was an old mule. The tins of chocolate pudding clicked in my pockets keeping time with the truck driver's grunts. He shivered twice. The inside of my thighs got wet. He pulled up his pants. I let down my shift. He went out the back door, the truck roared, and that was that. No hug afterward, not even a handshake. If he would have just slapped my ass, that would have told me something. Well so much for love. The pudding was bland too. Next time I'm going to let Stella or Della have that trick. That's all he was.

Love,
 Promise

Dear LaKeisha Ann:

The world is stranger than strange. When you and I were young girls, an older girl who didn't want her baby might leave it on a doorstep. You never heard of anyone throwing away a whole carload.

Out here parked at the gate the other day, was an old 1997 Chevy just as pregnant as could be with some little round-faced children. They were black and all of them had a widow's peak and were snaggle-toothed. They looked like little Vampires. There was a note on the windshield. It said, *"I'm Tired."* Wasn't signed Mom, Mother, Mammy, or whore. Just, "I'm tired."

The oldest was a girl six. She said her name was Mona and she lived on Bishon Street in Lousiana. A man named Oscar drove them there and was gone to get some soda water. Oscar and the soda water never came. She didn't know where her Mama was. She held a four month old baby, who was nursing what looked like clabber from a big baby bottle. He spit up all over his poor little big sister. In the back seat was two-year old twin boys both naked from the waist down. Remus and Demus is what Mona called them. But she didn't know who was who.

Doctor Bacon asked the "Little Mama" what city in Lousiana? She said, "Supper." Nobody ever heard of "Supper Lousiana." We all thought the child was saying "Supper" because she was hungry. She kept saying it was a "stinky town."

I remembered my Big mama's hometown of Cameroon Louisiana. It was all dust and crackling heat. Not far from Cameroon was a town called Sulphur. It was nicknamed "stink pot." I started to tell Dr. Bacon this, but I didn't. I wanted to wrap my arms around those children. We waited until dusk for "Oscar" to return. I was glad to see the sky darken and there was no "Oscar in the purple clouds." Mona said her Mother was named Doris. Isn't that old-fashioned?

Doctor Bacon sat in the big old clumsy car cuddling the twins as Big Fingers drove it to the main building. Me and the rest of the patients ran and jumped around the car as if we were a bunch of children ourselves. The children were like dolls to us. We fought over which one we wanted. We bathed them and combed their hair. Dr. Bacon sent Big Fingers out for pampers and ice cream. We dressed our babies as best we could in cut-off hospital gowns and let them play with our trinkets. Some women here have never seen their babies. The ones that get pregnant here and don't have any family to see about them, gets their babies snatched from between their thighs and shipped off. Some are too crazy to know that they're having a baby.

So for a brief moment that little brood had a family experience. I know "Little Mama" will never forget it. She cried and tried to hold onto Big Fingers and Doctor Bacon when the Child Welfare folks came. Poor child. I too miss my shiny moment of family, Charlie, Little Chester, and me. When "Little Mona" grows up and has her own family, I hope she keeps hers together better than I did.

Love,

Promise

PS. Bring me some big sweet pickles when you come out here again. For some reason I feel pregnant.

Dear LaKeisha Ann,

After the state come and got Little Mona, I snuck out and sat in the car they came in. They were waiting fr a tow truck ot come and get it. The velvet seats felt good to my naked ass. I think me and Charlie did something in the back seat of a car one time. I saw a piece of map on the floor. The top parts of Texas and Lousiana was torn off. Maybe they don't exist anymore. Who knows. A line dipped and zigzagged between Rust Hills And Lake Charles. Then it dropped to a dot name Sulphur. It was what Mona was trying to say. I knew it then and know it better when I saw the map. Something told me to hold on to that map. I stuffed it in my snatch and snuck back inside.

Love,
Promise

Dear LaKeisha Ann:

Pregnant! Yes! I told Charlie. I hoped that would make him want to divorce me. I danced around the room telling Charlie all about the little black man growing inside me and how he would be a better Doctor than him (Charlie)—a better everything. But Charlie said nothing about divorce. Water from his gray eyes ran down his red face. I heard doors slamming and white voices hot like jungle animals.

I'm going to name this baby Keish Jonathan. Keish Jonathan Silvers. Or if I get my old name back, Keish Jonathan Goodday. Some of your name and my brother's name.

Love,

Promise

PS. I'm knitting blue booties.

Dear LaKeisha Ann:

The revolution will not be televised. The revolution will not be televised. The revolution will not be televised. Girl, this ol' stupid phrase whistled through my head all morning.

I kept wondering where had I heard that silly mess. What revolution? Then I remembered this so-called revolution erupting from my mama's simulated wood stereo. Some boy named Gil Scott something was the singer of this revolution. I remember my Uncle Bobo and my Mama raising their fists in salute to that old record crackling on the record player. It was mixed in with some old James Brown songs and some Marvin Gay songs. We thought James Brown was ugly, but Marvin Gay was pretty and we wanted him to be our husband. But nothing changed for Mama and Bobo except that President Reagan, who killed the food stamps. Uncle Bobo got fired from driving Mr. Fritz's car. Fritz died. The car didn't die. But there wasn't enough money in the will to pay Bobo to drive Fritz's wife. Nothing left for Uncle Bobo to do but play security guard here and there. And Mama, bless her heart, the bottle is her shield and sword in her war to forget the past, so much for their revolution.

Change, girl. That's what a revolution is all about. You know a revolution is always violent. And the violence is what liberates the oppressed. Me killing my child liberated me from domesticity. Jonathan's disease, which savagely destroyed his body liberated him from a life of unhappiness. Blood cleanses. That's the theme of the new testament. Poor limp haired Jesus, shedding his blood so that needy souls from Albania and Alabama, India and Iowa could make it to heaven.

Now Big Fingers, he will learn of the cleansing power of blood. He will learn that violence is a liberator. The punisher will become the punished. We have received the full force of his strap. It has cut more than skin. The pain's gone to the soul and strangled our will, but it hasn't crushed it. My turn is coming soon. Big Fingers is slipping. He's falling in love with me. He's kissing my breasts as they swell right along with my belly. Keish Jonathan will be my Cinque or my Toussaint. We're going to make sure Big Fingers suffers more than Christ ever did.

Love,
Promise

Dear Big Mama:

Lord, I need some church this morning. I want some shouting music. There's an ache in my loins that only your Jesus can cure, Big Mama. I desire a touch from his bleeding hands. I want his frothy mouthed big black apostle to lick my ears with sweet words. Oh Big Mama, do you hear me. Won't somebody shout amen!

Big Mama, when I was little I didn't know how much I loved you and your church women cloaked in the white purity of nurse's uniforms and winged caps. I need you now. I need your hands placed on me. Touch the places filthy men have touched with their hands and electrodes. (Yesterday I forgot my name for two hours when they removed the electrodes from my temples.)

Looking at you with thirty plus year-old eyes, I can see you better. You were a paradox. You didn't mean to be mean. When a woman comes into this world, she is instantly one step behind everything in this world. There are men who love their dogs more than us. And yet we have to love them—bear their children, their angst, their bad habits. And some of them with their sweet cat eyes we just have to love. I see the burden you bore. The pain of cancer and the drugs that were supposed to shield you from the pain, could not sweep away the vision of the man you loved hanging from a tree. Your eyes saw the thorny flames and your nostrils breathed in the sweetness of burnt maple and flesh. I would get irritated when you all the time asked me if I was frying bacon. Forgive me.

And yet you loved Jesus who looked so much like the men around that tree—the ones throwing liquor and kerosene at the fire. You worked in many a white woman's kitchen, preparing meals for her and her husband while keeping the arsenic in your veins from leaking out and poisoning the food. All of that baggage would burden anyone. I inherited some of your burden and created my own. Here I sit craving you, your church women and your Jesus. "*Jesus is on the mainline! Jesus will make it all right,*" you used to shout. Well lord, touch me, and touch the seed that grows in me. Big Mama, please come down here and hold my hand. Don't let me hurt my child. I want a second chance.

I shouldn't have burned your letter. But I was being a sassy gal. Burned all your history. You loved you some Bud. Did you love the thing that gave you Aunt Susan? Imagine all them blue/gray eyes seering the flesh of your husband and them same eyes hovering over you as they pounded a child into your belly. How did you manage that contradiction? Black church women seem to manage their contradictions just fine on Sunday morning, I guess.

I'm sorry I made you eat mashed up sweet potatoes. You were right about Suliman. He was no good for a grown woman. Okay for a daddy when he was around. I learned about Sulphur, Louisiana and that land from some children abandoned here at Rust Hills. Supper Louisiana—bless poor Mona's heart heart. I wonder what happened to her.

I married a man who was a gynecologist. He helped fix up my pussy that that bus driver almost destroyed. But I showed my gratitude by destroying our son. But another is coming from the AMCO man. I'll make a good mother. Look down from Heaven one day, and you'll see me being a good mother either at Astroworld or on that land in "*Supper.*" You'll see I'm not a poisoned child.

Love,
   Promise
   PS. Bring me some pickles and some of them winged hatted Church Sisters with you.

Dear LaKeisha Ann:

Yesterday—first let me say that Charlie is a mother fucking son-of-a-bitch. I know that the demons in hell are preparing a cauldron of boiling blood in which to cook his ass forever.

Yesterday the sky turned black all at once. Big Fingers was talking to me, then poof! I awoke up to find my ankles chained to stirrups on an examining table. My hands were tied to rails. My gut ached as if it had been shredded. I looked to my right. In a pan there was a pile of bloody tissue. I asked myself, "Who in the hell shredded that liver? I hope they don't think I'm going to eat that shit." Suddenly I was aware of a tiny arm attached to this what-I-thought-was liver. The arm twitched and groped like the leg of an insect. Then it stopped. I then realized that mass of tissue was my child. He had been wrenched from me. My Keish Jonathan! His shallow bed rested on a sheaf of white papers. I tried to read the writing on the papers, but all I could make out were x's and o's. In the middle of all of this code I saw a signature in bold straight up strokes charging across the paper. My husbands!

Yes, honey, that bastard signed for me to have an abortion. He probably held the forceps in his hand. Pulled all of my little Toussaint out of me.

I wanted so much to have this baby, to be a good Mother. I wanted to show the world that Promise and her child could survive rainy days intact. I wanted a vessel to hold and carry the blood of my dead brothers. But that will not come to pass. The blood of my future clots in a mass of tissue on a silver tray. Pray for me.

Love,
Promise

Dear LaKeisha Ann:

I woke up today with a thought. (I'm allowed to think in here after Big Fingers and his cronies have finished their tortures.) So my thought was about my abortionists. Maybe it was a good thing, me going under the knife to save my baby from the soul murdering disappointments of this world.

What are these murders? Well, to be born and not wanted. To love and not be loved back. To be spit at and sniffed at because your skin is ebony and your hair is lamb's wool. To be a slave. To have your Mother say, you ain't shit. To be called pussy lipped. To be burned at the stake because you never marry and have too many cats. To have a man call you a bitch. To be raped. To be put in an assylum. To have electrodes stuck to your breasts. To cry tears that come from the valley of your belly where the pain of living has settled and took root.

I hope you've never cried from your belly. Tears may flow from the tear ducts, but they come from the deep dark places where pain has rooted. And that kind of cry will drive you to bear the brief discomfort of arsenic or a rope around the neck.

So I guess Charlie was right.

Love,

Promise

PS. Don't forget to add abortionists to your prayer list. Praise god for them.

Middle Years

Dear Lakeisha Ann:

You're thinking about marriage you say. Well that's good I guess. All of us girls die for the chance to wear the white satin and lace uniform in June. Rose petals and Baby's Breaths rain out of the sad but brilliantly blue sky. And of course a fat punk must sing a love song proclaiming, "I will Love you forever." Don't forget the wedding cake that's so cakey it gives you the runs. Marriage is something every woman should do when she's finished with living her own life.

A man is a yoke and a leash. You can't do, you can't go, you can't this or that, because your husband won't like it. You wake up one morning desiring to drive to a little hidden garden and lie naked on the grass and just let the sun kiss your ass all over and have your husband suckle your nipples, but husband says, "I'm tired. What's for breakfast? When you get off from work, we'll go to the movies." To the movies to watch actors live fantasies that someone else invented.

Most women pick very dull men for husbands. They are sweet guys who can be yoked to mortgages and baby carriages out in the wilderness called suburbia. Those kind of men aren't going to yank you to Africa and take pictures of you naked in the Nile. Forget lunch in Paris. Those things take MONEY. Airfare to Paris costs more than a paycheck. It takes balls.

Think on these things, girl. You're not past fifty. You've spent your "younger" life raising your girls. Now it's time for you to have some fun. If you can't get to the Nile, find a mountaintop, get buck naked and let the sun kiss you all over. Then bend over and let the sun kiss you some more.

Love,

Promise

PS. If you must marry, I hope it's not to a Henry or George. Michael sounds sexy.

PPS Freedom for me is a line zigzagging and dipping. I'll be home soon. Jonathan said so.

Dear LaKeisha Ann:

Your impending enslavement made me think back to my marriage day. It was a killing heat day in June that I became Mrs. Silvers, wife of a new young Doctor. It rained that day and the rain hit the sizzling sidewalk, rose up and steamed our faces. I crammed too much cake into Charlie's mouth. No one paid too much attention to that. How could they suspect my darkness? To the witnesses I was just a bride a little on the nervous side. And anyway the sun did peep out again. That saved me.

You wondered if you should wear white. You've had children and don't feel so virginal. Well your heart isn't as black as mine was, and a white dress does hide a black heart well. So wear white. Let the audience cluck their tongues. Give them stones and invite the tongue cluckers who've sinned less than you to bash your teeth out. Watch the stones turn to boulders in their hands. Or watch them bash their own teeth.

You should have seen me all decked out in white. It masked my madness. Nobody knew what was to come. The least suspecting was Charlie. Poor guy had spent every day from high school to med school with his head crammed into some book. The only thing he knew about women was tubes and ovaries. He should have worn white. For he was truly a virgin for marrying a bitch like me. He soon found out how much it takes for a man to stay a man. Any chance I got I would de-ball him. I'd call him stupid. Make fun of his cock. Ask "Why does it curve so? Did Your mammy use a curling iron on it?" If men were smart they would fight all wars with their tongues.

But you know, you can only kill a man if he loves you. if he loves you, you can get close enough to wound him. So my friend, soon to be bride, wound the bastard sometimes. If he loves you he'll cry or knock your head off. My poor Charlie, even now he has tears left for me.

Love,

Promise.
PS. go easy on the wedding cake.

Dear LaKeisha Ann:

So how is the new bride? Did he, what's his name—Jesus—carry you over the threshold? Or did he point a gun at you and scream, "Walk, bitch!" You never know what you will get from a man named Jesus or as you call him "Hey Zoos." Even the one in the Bible wasn't mild and meek all the time. A man joked on television last night that marriage calms the savage beast. I know you know all the cards to play to keep your beast calm as a boiled egg.

In my house of marriage and husband, even when all was peaceful, there were times when I trembled with rage. Love was too much for me. I had to shake the rafters, make the roof fly off. I spent many a morning picking broken glass out of the carpet. One time we gave a party and I had to serve wine in plastic tumblers. All of my glassware was broken.

"Honey, I brought you some roses," Charlie might say standing in front of me, gray eyes darting with uncertainty, not knowing what bile might spew out of my mouth.

"What the fuck am I going to do with a bunch of funky flowers? Eat them? Give them to your Mammy!" Or I might gracefully sweep them from his hand, plant a deep kiss in his mouth, and place the roses in a thin Stueben vase or "vaahhhse" as the country club set calls it. Then I'd cook up something spicy and me and Charlie would ride each other until five in the morning.

A few days later I would wrap my hands tight around the roses' stems and let the thorns dig into my palms. Not even Charlie the figured out why the water in the "vaahhhse" suddenly matched the color of the red rose. I told him the water was draining the color from the rose and the bandage on my hands was from picking up broken glass. Charlie was easy.

The baby calmed me a little. The ferocious sucking mouth and fingers squeezing my nipples gave me pain and pleasure. It was like having a new man plunging his new cock into you, slapping you with a new hand. But then it wears off. I grew weary of Little Chester. Soon I was making the walls vibrate again. Lord, Lord the tongue can move mountains.

Baby, I hope your house of marriage and husband is calm and peaceful. You deserve that. Keep yourself and Jesus happy. Just don't abandon me.

Love,

Promise

Dear LaKeisha Ann:

I hope your husband isn't a round man. A man needs a squareish face. His shoulders should be broad and boxy. My Charlie was no statue of David, but he leaves no doubt to the eye that he was a man.

Now this Big Fingers creature employed here as "Orderly in Charge" and you may translate that to head nigger in charge is quite fat and roundish. He's gotten fatter since I've been here. Well you've seen him. He gets fat and the patients get skinny. He reminds me of a woman. Remember Bella the *"funny"* woman in our block? Black Bella in her Wrangler jeans and construction boots and earrings? This is who Big Fingers reminds me of. Except he has a mustache.

The other day a patient bit him on the arm and he shrieked like a woman. Or maybe it was an ape's shriek. But it sounded feminine.

That woman stands up in the diningroom to eat now. Piss runs down her leg. All Big Fingers has to do is walk by with strap in hand, and the piss flows out of Audrine like she has a water faucet under her dress.

She was a pretty woman at one time. I think I remember her from college. Almond skin and auburn hair. Gray eyes. A male chorus always calling out to her and singing her praises.

"Yo, yo what's up, Audrine . . .Audrine you got it goin' on . . .If you was my lady, I'd buy you the White House . . . That's a fine sexy bitch there . . . I wanta snatch them panties off and eat all that ass . . ."

Audrine was always riding in some man's BMW or Lexus. Audrine lived off campus in a condo she shared with a nerd who was away at Princeton. If Audrine had had brains, she would have been at Princeton. If she had any brains now she would be able to sit down and eat. You don't fuck with the hired help around here.

I always thought Audrine was just pussy with a pretty face. Now she's crazy pussy with an ugly face standing up in piss so she can eat. But I'll bet she won't try to eat Big Fingers's anymore.

Love,

Promise

Dear LaKeisha Ann:
The madness continues unabated, unshackled.
For a moment, we were wild horses and
"Injuns" full of liquor. We went nuts!

For real we did go nuts. Last month Big Fingers took me, Stella, Della, Audrine, and a mute girl named Pauline to the beach. He woke up early Sunday morning bellowing, "We gone have a whang dang doodle all day long! We headin to the beach!"

I told Big Fingers that we didn't have any bathing suits. He said the sky was going to be our suits and the ground our shoes. He herded us into the showers. When we got through showering, he handed us towels and small bottles of oil. He watched and instructed us where to oil. Poor Audrine forgot where her breasts were. Big Fingers slapped her hands away from her ears and oiled her breasts himself. He pointed to Pauline's body parts and she obeyed real good.

When we were all oiled, he had us put on red loose fitting shifts. I felt something scratching my bust. I pulled out a tag and it said *"Walmart Markdown—$3.99"* Can you imagine anywhere on this planet buying a dress for $3.99? Besides I thought the Japanese moved all the Walmarts to Tokyo in the belly of huge cargo planes. Child, the rumors you here in this place. But back to my point. Our shifts fit us real nice. Except for poor Stella. Nothing is loose on her. She looked like a big red birthday balloon. Big Fingers stuffed us into Dr. Bacon's bus and gave us each a can of Bull malt liquor.He told me to drive. That shocked my ass more than electricity. I looked at the wheel and gauges like they were on a space ship. Big Fingers coughed. I turned the key put the stick thing on R and the bus lurched backwards.

"D, fool," Big Fingers barked. I put the stick on D. Pauline coughed and the beer ran out of her nose and down the front of her dress. We lurched forward. It all came back to me how everything rushes by like in a movie. He gave directions like somebody in the army.

We got to the beach in one piece, by the grace of God moving a big truck out of Big Finger's way just in time. He had been hitting the Bull very hard himself.

Honey, the beach was naked. Breasts jiggled. Cocks swung like pendulums. We all got naked too after Big Fingers threatened to get his strap. He didn't get naked. He slipped off his pants, but kept his t-shirt and boxers on. He blew up a huge beach ball and planted himself square and squat in the sand like a boulder. He tossed us the ball and yelled for us to "keep it in the air, Girls!" The light from the minicam bounced along with us. Soon we were shrieking like high school girls. Even Pauline barked, "ugh! ugh! ugh!" She sounded like a dog with a sore throat. Big Fingers propped the camera between his thighs. He crossed his arms and smiled as if he was Jesus watching babies. Soon he was snoring.

We started to draw a crowd. The naked people pointed at us. Audrine by now who was feeling her old sassy college girl self, pointed back at them. After all they were naked too. But their eyes wasn't full of fun making and laughter. Their eyes were question marks. One woman shook her head and looked down as if we were a funeral instead of a bunch of girls having fun. We girls started to feel more naked than the rest of the folks. We dropped the beach ball and it went thump against Big Finger's toe. He jumped and looked at us standing around with our heads hung down. His hand made a motion to pull his strap from under his ass until he saw the crowd around us.

A stout woman with small lemon-sized breasts approached us. She talked softly as she ran her fingers over the marks on our backs and thighs. The woman touched a fresh scar on Audrine's ass and Audrine trembled and started to cry. Suddenly the woman screamed, "Who did this to you women? What beast did this?" She looked squarely at Big Fingers. He said he didn't even know who we was. He denied us ten times more than Peter denied Christ. And before the beach police got there, he was gone.

It took two sheriff cars to bring our crying selves back home. Home? Well it's home to us. "Home is where the hurt is," I heard a singer sing once. Men and women in suits came and visited our home. I helped Dr. Bacon type reports that verified our scars were consistent with us fighting, falling, and mutilating ourselves. I even helped Dr. Bacon make up my own story that showed I would light cigarette butts and try to sit on them for as long as I could. A very tart investigator asked Dr. Bacon was we some kind of religious order that practiced self-mutilation. Dr. Bacon made late night calls to the Governor's office. The men and women in suits stopped coming. Some new orderlies were hired. We gave a carnival and opened our doors to all the television cameras we could find. It was as if Astroworld had landed in our grounds. But then I heard your voice in my head saying, "Silly Bitch, Astroworld don't come to you. You got to catch a bus with a one on it. A big fat one in the window." So I knew it wasn't Astroworld. And then . . .

I opened the door the Doctor Bacon's office one night and Big Fingers stood before her. His big head was bowed over as if it was going to fall off his body. *"I only meant to do good, Dr. Bacon. I only meant to do good. Please, Ma'm, take me back. I need my job. And you Alice need me."* Dr. Bacon closed her eyes, sighed, and nodded her head.

So girl, that's the scoop here. What's going on in your world? Write soon.

Love,
Promise

Dear LaKeisha Ann:

He never fucks us. Big Fingers beats us, bathes us, feeds us, but never fucks us. Old Lady Sykes who ain't too reliable in the truth department, but who has been here for years, says that one day Big Fingers and Doctor Bacon was playing Cowgirl and horsy naked. Dr. Bacon lassoed Big Fingers and the lasso caught his "johnson" and yanked it off. She says, "he ain't a bit more got nothing down there than a newborn baby girl. hah! Hah! Hah!"

Love,

Promise

PS. Speaking of johnsons, Is your new husband anything like that boy Saul? Remember when he used to open his pants and pull it out and chase us around the projects? He was a War Boy, I think. You nicknamed him Black Beauty. He sure was black. Didn't he get you pregnant first?

Dear LaKeisha Ann:

Audrine died today. They found her in the bathroom sitting on the commode. Bloody shit all over the commode. The funeral Director will make her pretty again. Her auburn hair will be swept back from her head and styled like a burnished shell. A satin shroud or perhaps her wedding dress will hide the damage Big Fingers inflicted on her frail body from prying eyes. The old "college boys" will lean their fat bellies over the edge of her casket and marvel once more at Audrine. And some of those freaky devils will want to . . . well I'd better not say that, but some men will do anything when the lights go out.

I will miss Audrine. Her hungry mouth and bosom was a comfort when they didn't have her too drugged up.

Love,

Promise

Change

Dear Somebody:

What is this place, this Rust Hills doing to me? The nigga who drives the delivery truck that brings the shit we eat is disappearing. Slowly one piece at a time—an arm, a leg, a piece of his ear. There is fog where his eyes used to be. I tell you, the nigger is leaving. I can't even hear him. His patent leather boots that used to hit the sidewalk and make a cracking walnuts sound, is quiet. I can't smell his bitter sweat anymore. I know he comes everyday in his blue AMCO truck. I smell the gasoline, but my crotch is staying dry. I go hohum and keep digging in the garden or keep typing Dr. Bacon's letters.

Now the little white mailgirl—well I pause and misplace the alphabets in words when she walks in the office. But why?

Strangely,
Promise

Dear LaKeisha Ann:
Yesterday. yesterday
they touched hot
light bulbs to my
titties. Good god!
that baby's lips
was blistering.

Do you think, girl, that my baby went to hell? (I'm speaking of Little Chester) I mean why else would his lips be so hot? I loved my baby. Now I say this and I mean it, If the bus company caused my child to go to hell, I will sue the shit out of them. Girl, I will own Metro. And if I owned Metro, I could fire the men drivers and hire just women. Wouldn't that be good? You could come and work for me. We could play husband and wife like we used to. I play husband and wife with my self sometimes. I stole a big yellow squash from the kitchen. That's my husband. And me, I'm the wife. My husband sure is good to me. Ol' Big Fingers be watchin' through the slits in the door when I play husband and wife. But I don't pay him no mind.

When you come and see me next week, I'll let you meet my husband. Now like all men, he's kind of starting to turn rotten on me. I'll make sure he washes real good for my best friend. Also when you visit, bring me some Now-Laters. It's been a long time since I had any Now-Laters.

Love,
Promise

Dear LaKeisha Ann:

When we were kids, I once called you black. Now when you visit me, you are my light. I wish I could get you to go with me when I'm put in isolation. In that dark room, your face would be a moon to me. My personal moon. The isolation room is so black, the blackness presses heavily against my naked back. I cover my breasts and twine my legs together to keep from getting ravished by the darkness.

I called Dr. Bacon's dog a bitch last week—her dog mind you, and they threw me in isolation. They said I was "uncontrollable." Isolation is well padded. If it weren't so cold, you would think you were back in your Mother's womb. Of course you don't funk up your Mother's womb with shit and piss. Well maybe you do. But there's plumbing to wash it all away.

You were not there to help me, but I found a way to keep from drowning in the murky waters. I closed my eyes and visualized stuff. I was on a bus. The city was bathed in a strange mixture of moonlight and sunlight. The sky was cobalt blue and the grass lime green. There were only women in my city. They wore pastel tunics. In their pinks, yellows, blues, and reds, they look like walking flowers. They moved with urgency along the sidewalks, in granite bank lobbies, in libraries. They climbed telephone poles. They slung wires and dug holes. They leaned out of apartment windows. They walked dogs. They frisked bad girls. They put out fires and filed each other's nails. I leaped out of the darkness and joined them.

I greased my hair with the hard fat that crusted on top of the soup. I rolled it with old chicken bones. I painted my lips with egg yolk and rouged my cheeks with jelly. I manicured my fingernails with my teeth. I buried my hands between my thighs for warmth. A woman named Arlene picked me up one cool afternoon. She was driving a red convertible. We went to her apartment building. A doorwoman opened wide the gold framed doors for Arlene and I. A stained glass elevator swooped us up forty floors above the street.

Arlene's apartment was all hot red. The red walls cast pink shadows over the clouds that floated through the open glass doors. She fixed us roast beef sandwiches and pickles. She taught me how two women devour huge dill pickles. You wrap them in cellophane so that the vinegar and salt doesn't burn your vaginas. You put one end of the pickle into you and one end into your partner. You ride and you ride until the pickles become broken masticated victims of lust. Thank god we were two girls with flat stomachs.

When Big Fingers and his goons threw open the doors and the light rushed in at me like a hundred silver knives, I was not blinded. I did not flop along like a fish out of water. Baby, I walked like the queen of the Zulus. I had survived thanks to Arlene.

Love,

Promise

PS. Maybe one day you will take the place of Arlene.

Dear LaKeisha Ann:

Well you certainly looked dolled the other day. In fact you were beautiful—beautiful and grotesque in the plastering of your face and the coloring of your eyelids orange. After you left, me and some white girls decided our bodies needed a little coloring. There were men here rewiring the electricity. (The therapy they give us is quite hard on the wires) Men do bring out the worst in us girls. So we sneaked some food coloring and dyed our breasts. I dyed mine red. They looked like dark red apples. Maureen's looked like mangos. Earline colored hers brown. We called her the white woman with the "Queen Nerfiti" breasts. Every morning we stood in the window waiting for the electricians. When they arrived we commenced to jumping up and down. Well we did make them smile. We paid for it later when Big Fingers saw us in the showers. Isolation, beatings, and an increase in medications were the crosses we had to bear for making ourselves beautiful.

For the most part though I'm very happy to be in this all womens place. Outside of that one larkish experience we don't preen for the attention of men. It's all right and even expected that we look like a bunch of rag mops. If we smell each other's pussies, there is no shame, no rush to grab the FDS or vinegar bottle. We can just be and be and be.

Love,
Promise

Dear Bitch:

What do you mean not to send anymore letters to your house? You say you afraid your granddaughters will get a hold of them? Fuck you and those whores. I heard y'all sit around and play with each others snatches anyway. What the hell can my letters do to the daughters of a cunt ruled by a cunt matriarch? Fuck you fuck you fuck you.

Fuck you,
Promise Goodday-Silvers

Dear Lakeisha Ann

Fuck you, bitch. Show these whores the letters I've been writing. I don't give a damn. What are they going to do, lock me up? I'm Crazy, bitch. I'll cut your fucking head off. You dead bitch.

Fuck you,
   Promise

Dear LaKeisha Ann:

It is funny. In the prison in thr next county over men are always escaping. The high fence, razor wire, and moat full of piranha can't hold those souls. There is a rumor that one man escaped by killing then hacking off the leg of his cellmate. When he got to the moat, he threw the leg at one end, drawing the fish toward it. He then just walked across the water. Not with the same sure footing of Jesus, but still he got over.

For some reason no one has ever tried to escape Rust Hills. As you know this isn't Fort Knox. Hah! A chicken wire fence surrounds the perimeter. A gate once ruled by electric nerves, now swings at the mercy of the wind. But there is a wall here that no wind can knock down. That wall is fear. The Great Wall of China was built on a foundation of fear and sweat, I remember a professor of Chinese history saying. But there is no wall of mortar here at Rust Hills. The staff here uses the stuff of our nightmares to keep us behind invisble walls. Our nightmares are our gods. That's the difference between us nuts and you on the outside. A nightmare is just a nuisance to you. Robs you of a bit of sleep and security. To us, our nightmares are our constant shadows, is the air we breathe.

When I first got here, I would wake up at night screaming at the headless children chasing me. Instead of allaying my fears with words or medications, Dr. Bacon played into them by telling me headless children resided "just over the other side." And of course I wouldn't go "just over the other side". Audrine who was in here because she killed her Mother was told that the dead woman was "just over the other side." waiting for her with a butcher's knife. There's a whole assortment of monsters just over the other side waiting for us. And it works this fear of the unknown.

Churches get rich exploiting this fear of the "other side," which they call hell. And don't you dare question the other side of your gender. Society's wrath plows into you like a bus.

When you were a girl, even though you were a little whorish, you were so masculine. You had a long skinny black neck that you snapped when you "read" us. You lips were so pink and sweet from the bubblegum you smacked. You weren't a good girl, but I loved you. Now you've caved in. I suspect you're begining to worry about that "other side. You're turning yourself into a cream puff of a woman. Puff! Puff! Puff! Too much powder on your face. You look like a powdered donut. All of that is not for me. I've discovered the "other side" in me. I'm going over the wall. If it takes cutting off someone's leg to get out of here, then so be it.

Love,

Promise

PS. I'm sorry my last letters was so vitriolic. That what Dr. Bacon said the other day, I was full of vitriol, vitriolic. Sounds like some kind of motor oil.

Dear LaKeisha Ann:

A word rumbles through my head. It repeats itself constantly. The word strokes me as if it's sex. I stand at a podium in front of young men and women and I spit the word at them and it softly licks their ears. The word is "vicariously." I love it. It came to me this way.

A group of sissies came out here to entertain us. And entertain they did. There were four of them. I looked for Jonathan, but he wasn't there. He should have been with them, dressed in Big Mama's old faded flower house dress, shouting and speaking in tongues, or as he called it, "pig latin dipped in collard green juice." Anyway, the sissies did a skit called "Divas on Parade." They dressed in sequinned gowns, feathers, heels, and cheap dime store jewelry. They pretended to be singers from long ago—The Supremes, Aretha Franklin, and Anita Baker, Jonathan's favorite. The older sissy went way back to the days of Sarah Vaughn. I'm not sure who that is, but close your eyes and dream of a man moaning in your ear in the dark smoke of night. Big Fingers reminds me of some Sarah Vaughn when he whispers in my ear, "Come on, Baby, let me make you feel good."

When the show was over someone sharp enough to ask questions asked the "Divas" why they did this. One answered that it allowed him to live vicariously the life of a woman for a few moments. And he was so glad to do it in front of the inmates of the asylum. He meant to be funny. He was trying to say he was as crazy as us. And he was funny. Vicariously—I love that word. When the sissies hugged me, I shut my eyes and it was Jonathan hugging me.

That night I slept with my eyes opened and let the pictures run through my head. And then I stopped on one picture. My Father black and buck naked plowing into my Mother. His ass like a horse's ass. His balls like a sack of red blood beating against my Mother. Vicariously. I got up and took off my clothes. I rolled my pillow up tight and straddled it. Vicariously I fucked my Mother. Fucked her until she was red and bloody and they had to dash cold water in my face to make me stop.

You can live in your own body, but sometimes you have to live in somebody else's soul. Especially if your own soul is very lackluster. Pete Chesterfield must have been inhabiting a lackluster soul. I wonder whose soul that man was living through that made him want some ol' skinny runt like me? Maybe he thought he was a boy again. But I'm also bothered by all of this vicarious living. If you assume someone's life, don't you assume their death also? Imagine imagining yourself as Joan of Arc. Lord, Lord!

Love,

Promise

PS. When you come out here again, let me whisper some Sara Vaughn in your ear.

Dear Jonathan:

I caught myself buck naked in the reflection of the stainless steel doors to the shock room last week and fell in love with the girl who looked back at me. I loved her pointed chin and her sparkling ebony pupils. I loved her broad nose and the thick "pussy" lips. I touched her breasts. Her fingers found my thighs. They healed the bruises left by Big Fingers.

Now I understand your desire for the familiar. The opposite sex is an invading force. It's a conqueror that never feels comfortable with the village that has surrendered herself to him. What I'm saying is that a man can never truly love a woman and vice versa. They just spend decades trying to anihilate each other. The Beast Big Fingers has declared war on my body. I can't fight back. I try to keep my most prized possesion, my soul out of his clutches.

I've found comfort in my two women. I am smothered sweetly by their softness. A woman needs that. Just as men need each other's hardness. The hardness of their cocks. But of course you guys never pierce the shell around your hearts. Poor Brother, your shell was fragile. You wanted to love a man, but not enough men wanted to love you. But a woman she's soft to begin with. That's why we aren't born with any spears between our legs. We have no armor to pierce when we love each other.

Jonathan, Big Mama was so ugly toward you, when you were on your sick bed. I hope you have forgiven her. Fear drove her actions. The poor woman had known so much death. Imagine seeing the love of your life, your future dangling from a tree. Imagine seeing your Grandsons buried before the hair could sprout thick on their faces. Gruffness was her shield.

You two are up there in the heavens. I know this. And if God is a woman, leave her for me to worship. And I give you your Jesus.

Love Your little sister,
Promise

Dear LaKeisha Ann:

Do you remember that rainy day, when the rain trapped you in my house, (when the rain was to me like Christmas tinsel and not razor blades), and we played husband and wife? Do you remember that day? My Big Mama dozed in front of the TV as "Another World" flickered in front of her closed eyes. Jonathan snoozed. The sheets formed a tent from his erection. We watched that tent rise and fall in time with his breathing. I didn't know then, but now I know why we all of a sudden wanted to play husband and wife. The rain fills people with romantic notions. That's why I can forgive a certain bus driver.

We argued over who was going to be the husband coming in from the rain from working hard on the job. You won when you said the husband had to be a boy. Why I thought a woman could be a husband, I don't know. I didn't want to be no boy.

You wore my Mother's colander for a hard hat and a "Ninja Turtles" lunch kit was your tool box. You went outside on the front porch and stood for a few minutes while I pretended to be the wife inside the house washing dishes. You kept coming in before your time and I had to keep sending you out.

"Wait a minute, boy, I'm washing dishes . . . No you can't come in yet, I'm watching 'The Young and the Restless' . . . Okay now you can come in 'cause I'm cooking your supper . . ."

You came in and pecked me on the cheek, looked in my pot at the imaginary beans an rice and said they smelled good. Then you said you had to get out of your wet clothes. I said "you can't get naked in the kitchen. You got to go in the bathroom or the bedroom." And you said, "where they at?" And I said, "silly husband, you don't know where your bedroom or bathroom is?" You twisted my arm and made me tell you. Behind a big old blue vinyl dinette chair where Big Mama had some red flower pots, was the bathroom. You said you had never seen a red commode. I said pretend it's white. Underneath the kitchen table was our bedroom.

You went into the "bathroom" and took off all of your clothes down to your panties and pretended to take a shower. I stopped cooking to look at you. You said, "Woman, you can't see when I'm taking a shower because there's a wall there." I said, "the wall fell down. Our bad children knocked it down." You said, Okay you was going to whip them when you got out of the shower. So you got through showering and put a dish towel around your waist and came back into the kitchen and asked which one of our children knocked down the wall? I pointed to my dolls and said all of them did. You told the dolls "I'm going to whip you for knocking down that wall." All the dolls that had on panties, you pulled their panties off and spanked them with your hand. The ones that didn't have on panties, you whipped them harder with an extension cord because they were nasty for not wearing panties and had been doing the "nasty" with some boys.

Then you tried to whip me with the extension cord. But I told you you couldn't whip me like that because I was a grown woman and your wife. You said okay, but I got to beat you 'cause you let the children tear down the wall and you don't have my supper ready. And I said okay, but a man beats a lady with his fists. You pushed me around and pretended to give me a black eye. I found a Magic marker and drew a half moon under my eye. After you beat me I went out on the porch and acted like I was crying. You came out on the porch still wearing our dish towel. I forgot we was playing and said, "Girl, you can't come out on the porch in a dish towel!" You said a man can go on the porch in a towel or his drawers as long as he ain't naked. I said, Okay.

I pretended to cry some more. I said I was going to go to a woman's shelter. You said, "baby come back in the house. I'm sorry I beat you." So we hugged and made up and we went back into the

house and I finished cooking your supper. You sat down at the table
in the dish towel. I said hold on wait a minute, you can't sit at the
table in a towel in front of the children. You said I'm a man, I can do
whatever I want. And I said I'm the woman of the house, and I say
a man has to be dressed when he eats in front of the children. You
never see the daddy on the "Cosby Show" eating in a towel in front
of his children. And he don't beat his wife. You said yes he do when
nobody's looking.

I started to cry for real and said, "Please LaKeisha Ann, play fair!
You never want to do things the way I want to do them. And you
said, "Shut up, silly bitch. I don't want to be your husband anyway.
Next thing, you'll want me to put a carrot between my legs and poke
you in your snatch."

You whipped off the dish towel, put on your clothes, and went
home. The sun came out and painted the kitchen gold. But all I could
do was sit down at the table and cry. I cried and the dolls cried too
because they wanted their Daddy. And ever since that day I've been
curious about carrots. They served some here the other day and it
made me think of you.

Love,

Promise

*PS. I told the story to Big Fingers and he said a carrot is a poor
substitute for a man, but he like the part about us playing husband and
wife.*

*PPS: You were wet and shined like Karo syrup. I got my ass beat
that night for drinking from the bottle of Karo syrup. Imagine, we got
a way with playing husband and wife. My whipping was for drinking
your sweetness.*

Dear Charlie:

What can I say? You're a man and I'm a man. Please divorce me. Give me back my name.

Love,

Promise

Dear Charlie:

Your lawyer was very efficient and very kind. Although his suit was a little ill-fitting. He had all the papers x'ed and laid out for me to sign when Big Fingers led me into the room. The lawyer gently patted my hand as he pointed to each x. When Big Fingers led him out, I thought to myself, there goes Mister Turtle following Mister Gorilla.

Doctor Bacon asked me if I needed to talk. I told her I was fine. Glad to be Miss Goodday again. But she still had me locked naked in an isolation cell "for my own good." Sometimes the world won't let you be happy.

Love,

Promise Goodday

PS: I held onto Big Mama's land. Dr. Bacon said something about a trust held by Rust Hills. I said trust my ass. Marked through that line. The turtle lawyer shrugged and threw that piece of the paper away. I ain't as crazy as I look.

Dear La Keisha Ann:

I don't know what it is, but you call it "peculiar." I say I love you and you say I'm acting peculiar. Peculiar. It's a word that makes me knit my eyebrows together. In just saying the word you wrinkle your nose for one brief second as if you're smelling shit. And you have the nerve to assign the love I have for you to such a word?

An obstetrician Charlie and I knew, used that word to describe a two-headed baby he had delivered. It was actually two babies. One kind of sprouted from the other's rib cage like a tree going off into its branches. Well "peculiar" fits that kind of thing. Along with three-legged horses and six-legged cows. But it doesn't fit two women reaching toward each other to form a union of spirituality and intimacy.

The physiologists speak of a connective tissue in the sockets between bones. Love to me is the connective tissue between the bones of one woman and the bones of another. But you call it peculiar. Well my journey will soon begin. Perhaps alone I will go. I suppose if I don't find love on the road to Astroworld, I'll find something very peculiar.

Peculiar,
Promise

Dear LaKeisha Ann:

Do you remember my Big Mama's friend Miss Lucille and how black she was? God wasn't that woman black? "Black as a rotten heart drying in the sun," Big Mama used to say. Well, child, if you could see my two money makers Stella and Della, you'd swear they were Miss Lucille's offspring. Child these girls are so black their menses are purple. I kid you not.

Their blackness makes the night darker and makes the men feel invisible and sinless as they lay money in our palms. Very useful.

Love,

Promise

PS The road home is a dip and and a zigzag. I'll be home soon.

Dear LaKeisha Ann:

There is a highway that runs close to the place. I discovered the highway by mistake. All of the time I assumed that that loud whoosh I heard everynight was a flock of birds, until I sneaked out the gate and went past Dr. Bacon's cottage. White girls have tried to sneak past Dr. Bacon's window, but the full moon bounces off their bodies and lights up Dr. Bacon's room and wakes her. But I got naked, absorbed the moonlight, and Dr. Bacon's room stayed dark. And of course highways are full of traveling men.

Stella, Della, and I tuck our gowns under our arms and sneak naked past Dr. Bacon's window. We stand by the road in our short gowns. A car stops. I do all the negotiating. There's a field not far from the road. Under the bushes, the ground is soft with crushed Lilies and leaves. The girls are fat. Sometimes the men fall asleep on top of the girls with thumbs or nipples in their mouths. I don't always roust them right away. Let sleeping dogs lie sometimes.

Some nights we get fifty bucks in change and dirt covered bills. The road to freedom is a long one. I hope God keeps these two mules kicking. I want to fill two dozen pairs of panties at least.

Love,

Promise

PS A dip and a zigzag on a map. A treasure map/

Dear LaKeisha Ann:

The quarters are piling up. I sewed together the leg holes of some extra large panties and girl, it's half full already of quarters. Della and Stella have been working overtime and it hasn't been a month. When I get out of here, I'm going to open up me a store or beauty shop.

Love,

Queen Promise

Dear Mr. Shadrach Chesterfield:

I will soon be leaving here. I remember your visit from some time ago. I hope this letter reaches you at the address that you left for me at that time. I think when you came to visit me then, you asked me to forgive your father. I don't know how I responded then. Did I answer you? Did you know the county didn't bury him right away? My mother didn't bury my sister Nettie. But nothing needs to be buried in order for us to move on. All we have to do is forgive.

I don't remember your face too much. You are tall. Your head blocked out the naked sun bulb in the sky. But I will never forget your arms. I don't know why, but I rolled up your sleeve. The attendant had left us. I traced my fingers along the needle marks in your flesh. Some crisscrossed each other. I don't know if I said so then, but your arm reminded me of a map. I've been studying maps lately. And of course the lines in a map lead to somewhere. This "somewhere" should be a place where we find peace and forgiveness. My journey starts with a zigzag and a dip. A little girl named Mona gave me the map to my peace—my grandmother's land. Well healing is a journey and it ends at the mountain of forgiveness. I forgive your Father. Tears and more tears after your visit began to rain from my eyes. Soon the hate filled valley was flooded and I floated up to the mountain. It took some some, but I got there. You are my brother in suffering and I must forgive our Father.

You too must do the same. Pick a rainy day to go to your Father's grave. Roll up your sleeves. Stand in the rain and let your tears and God's tears wash away the scars that criss cross your soul. Men must shed tears or the world will end.

Love,

Promise

PS. You never came back to visit me. I hope I didn't offend you in some way.

Dear Uncle Jonathan:

I'm having fun today. My name is Chester. I'm your nephew. My Mommy's name is Promise. I'm having a lot of fun. We are at AstroWorld. We ride on a lot of stuff. The rides spin us around and flop us upside down, but only for a little while. The most fun is Mommy.

Mommy has me by the hand. She's twirling me around in the air. She lets go of my hand and grabs my ankle. It's fun to see the trees upside down, and to see the sun upside down. Mommy twirls faster and faster. I yell for her to stop. Stop Mommy! Stop, Mommy! But she keeps on twirling me. I see something coming at my head. Mommy ! Mommy! Mommy! I scream over and over. But Mommy doesn't jerk me back. She keeps on twirling me like she's a witch. Then my head is on fire. I don't see Mommy no more. Come back Mommy. I love you.

Love Chester

Well, Brother, how do you like what your nephew wrote? It was Dr. Bacon's idea. She has victimized me constantly with this "confront and be cured" stuff. Well it works. I threw up and my bowels emptied after "my child" wrote you that letter. I am a cold blooded murderer. I cannot hide that fact in anymore self delusions of good-Mother-liberating-her-child-from-a-life-of-pain bullshit. I am a murderer. Lord, lord. I have to live with the fact that I'm a murderer. And it is a relief. My soul is rotten to the core. I am the imp that Big Mama said I was. I'm a whorish pimp. And you know what? I love myself. I love the truth about me. This truth strengthens me. When you know yourself, you can control yourself. If people knew themselves and accepted the truth about themselves, there would be fewer suicides. We may be victims of beasts, but we are just as much beast. Pete Chesterfield should have realized his truth. He would have lived and could have looked me in the eye and said, "I'm sorry."

I remember your brush with truth the day you acknowledged that you had AIDS. You cursed us and the men you slept with. You cursed the world for making your love ugly and for dooming you to filthy back rooms. Then you went to sleep. Mama secretly packed your clothes twice that day. Then she would break down and get me to help her unpack them and put them back so you would never know. I think Big Mama was urging her to put you out. There was talk of plastic dishes and rubber suits.

When you woke up, you apologized and kiss us all—except Big Mama didn't let you kiss her. You said it wasn't the dying you were afraid of. It was the getting there that was a Mother Fucker. You had seen others make that journey. But you were ready and would not cut short the trip.

You were so right. The final destination isn't so bad. It's the journey. It has been a long journey. It had better not be a letdown, because the road to get there has been hell. LaKeisha Ann lied. All yellow buses with a "ten" on them do not go to Astroworld. I found out the hard way. I'm going to Supper as Mona—ah! You don't know Mona—called it. Well, it's Sulphur that "old stinking" land Mama and Big Mama used to fuss about. I wish I had your bones, Nettie's bones, and Big Mama's bones to take with me. I wish I had Uncle Bobo and all my uncles.

Love,

Promise

PS. If you're at the bosom of Jesus, which if I know you, (smile) ask him to keep me safe.

Dear Jonathan:

Brother, remember when I used to tell you my dreams?

Or was it the nightmares? Here is the picture.

Iron door cage. The floor is cotton and the walls are covered with down. The ceiling is a fluffy blue sky. Snakes rattle and writhe around my ankles. They bind them together. The snakes are the color of rainbows and have eyes of black opal. I cannot get out of the soft room. A man bars the door. Hot light bulbs seer my soul. Little Chester, he, he is naked in front of me. He has grown a large cock. It looks like yours. I reach for it, but snakes have bound my wrists. Chester pees and my eyes pee too. The pee stings my ass, but I can't get up. A tree grows in the room. Big Mama's husband Bud swings from the tree. I wish the rope was around my neck. I cry out to myself, "Lord, lord, two things I want the most, I cant't have." Big Mama's church answers, "Lord, what must I do to be saved?"

So that, Brother, was the dream.

Love,

Promise

Dear Jonathan:

Last night I dreamed a dream in which a large black dog was pissing on a pile of money. Boy, the dreams these drugs make you dream! Speaking of dreams, Brother, I want to ask you, do you dream in your cold grave? Do you see Bobo and Poochie? Even though Nettie wasn't buried, did she make it? Did the Lord Jesus save you like you asked him to when you blew out your last breath? Is your black ass swimming buck naked in a river of milk? Are boy angels licking the sticky honey off your ear lobes and toes? Is there a little sand colored boy, who you've never seen before, looking into your eyes and calling you Uncle? I'm sure his bashed in head repulses you, but he is a good child. Will always be a good child. Never got to suffer and turn bitter. Even while dying he never suffered. The medical examiner said the first blow struck him dead. He was a lucky child. Kiss him for me.

Love,
Promise

Dear LaKeisha Ann:

Girl, you must be getting old. I asked you for a book of lesbian poetry, and you send me a Bible. I must say though, that Judith made me pause. Big Fingers needs to meet his Judith. And if it's not his head that gets cut off, his balls will do.

Love,
Promise

Dear Jonathan:

Big Fingers gave me a dollar today. I don't know why. He just up and gave me a limp and torn dollar bill. It reminded me of the wilted spinach in Kwong's Market. It also reminded me of the green jello you vomited before you died. It was like liquid money only it was foul smelling. Big Mama came running into the room scolding and cussing. She raised her hand and hit you, but you had already left this earth. Did you feel her lick? I told myself as she kneeled in your vomit screaming that I would hit her when she died. I didn't get a chance to because they took her to the hospital. I got punches in before she died as she lay in the bed squalling and talking out of her head. Had to quiet her, or else she would have run the boys with their dollars off Nettie. It was a lot of wilted spinach and green vomit I was stuffing into my old dolls and stuffed animals. I wonder did Big Fingers call himself paying me? Or is he falling in love with his whore?

Dr. Bacon is getting suspicious. She wonders why the trips to pick up supplies is taking so long. Big Fingers says road construction. But that dollar tells the truth. We park in an alcove of trees and he sucks my titties like a newborn baby. Freak.

Love
Promise

Dear LaKeisha Ann:

Girl, thanks for the Nowlaters. A whole case of rainbows colors and sweetness, I thought to myself, as my eyes took in the lime greens, reds, pinks, and my favorite color purple. Eat some now save some for later. Life is like that. Live some now and hope there is some later. Of course life is not sweet as candy.

When I leave here I won't try to see you as you requested. I know you do not make that request out of hate or bitterness toward me. But it is one of fear. Love is built on a foundation of fear. We fear to love the forbidden thing we yearn for the most. So I know deep down that you have a powerful love for me. The unrequited flame is the flame that burns longer and hotter. So maybe when we're old ladies lying side by side in some nursing home, we can through whispers and loud death rattles declare our love for each other. And maybe we can stroke each others cooling limbs if the staff pushes our beds close together. Yes I'm a sentimental bitch. Take care.

Love,
Promise
PS Life is a dip and a zigzag. I'll be home soon. Jonathan said so.

Dear Little Chester, my baby:

Your Mommy is going to a fun place tomorrow. She's going to Astroworld. Astroworld is a big park with fun things to do and fun things to eat. There are clowns and people dressed as furry and feathery animals. All of the ice cream in the world is there. You can climb up a big ol' mountain of strawberry ice cream. You can swim in chocolate milk and bathe in lemonade. The soap is made out of candy. I know you'll be eager to take a bath for mommy if, well . . . They have your favorite apple sauce too. Big glass jars of the stuff. You won't see Great Uncle Bud strung up and on fire. You won't see people with blazing blue eyes pointing and laughing. It will be all fun things on Big Mama's land.

I know you want to come to AstroWorld with me, but you have to wait until you're a big boy. Don't cry now. Big boys don't cry. When I was little I wanted to go to Astroworld too. But I cried and couldn't go. I sat on the bus and cried. My tears filled up the bus and drowned the bus driver. And so I never got to go to Astroworld.

Mommy doesn't want to see her boy drown people with his tears. The older you get, you learn how to shut off those tears. That's what big boys and girls do.

I know you will be asleep when you get this letter, but I will bring you back some magic dust. I'll sprinkle it on your bed and when you wake up you'll be a happy little boy. You'll be happy for ever and ever. Your eyes will sparkle like crystals and God will give you a sweet Mommy who will take you to Astroworld everyday.

Love,
your Mommy

To: Mr. Pete Chesterfield

Dear Sir:

Is it true that the rains from heaven are the tears of children who have been tormented and killed? Is God in his mercy and big-heartness hugging these teary children to his bosom until their cries are hushed? Do those tears give life to the powerful Niagra Falls, the sleepy Nile, or that putrid whore the Rio Grande? If so, I hope your grave fills with water and you float in the misery you have caused. You cannot confront and be cured. All you can be is be punished.

Promise

Dear Doctor Bacon:
Hit the road, Jack
Don't come back
no mo no mo
Hit the road, Jack
Don't come back
no mo no mo
Hit the road, Jack
and dontcha come back
no mo.

Doctor Bacon, your hospitality was wonderful. Give my regards to Big Fingers and company. Lord, Big Fingers! I regret I can't take her hands with me. Right now my heart could use a little cupping. But I got her drawers to remember her by. If I were a ship's Captain like you, Madam, I would hoist them from the crow's nest and watch them flap in the breeze. But I'm not a Captain. I'm just Promise.

Now my question to you Doctor Bacon is this: When did you castrate Big Fingers and turn him into a woman? When we stripped him, well her, naked, I expected to find a cannon of a cock loaded and pointed at me. But lo and behold all I found was a dark tunnel. The gates to the tunnel were loose and floppy as if a bunch of babies had kicked them down. No wonder "he" never poked me.

I hope you had nothing to with that mutilation. You had very little to do with my cure.

Take care,
Promise

Dear Big Mama:

On the road to God I go. Not in the belly of a silver plane or the new plutonium rocket ships I've heard so much about, but in a rickety old bus filled with nutty lesbian whores. We just might plant some "sweet taters" on your land. Wish me luck.

Love,

Promise

Chapter 20 – THE ROAD

Two hills rose behind the hospital like the heads of fat cabbages. Through the hillside trees, the highway gleamed in broken strips of graphite. Cars scurried along like jeweled insects.

Promise scanned the bluffs and wondered which ridge concealed Houston—and Astroworld. It was early Sunday morning. The moon was white dust; the sun, pale corn.

There was no funeral today to stop her heart, no bus driver pressing his musk-soaked body against her, no suffocating shadow. Today, she could imagine herself falling into a mountain of blue cotton candy, sticky sweetness clinging to every inch of her skin.

"Party! Party!" Two shrill voices cut into her quiet moment.

Stella and Della popped their fingers and gyrated, their bodies still soaked in music that had seeped into bone and blood like liquor. "Blues! Blues!" they chanted, sheets dyed wet and bright wrapped around them.

Lord, what a party it had been.

****

It began with eggs. Dozens of eggs piled into pyramids, boiled and waiting. Pots of dye cooled on the stove, sending up streams of blue, yellow, purple, green, and red steam.

They were meant for baskets—eggs nestled into shredded grass with lemon and apple jellybeans, hollow chocolate bunnies, and cellophane-wrapped rabbits packed in straw.

But a cut across Promise's back stung with memory—Big Fingers, raging, whipping her and the girls with an electrical cord when they dropped too many eggs. "This is your payback, bitch!" he'd spat into her ear.

The party itself was an accident. Stella, clumsy as always, spilled a pot of baby-blue dye. It spread like a flood. Walls, floor, ceiling, even their skin—dotted blue.

Promise thought of the linen room—those thick white sheets, hoarded for the doctors, never for the patients. She had seen them cover corpses, making the morgue gleam like fields of snow. They needed those sheets.

On the way, they passed the staff lounge. Old gurneys, stale smoke, men slouched, an ancient record player spinning blues.

Promise stopped. On the album cover, a bear of a woman howled and wept in the same breath. *This is the blues,* Promise thought. She tucked the record under her arm, ordered Della to carry the player, and marched them on.

****

We gonna have
   a whang dang doodle
   all night long...
The record screamed, and the music overtook them.

They stripped out of drab green hospital gowns, wrapped themselves in sheets, hurled fistfuls of dye until they shone like stained-glass saints. They laughed, pinched, danced, their hips undulating, their arms flailing between gospel and burlesque.

Promise melted lard, pressed their hair with a comb, tied it with red ribbons snatched from Easter baskets. They gorged on jellybeans, washed it down with sugar-water over ice. The frenzy deepened—crying, scratching, hugging, fighting, kissing.

Until the door darkened.

"My bitches."

Big Fingers stood there, chest heaving, cord coiled in his hand, his eyes like chips of broken glass. "Clean this shit up!"

The girls froze. Old wounds tingled alive again. Stella and Della wept. Promise felt her spirit retreat, her body sink toward the floor.

But a voice rose from somewhere deeper. Big Mama's deathbed supplication surged out of Promise's mouth:

Lord, ain't you whipped me enough? I tried to serve you, Jesus. I raised my children right. I didn't curse you when you took my man, my grandsons. I steeled myself and held on to the hem of your garment. But a woman can only take so much. Steel me, Lord! Steel me against this pain.

Her body stiffened. A cool hand pressed her back.

Promise charged. Nails into flesh, fists pummeling. The cord lashed her, bit deep, but Stella and Della swarmed him too—scratching, biting, screaming until his voice broke beneath theirs and he crumpled.

****

Whimpering on the floor, Big Fingers clutched his chest, the cord still looped through bent fingers.

Promise reached for him—and saw the cloth binding his torso, fastened with Velcro. Like the bandages Big Mama wore after her breasts were cut away.

She unraveled it, circling him like a child playing with a spool. He sagged, heavy and shamed, until at last the cloth dropped away and what was left was not a man, but a mound of flesh. Heavy breasts. A small head atop a swollen body.

"A she-Buddha," Promise thought.

Tears streamed down the woman's cheeks. Stella yanked down her pants; there was nothing between her thighs but folds of flesh.

Promise saw the hands that had known her body so cruelly well. For a heartbeat, she wanted to comfort. But the cord lay coiled at the woman's feet, and memories of Nancy, Audrine, tiny Collette, beat to death for shortening her name, flooded back.

She raised the cord high. The whistle through the air, the animal screams. Ghosts of tortured women filled the kitchen. Pots boiled over with entrails. Seven girls bore a tray on their shoulders. A man's head sat on it, a bus driver's cap perched above silver eyes. Dr. Bacon's face glowed like a pale moon.

When Promise opened her eyes, the floor was streaked with blood. She wiped her sweaty palms down her dress. Stella and Della followed as she left the kitchen, food coloring jars in hand.

****

At dawn, Dr. Bacon's bus stood waiting, pink under the rising light, blotched with food-dye flowers. Promise smeared her bloody hands across its side and christened it *Miss Piggy*.

They loaded it with sacks of panties fat with earnings, fastened with blue ribbons. Stella and Della tied red ribbons in their hair. Promise smiled at them. They smiled back.

The road out twisted like a snake. The girls clapped and sang. Promise gripped the wheel.

The highway split—arrows pointing left and right.

Left: a billboard, fading letters—*HOUSTON.* Below it, a washed-out Ferris wheel. *STROWORLD,* the missing "A" long torn away.

Right: flashing cones, a gap in the guardrail, and beyond it, the emblem of Louisiana: a pelican feeding her young.

Rain broke suddenly, hard and furious. Promise's heart fluttered. She swerved, wheels locking, spinning, until the bus pointed left again. She gunned the engine.

The sun burst through. The rain was gone.

Beside her, she felt a presence—the scent of bitter roses, the cologne Jonathan once wore. She smiled. Forgiveness. A hand, perhaps his, on the wheel.

Stella and Della burst into song as the bus roared past the sign:

COME HOME TO LOUISIANA.

Epilogue

Yellow police tape fluttering from the Ferris wheel causes drivers to slow down as they pass the abandoned amusement park. Their eyes take in the spot where the *Leaky Eye* lost his life.

"They should tear it down," A driver remarks.

"Leave it up," his passenger answers. "He should be hanging there, too—dirty dog."

****

A few miles away, LaKeisha Ann sat at her kitchen table, a shoebox between her and the visitors. Dr. Bacon's blue eyes were steady, patient. The two police officers leaned back, restless, as if their time were being wasted.

"I kept all of her letters," LaKeisha Ann said, her hand resting on the box lid. Her nails clicked once, twice, before she opened it. A neat bundle of envelopes, tied with faded ribbon, sat inside.

She hesitated, wondering if she was betraying Promise. The cops cleared their throats.

She slid the letters forward. "If that thing at Rust Hills hurt her, she deserved to hurt it back."

The younger officer sighed, plucked up one envelope, and skimmed a few lines before tossing it back. "She sounds crazy. Just proves what we already knew. How are we gonna get any clues to her whereabouts out of this?"

Dr. Bacon didn't touch the letters at first. She studied them like they were relics. Finally, she lifted one, unfolded the pages slowly, and read. Her lips moved without sound, her eyes tightening as she scanned the last letter.

"You're right. These won't help much, Dr. Bacon said softly. "All she says is she's going to supper. Doesn't make sense."

LaKeisha Ann swallowed—grateful that Dr. Bacon was throwing the cops off Promise's scent.

"I couldn't make much sense of them either."

The room was quiet. The refrigerator hummed. The cops shifted, impatient, but Dr. Bacon kept reading.

****

Outside, kids ran past the house, their laughter sharp and bright. For a moment, LaKeisha Ann imagined Promise among them—barefoot, hair wild, shouting to be heard above the noise.

++++++++++++++++

Notes

Author's Note

The world Promise inhabits is one of institutions, memory, and survival. The letters, misnamed medicines, and fractured images are not meant as sensationalism but as part of her truth: a truth filtered through trauma, faith, and longing.

Promise's letters are written as she might have remembered or misremembered—sometimes distorted, sometimes raw. The misnamed drugs, the heightened imagery, and the fractured voice are deliberate choices to capture her trauma and survival. This is fiction, but it is meant with respect for those who lived through such places and times.

*Adrian Johnson was a Black Houston teenager who, in the mid-1980s, was wrongfully accused of the murder of a white woman. His case became notorious locally because:

- **Police misidentification** — HPD initially believed they had the right suspect, only to discover later they had the wrong man in custody.
- **Coercive interrogation tactics** — reports said detectives used aggressive, racially charged questioning, similar to what's depicted in your chapter.
- **Racial overtones** — the case stirred tension because of how quickly the justice system moved against a young Black suspect without credible evidence.

**Note on Medications

In several passages, Promise refers to "Lythum" (Lithium) and "howl-doll" (Haldol). These are her misnamings, left intentionally to reflect her voice. Both drugs were widely used in psychiatric institutions during the late 20th century. Lithium was prescribed primarily for mood stabilization, while Haldol (Haloperidol) was a powerful antipsychotic with heavy sedative side effects. Their effects were often both numbing and profoundly altering, and in many cases left patients in a haze rather than truly healed.

About the Author

Charles W. Harvey is a native Houstonian and a graduate of the University of Houston. Charles was a 1st place prize recipient of PEN/Discovery for Cheeseburger, which went on to be published in the Ontario Review. Harvey was also awarded the Cultural Arts Council of Houston Grant for Writers and Artists. Charles has been published in Soulfires, Story Magazine SHADE, High Infidelity, The James White Review, and recently NEWVERSENEWS. He is the author of the novels The Butterfly Killer, The Road to Astroworld, and Antoine's Double Trouble. He is also the author of several stories and poetry collections.

Book Catalog[1]

1.	*https://books2read.com/ap/xbo9BR/Charles-Harvey?edit=maybe-later*

◈ Let's Stay Connected

Thank you for reading *The Road to Astroworld*. If this book spoke to you, I'd love to stay in touch and share what's next. Also, your honest reviews are welcomed and encouraged.

◈ **Join my mailing list** for updates and exclusive content:
https://charlesharveyauthor.wordpress.com/signup/

◈ **Visit my website and blog**:
https://charlesharveyauthor.wordpress.com/

◈ **Follow me on BookBub** to get alerts on new releases across major retailers:
https://www.bookbub.com/profile/charles-harvey

◈ **Follow me on X (Twitter)**:
https://x.com/CharlesHarvey99

◈ **Follow me on Instagram**:
https://www.instagram.com/charlesharveyauthor99/

Don't miss out!

Visit the website below and you can sign up to receive emails whenever Charles Harvey publishes a new book. There's no charge and no obligation.

https://books2read.com/r/B-A-EWG-TLUWG

BOOKS 2 READ

Connecting independent readers to independent writers.

Did you love *The Road to Astroworld*? Then you should read *David and Jonathan: The Price of Shame*[1] by Charles Harvey!

David and Jonathan: The Price of Shame*A Novella by Charles Harvey*

In a small Southern town in the late 1950s, Ruth believes the Lord spared her son for a reason.

From the night David is born, a warning shadows her joy: shame will sit at her table if she lets him wander too far. Years later, when David's closeness with another young man begins to stir unease in their community, Ruth becomes convinced that she alone must protect her son from what the world and God might do to him.

But protection can harden into fear. And fear can turn an ordinary Sunday into something irrevocable.

1. https://books2read.com/u/3RAeJx

2. https://books2read.com/u/3RAeJx

Set against the quiet pressures of family and expectation, *David and Jonathan* is a literary novella about love constrained by silence and the devastating cost of believing you are right. Written in the tradition of **James Baldwin's moral dramas**, it explores forbidden love and religious fear in the rural American South.

Read more at https://charlesharveyauthor.wordpress.com.

Also by Charles Harvey

Astroworld
Promise:Short Stories From The Road to Astroworld
Promise's Letters From the Road to Astroworld
The Road to Astroworld

Buck Wile Stories
Buck Wile is Punk'd Out On Da Downlow
Buck Wile is Butt Naked In Da City: Not Always a Gentleman, but
Always a Ladies' Man

Catnip
Catnip Gray Cat Detective: The Tabitha Davenport Affair

Dogs Bark
When Dogs Bark the Short Story
Bark Too

Kiss
The Beginning of John Henry and Alphonse

Poetic Journeys
Americana: Memory, Resistance, and America
3AM:Poems From the Sleepless Hours
The Last Supper: Poems of The Body,Truth, and Survival
Rough Cut Until I Bleed: Poems of Love, Hurt, and Want

Roommates
Roommates and The Old Dead Seaman
Roommates and Other Stories

Standalone
Coming Home Tomorrow: When Caring Becomes Too Much
My Manhood is Very Important to Me: How Far Will He Go to
Prove He's a Man?
Betty's House: Love and Deception
Black Queen: Is the Party Over?
How I Got Over
Insects and Elephants: What Happens When the Government
Goes Quirky
Minister Q: What Sis Gloria Knew
Othello Jones
The Blue Train To Heaven: A Burial and the Burden of Old
Resentments

The Power Plant: Men Under Pressure
We Are Here: Poetry of Pride and Presence
Ebenezer Jenkins' Christmas in Chicago
Unfucked
Q is a Bad Letter and Other QQ Crazy Stories
Antoine's Double Trouble: One Man Living Two Lives
Maura And Her Two Husbands: A Novel of Love and Trouble
No Satisfaction
Urban Tales
Into the Murky Waters
Red Underwear
Cheeseburger and Other Stories
Kirby Bob Understands Heaven
A Foursome Plus Poems: Twisted Gay Humor
Cruising in the Name of Love: A Gay Dramatic Monologue
Ungefickt: Ein Gedicht
David and Jonathan: The Price of Shame
The Butterfly Killer: A Psychological Crime Thriller

Watch for more at https://charlesharveyauthor.wordpress.com.

About the Author

Charles W. Harvey is a native Houstonian and a graduate of the University of Houston. At UofH he studied fiction under the guidance of Rosellen Brown and Chitra Divakaruni. In 1987, Charles was a 1st place prize recipient of PEN/Discovery for his short story Cheeseburger, which went on to be published in the Ontario Review. In 1989 Charles Harvey was awarded the Cultural Arts Council of Houston Grant for Writers and Artists. Also in 1989 he was a finalist in the MacDonald's Literary Achievement Awards. Charles has been published in Soulfires, Story Magazine SHADE, High Infidelity, The James White Review, and others. He is the author of the novels The Butterfly Killer, The Road to Astroworld, and Antoine's Double Trouble. He is also the author of several story and poetry collections. He also writes for the stage and screen.

Read more at https://charlesharveyauthor.wordpress.com.